Dangerous Lessons

"You want a position as a Spanish teacher?" Lord Jeremy Danbridge asked. "Then tell me, how do I say, 'You are as beautiful as flowers in a meadow or stars in the sky'?"

"There are more useful phrases we could begin with," Falcon protested. Then, as Jeremy positioned her in a corner with nowhere to escape, she said, "Lord Danbridge, please."

"That doesn't sound like Spanish," he said. "How do I say, 'I want to make love to you'? Teach me!"

When she said nothing, he went on, "You want a recommendation, do you not? All I want is one kiss."

Falcon saw she had no choice. "All right," she said, prepared to accept the worst to get the best position she could hope for.

But as Jeremy gently touched her lips with his, while pulling her firmly against him, she realized that he not only excelled in language lessons—but also in the language of love. . . .

D1711321

SIGNET REGENCY ROMANCE
Coming in October 1997

Eileen Putman
The Perfect Bride

Barbara Allister
A Marriage of Convenience

Dawn Lindsey
Foolish Fancy

1-800-253-6476
ORDER DIRECTLY
WITH VISA OR MASTERCARD

SIGNET
Published by the Penguin Group
Penguin Putnam Inc., 375 Hudson Street,
New York, New York 10014, U.S.A.
Penguin Books Ltd, 27 Wrights Lane,
London W8 5TZ, England
Penguin Books Australia Ltd,
Ringwood, Victoria, Australia
Penguin Books Canada Ltd, 10 Alcorn Avenue,
Toronto, Ontario, Canada M4V 3B2
Penguin Books (N.Z.) Ltd, 182-190 Wairau Road,
Auckland 10, New Zealand

Penguin Books Ltd, Registered Offices:
Harmondsworth, Middlesex, England

First published by Signet, an imprint of Dutton Signet,
a member of Penguin Putnam Inc.

First Printing, September, 1997
10 9 8 7 6 5 4 3 2 1

Copyright © Gail Eastwood-Stokes, 1997
All rights reserved

 REGISTERED TRADEMARK—MARCA REGISTRADA

Printed in the United States of America

Without limiting the rights under copyright reserved above, no part of this
publication may be reproduced, stored in or introduced into a retrieval system, or
transmitted, in any form, or by any means (electronic, mechanical, photocopying,
recording, or otherwise), without the prior written permission of both the copyright
owner and the above publisher of this book.

BOOKS ARE AVAILABLE AT QUANTITY DISCOUNTS WHEN USED TO PROMOTE PRODUCTS OR
SERVICES. FOR INFORMATION PLEASE WRITE TO PREMIUM MARKETING DIVISION, PENGUIN
PUTNAM INC., 375 HUDSON STREET, NEW YORK, NY 10014.

If you purchased this book without a cover you should be aware that this book is
stolen property. It was reported as "unsold and destroyed" to the publisher and
neither the author nor the publisher has received any payment for this "stripped
book."

The Lady from Spain

by

Gail Eastwood

A SIGNET BOOK

Chapter One

People were staring. The young woman standing by the parlor desk in the Plough and Hammer Inn could sense it even without turning, as if their curious looks touched her like so many inquisitive hands. Murmured fragments of conversation fluttered about at the edges of the room, and she held little doubt that they centered on her. *It does me no harm,* she reminded herself, straightening her stance just a little. *Let them look.*

She had known her peculiar dress and speech would attract notice in this tiny Wiltshire village, although certainly she had never expected the inn to be so busy. It appeared that half the population of Wickenden had business there on this fine spring day, along with passengers from several coaches. But at least the people around her had the grace not to confront her openly, unlike the proprietor of the inn. Haloed by light from the window behind him and safely situated behind the parlor desk, the large, ruddy-faced fellow eyed her silently, inspecting her through a haze of pipe smoke as if he had not heard a single word she'd just said.

Falcon Colburne did not believe for a minute that the man in front of her was deaf. Raising her chin an eloquent fraction of an inch, she answered his rude stare with a determined stare of her own. For now it suited her purposes to be taken for a foreigner—as long as it did not cost her a bed to sleep in. But if this man thought that he might deny her a room just because she appeared to be cut from a different cloth than his usual patrons, he had better think again!

"Two adjoining rooms with a parlor," she repeated, giving her words a definite Spanish inflection. This time she summoned a tone of severe authority that gave a cutting edge to her voice. In her nineteen years she had overcome far greater

obstacles than this plump, pompous, pipe-smoking proprietor.
She wanted him to know it.

"Ahem. Yes, well, madam," the man said at last, finally removing the pipe from his mouth and lowering his gaze to the
desk. "Happens I do still have two adjoining rooms, although
I don't know as you'll find them suitable. And the best I can
give you is a parlor across the passage from them." He
sounded as if he hoped she would refuse.

The rooms were probably tiny or above the kitchen, but
Falcon did not care. They represented a small victory nonetheless. She nodded.

"Sign on the line, then, if you please. The girl will show
you up." He slid the register over to her with an air of resigna-
tion.

Falcon drew the folds of the black lace mantilla covering
her hair and part of her face a little closer around her. *Sign on
the line!* It was such a simple act, for most people. But Miss
Falcarrah Sophia Colburne, nicknamed "Falcon" by her father's
regiment, was supposed to be dead.

Resolutely she dipped the pen in the ink, but she hesitated
when she looked down at the book. The blank space in the
register spoke volumes to her, seeming to symbolize all that
she had lost. For a moment she fought to quell the sudden
heartache that assailed her. Would she never become used to
these awkward moments? Why should she care what she
wrote in the book? Finally with a decisive flourish she filled
the space with the name she had used during her journey from
Spain and on her arrival in Portsmouth just the previous night.

"Doña Sofia Christina Ynez Alomar de Montero," the
innkeeper read aloud as he turned the book around to view her
signature. "That's a considerable name." He cocked an eyebrow skeptically as he eyed Falcon again. "We don't see too
many foreigners passing through here." He paused as if waiting for her to explain herself or reconsider.

Falcon said nothing. Who she was and what she was doing
there was no concern of his. She let her gaze stray to the window beyond him, which afforded a view of the stableyard.
She could see her manservant Carlos unloading trunks and
boxes from their hired carriage. Could he manage it all alone?
Where were the porters? *At least here we need not fear*

thieves around every corner as we did in war-ravaged Spain, she thought.

"I hope you'll find everything that you need here and enjoy your stay," the innkeeper finished lamely when she continued to remain silent. He nodded to the young maid who was waiting to escort the guests upstairs.

I hope so, too, Falcon agreed silently as she turned to follow the girl, although in her mind "here" meant in England and enjoyment was far removed from her purpose in coming.

As she moved away the scent of pipe tobacco blended into a mix of other smells—an overpowering scent of lavender water from one middle-aged woman, the smell of horse and sweat from a small beady-eyed man. She found it easier to keep her eyes straight ahead on the maid than to meet the stares of all the people who filled the small parlor. Only once did she glance up. The maid, sashaying through the crowd, paused to direct a saucy toss of her head toward one particular gentleman, and Falcon was overcome by curiosity to see who had merited such special recognition.

There was no mistaking the girl's intended target. He was a little taller than the other men standing around him, although not enough so to make him stand out by this alone. From the collar points and coat Falcon could glimpse through the crowd, his clothes appeared to be somewhat more fashionable than those around him, but again, not so much as would make him distinctive. It was his posture that she noticed at once. Even in that crowded room he had a military bearing that she was certain she could recognize anywhere—a proud, erect stance that no country farmer could ever match. His brown hair looked touched by sunlight, and his angular face showed a strength that made her think at once of army officers she had known in Spain.

That must be why he seems familiar, she thought. It was highly unlikely that she would have seen him anywhere before—after all, she had only arrived in England yesterday! Unless, of course, he had served in Spain in the early days of Napoleon's war. However, thinking of officers and the military reminded her suddenly of the one thing she had forgotten to do. With no other warning than a small exclamation of surprise she turned and reversed her course.

* * *

Lieutenant Major Jeremy Hazelton, Lord Danebridge, would undoubtedly have ducked into the nearest shadowed corner had there been one available at the moment he discovered the young señora's gaze upon him. He had been watching her with particular care, it was true, but he had the best of reasons not to wish to attract her notice. He did not know whether to be relieved or alarmed when she suddenly whirled around and headed back toward the innkeeper. *What the devil was she doing?*

She did not get far. She no sooner turned than she collided with the first of two women who had dutifully fallen into step behind her. Jeremy suppressed a chuckle. Could she really be so impulsive and forgetful? A moment earlier he had been admiring her proud and competent handling of the innkeeper. Surely she knew the women were behind her—he assumed that they were her servants. One was a tall, sharp-featured woman with a slight limp; the other was a small, dark, nervous woman clutching a basket and several wrapped parcels.

"Saints preserve us, child!" the tall woman exclaimed in an unmistakably Irish brogue. "What are ye about?"

The young "señora" reached out to steady her, apologizing and whispering, "I forgot to ask for directions!" *"Olvide que queria preguntar direcciones,"* she belatedly repeated in Spanish.

Jeremy did not fail to note that English had come to the young woman's mind first. Her accent had also diminished noticeably. Both observations merely reinforced the ones he had made about her in Portsmouth the previous evening. *Doña Alomar de Montero, indeed,* he thought. *You are no more Spanish than I am.*

He believed that she might well be a nobleman's wife. There was something aristocratic about her bearing and speech, and a hint of expense in the fine black satin and exquisite, form-fitting cut of her fringed Spanish gown. Perhaps a widow, although black was a fashionable color for Spanish women regardless of mourning or marital state.

He also suspected that she was beautiful. She kept her mantilla, draped in generous folds from a tall comb at the back of her head, drawn partly across her face to hide her features, as

was the custom in Spain. The seductive glimpses of smooth skin and luminescent eyes that it allowed tantalized and piqued his curiosity while frustrating his attempts to gain a good look at her.

Still, he had seen enough to know that she did not have the famous dark eyes of classic Spain, nor was her skin the dusky, golden Spanish color. No indeed, her skin was the color of fine porcelain, and her eyes were a light, clear, enchanting green. *A magnificent green—like sunlight on the leaves in a forest.*

He pushed the thought away instantly, chastising himself. He must not allow himself to be distracted by a pair of eyes—or anything else for that matter. If the doña was not a Spanish lady, then who was she? What was she doing here? Unfortunately for him, the government had made it his business to find out.

She had returned to the innkeeper.

"Excuse me," she said in Spanish, clearly assuming that the innkeeper would understand her. Then in flawless, accented English she proceeded to inquire after one of the residents of the village.

"I am certain you must know him," she finished. "He is a war veteran, a Cornishman who lives here now. Can you direct me to his house?"

If the innkeeper's eyebrows had been raised in curiosity before this, now they nearly shot off the top of his head. Jeremy was tempted to check the position of his own—he was simply astonished that this young woman would make her affairs known so publicly, no matter who or what she was.

The beefy hosteler took a deep, thoughtful pull on his pipe. "Old Martin Triss, eh? Now what would you be wanting with the likes of him?" The man narrowed his eyes in suspicion. "How do I know he would want me telling you where he lives?"

The young woman sighed in exasperation and fished a coin out of her reticule. "He is expecting me," she said with only the slightest hint of hesitation. "He will thank you for helping me."

Clamping the thin stem of his pipe between his teeth, the innkeeper tore a scrap out of his receipt book and wrote on the back of it.

"Cottram Row?" she asked, peering at it. "How would I find that?"

The man sighed, as if she had asked far too much. Only the reward of another coin convinced him to explain how she should go.

"*Gracias.* Thank you."

Jeremy echoed the sentiment in his mind as he watched his subject turn and thread her way back through the room, apparently unmindful of the additional stir she had created among the crowd. She did not appear to look his way again, for which he was also grateful. Perhaps he was mistaken in thinking she had taken note of him. Certainly she could not have done a better job of providing him with information he wanted to know.

He continued to stare after she rejoined the other women at the doorway and moved out of sight. Was she extremely clever, or extremely careless? She seemed to make many mistakes. He had noticed her hesitation before she signed her name in the register. He had also observed her nervous glance toward the window, which had called his attention to her luggage and the servant unloading it outside. The anxiety he'd read in that glance told him to inspect her baggage as soon as possible, for it could prove a rich source of information.

Should I believe that she is truly going to call on this Cornishman? he asked himself. If the fellow was a contact, did she hope to lend innocence to their meeting by her openness? Or was this public revelation a ruse to distract from her real purpose in Wickenham? What would a foreign agent be doing in this little village? Perhaps there was some other explanation for all this, although he could not fathom what it might be. If, however, she was merely confident that there was no one here who might be interested in her affairs, she was quite mistaken.

The lieutenant major turned his attention back to the matter of booking his own room, wondering how much time he had before the mysterious señora might set out to attend to her business. He was confident that the friendly young chambermaid, offered the proper incentive, would not hesitate to divulge the location of the "Spanish lady's" rooms.

Chapter Two

"This Sergeant Triss and yourself'll be the talk o' the town tonight—the topic o' the evenin' round every hearth," the Irishwoman fussed at Falcon as the little party of women made their way along the dark inner passage of the Plow and Hammer's upper floor.

"'Tisn't proper for a respectable young lady such as ye are to go traipsin' off to that Cornishman's cottage, for one thing. And to make it plain in front of all those people! What of your reputation? I don't know how I ever let ye go in there to be bookin' the rooms for yourself in the first place. 'Tisn't proper at all!"

Falcon smiled, knowing full well that she had not given her Irish duenna any say in the matter. She did not reply, however, as the maid leading the way in front of them stopped just then by a door near the far end of the passage.

Over the kitchens, indeed, Falcon thought with a grim smile as she noticed their proximity to the service stairs. For once she would have liked to be wrong. However, as she followed the girl into the indicated room, she found that it appeared to be perfectly serviceable. It was plain but large enough to boast two windows, and it contained a pair of chairs and a small table in addition to a bed large enough for her to share comfortably with Maggie. A door led to an adjoining small room for Benita, her Spanish maid.

"Parlor's just across the passage there," the chambermaid said with a nod toward the room entrance. "Shall you be wantin' tea sent up?"

Falcon shook her head and dismissed the girl, requesting only wash water and fresh towels. She turned then to her two companions, but at once the Irishwoman began to sputter again.

"No tea? Never tell me ye expect to be goin' off at this hour to call on that man! Ye've not had so much as a night's rest or a drop o' China broth to restore ye, child! What's more, 'tisn't right to go appearin' on his doorstep when he hasn't a notion what day or even what week to be expectin' ye. At the least ye should send round a note to him."

Well used to her traveling companion's occasional rants, Falcon chuckled. The older woman's strong opinions were as much a part of her as the Irish twinkle in her eye. "Don't be a scold, Maggie. You know very well how long I have waited for this reunion. Do you truly believe that I would put off making this call for even another quarter hour, now that we are finally here?"

"I believe as ye've waited this long already, it would not harm ye to wait a bit longer. Send for the man to call on ye here, as is proper."

"Ah, Maggie, after some of what you've been through, I never thought I'd see you daunted by the prospect of taking a little stroll without some tea to fortify you," Falcon said, cocking an eyebrow and holding back her laughter.

As she expected, the Irish woman's pride rose to her challenge. "Whisht, now! As if that would ever stop Margaret Meara. Me grandfather would roll over in his grave . . ."

"Good, then. As soon as we have washed up, we can start off." She held up a hand to forestall any further protests. "I believe it is perfectly proper for a woman to call on a gentleman about a matter of business, and this call is not only for pleasure. Triss should be on the lookout for us, for I sent a letter by the packet boat when we were only a week from making port to give him an idea when we might arrive. And as far as tea, why, we can have some when we return, if Triss does not do right by us, Maggie. Do you imagine that a mere Cornishman does not know his social duty? You had better not let him catch you thinking that way!"

Still chuckling, Falcon turned to the smaller woman who had been waiting quietly and spoke to her in rapid Spanish. *"Benita, no vamos a deshacer las maletas.* Once Carlos has brought up all the luggage, take out only what we'll need for tonight. There's no need to unpack everything as I hope we will be on our way again by tomorrow."

*   *   *

The lieutenant major sat waiting at a table by the ivy-clad window in the front of the taproom of the Plough and Hammer, precisely where he could observe all the comings and goings of the patrons of the inn. The open taproom doorway offered a perfect view of the stairs and entry passage, and he smiled when he saw the "Spanish" lady and her companion come down with a basket of packages and exit to the street.

They had certainly wasted little time embarking upon their errand, whatever it was. They had barely stayed in their rooms long enough for him to take care of certain details. Through the fronds of greenery that framed the window he watched them head down the street in the direction the innkeeper had indicated. Despite her limp, the tall woman walked at a businesslike pace, keeping up with the younger woman in black. The latter charged along with a stride that quite surprised him, especially considering the cut of her dress.

Most well-bred ladies in Jeremy's experience sauntered and strolled when they intended to go anywhere, making certain to stop upon occasion to strike an artful pose. His mysterious "Spanish" lady, however, moved with fluid, feminine grace yet still achieved a speed that could probably match most men's. Where had she learned to walk like that? She would no doubt reach her destination within the half hour.

He flicked open his pocket watch. *Time to stop admiring and get to work.* The two women could be back in less than an hour if their business was brief or the Cornishman wasn't home. Any attempt to follow them was bound to be fruitless, for once they left the village he would surely be seen. He would learn more by staying here.

He signaled to a barrel-chested blond man quaffing ale a few tables away, who promptly rose and disappeared in the direction of the kitchen and back stairs. Jeremy would give Nicholson ten—better make that fifteen—minutes to get the lady's servants out of the way. Then he would have a good look through her belongings.

He had not the slightest compunction about invading her privacy—he had performed similar tasks far too many times by now to give it any thought. He only hoped that he would find information that could close this case quickly. If not for this woman, he would have been well on his way home by now, not sitting here drinking ale from a chipped mug, preparing to search a stranger's room.

He waited the fifteen minutes. Checking his watch again, he tossed an appropriate handful of coins onto the table and headed for the stairs. The chambermaid had been quite helpful. He was glad now that he had not waited until evening to approach her. A few compliments, a few shillings and the promise of at least a drink to be purchased for her at the end of the night had been sufficient to procure the information he'd needed.

The "Spanish lady's" rooms were not the best, indeed. Situated where they were, they would be subject to noise from both the kitchen and the stableyard. But Jeremy appreciated their convenience to the back service stairs, which offered him easy access to his own room on the floor above.

He listened carefully as he approached along the passage. He had complete faith in Nicholson's ability to carry out orders, but unforeseen events were part of life. *Like this assignment,* he thought ruefully. Suppose the Spanish servants had refused to leave their post in favor of tea in the kitchens? Suppose they had been suspicious instead of delighted to meet a fellow servant who could speak their language? His assistant's persuasive powers were impressive but not foolproof.

He heard nothing from inside the rooms on either side of the passage. Assured by a quick glance that no one was coming, he slipped the skeleton key from his pocket and used it to let himself in the first door, quietly closing it behind him.

Falcon and Maggie had walked through the village with its modest stone buildings and then down a verdant country lane where white drifts of wild garlic in bloom along the lightly shaded banks spiced the air with their pungent scent.

"Everything seems so lush and soft, Maggie!" Falcon exclaimed, looking out over the green fields. "Even more so than I remember. It is so different from Spain."

"'Tis that, no question," Maggie replied, huffing as she tried to catch up to Falcon. The younger woman's pace had gradually become too much for her.

Falcon slowed instantly. "Forgive me. I'm like a hound on

the scent, all a-quiver to get there. Yet I'm growing increasingly nervous as we draw closer."

"'Tis only natural, child. Your anticipation puts all your other feelings up on edge."

"Yes." Falcon could not begin to articulate them. The hope of this reunion had kept her going for five long years of waiting and living among strangers. Now that it was imminent, she was not only excited and eager, she was afraid—mostly afraid that she had hoped for too much, but afraid, too, of the painful memories that she knew would come the moment she heard Triss's voice.

His cottage came into view at the next bend in the road. Like the houses in the village, it was built of gray stone with white-painted wooden window frames that gave it a neatly tailored appearance. It stood at the end of a long earthen path flanked by stone walls, as the innkeeper had described.

Hardly an instant after Falcon put her hand on the gate at the bottom of the path, the door of the cottage opened. A dear, familiar voice boomed out in greeting, "Falcon, is it you? O' course it must be. What other splendid señorita would be a-coming to my door? Welcome, welcome!"

A short-necked, bespectacled bulldog of a fellow came bustling out and down the path toward them, walking a bit lopsidedly but briskly nonetheless. His voice seemed to cut through time.

It was Triss—Corporal Martin Triss, as Falcon had known him, although he had become Sergeant Triss by the time he left the army, she had learned later from his letters. He looked hardly changed by the five years that had passed since she had last seen him—a bit less hair, more gray than she remembered, and the walk a bit more lopsided, perhaps, but that was all. He was dearer to Falcon than any other person alive.

She flew up the path toward him. "Triss! Oh, Triss!" All the long-harbored affection she felt for him seemed to well up until it spilled out of her as tears. She launched herself into his arms and clung to him as if she would never let go again.

"Well, look at you, missy!" Gently he set her back from him and adjusted the spectacles her energetic embrace had knocked askew. "'Ere, 'ere, now. Good thing this is not me best waistcoat, eh?" He reached inside his imperiled waistcoat and produced a large checkered handkerchief. "It seems that little girl I knew is still inside this very grown-up young lady, after all."

He offered the handkerchief with a tender smile. "It's all right, cry all you like, m'dear. You've 'ad a long road to travel. When you're good and ready, we'll go inside. I've a few things I want to show you."

At the inn, Jeremy had found nothing in the first room except a small cot—obviously the maid's quarters. A basket and several parcels lay on the coverlet, but for the moment he had ignored them. He moved into the main bedchamber, taking care to unlock the outer door of that room as well, as a precaution. He had learned long ago to make certain of his exits.

This room contained a double bed adorned with printed cotton hangings and a fireplace flanked by two windows. Two trunks sat on the faded carpet next to a pair of straight-backed chairs and a table that was scarcely bigger than a candlestand. Assorted boxes and a portmanteau sat between them.

He wasted no time, setting to work immediately on the lock of the larger trunk. He opened the lid carefully to avoid any sound and studied the way the contents had been packed so that he could replace everything exactly as it had been. Oh, there was no doubt he was a master at this game. But he had thought he was finished with it. When he had boarded his ship in France to come home he had believed all this was finally behind him.

More the fool you! he thought as he removed several neatly folded cambric nightdresses and a silk shawl from the trunk. His fingers skimmed through the remaining piles of folded garments, feeling for objects or papers. He listened for the telltale rustle that might lead him to a hidden document among the clothes. His probing released a scent of lavender from the depths of the trunk.

In the bottom he found a surprisingly small assortment of fans, brushes and haircombs, and a bulky object wrapped in blue silk. This proved to be a hand mirror set in an elaborately ornamented silver frame. It surprised him, for the clothing and other items in the trunk appeared to be for the most part very simple and such a mirror seemed out of place.

His training told him to break it. A message could easily have been hidden behind the glass, and such an out-of-place item was exactly the sort of clue he was looking for. The breakage would be attributed to the rigors of travel. But his instinct argued against the destructive act. He was not superstitious but he did appreciate fine craftsmanship, and the mirror was beautiful. He shook his head. He was losing his objectivity. Nevertheless he carefully rewrapped the hand glass and replaced it in the trunk.

Next to the mirror he found several pairs of white silk stockings, all neatly rolled. As his fingers grazed over their softness he winced. How often he had purchased fine stockings like those! His wife Anne had loved them. Sad, sweet memories washed over him, triggered by the combination of touch and smell.

Why was he thinking of Anne now? It was all bound up together, his not wanting this job, his wanting to be home, his not having been at home with Anne two years ago when she died. Blast! He should never have agreed to take this last assignment.

He forced himself to examine and replace each rolled pair of stockings as carefully and methodically as he did everything, but it required considerable concentration. Anger simmered inside him just beneath the surface. All he was doing here was wasting his time! So far, he had found nothing to indicate that this mystery woman was anything other than an ordinary person, certainly not an enemy of the Crown.

After repacking everything in the large trunk, Jeremy poked briefly through the boxes and the portmanteau, which seemed to contain bonnets, shoes and servants' clothing. Was there really a point to this? He opened up the smaller trunk and repeated the process of methodically examining the contents. He was taking too much time, he knew. In the bottom of the trunk, however, he finally came upon something of interest.

In a carved wooden box lined with green velvet he found an exquisite necklace of pearls set with a single, brilliant emerald at its center. There were earrings to match it and he caught himself thinking, *Of course, to match her eyes.* Among the plain, mostly black gowns in this trunk there was also one of green moiré—an evening dress or a ballgown, most certainly.

So, our mouse may at times play the peacock, eh? The discovery helped to bring back his focus. The box also held a locket with miniatures of a man in British regimental dress and a very beautiful woman. Who were they? It was an odd thing for someone supposedly Spanish to possess.

Delving further in the trunk he found a purse with a thick wad of bank notes drawn upon a bank in Madrid—a sizable fortune to be carrying in cash. Next to it was a book—the Holy Bible, in English, notably—and a second box, similar to the first one, containing a set of rosary beads with a crucifix.

Of course, she is Catholic! he thought with a sudden jolt of dismay. That was something he'd have to report, although it still could mean nothing. If she was a British subject who had married a Spanish don, it made sense that she might share his religion. It might explain everything. Many English Catholics emigrated. It did not have to mean she had designs against the government or was a foreign agent in league with those who did. But it made him wonder all the more about the man pictured in the locket. Catholics could not be commissioned officers.

Jeremy slid his fingers along the bottom of the trunk past the box with the rosary and at last encountered what he had most been seeking—a tied bundle of folded papers. *Ah,* he thought. *Here we'll have it.* The packet was too fat to lift out without upsetting all the other contents of the trunk, so he removed piles of clothing and set them on the floor.

How much longer did he dare to continue? Enough time had passed that the servants could return at any moment. He paused to listen for voices in the passage or the sound of footsteps on the backstairs. Hearing nothing yet, he turned his attention back to his discovery.

The papers appeared to be a collection of letters, sent to one person at various addresses in Spain. However, the name on the letters was not the one currently being used by his mysterious lady from Spain.

The lady in question, ashamed that she had given in to her surge of emotion, had meanwhile gathered herself together and even managed to introduce Maggie to the Cornish sergeant. Triss had served as batman to Falcon's father and had known her since her childhood.

Now the two women were seated in Triss's parlor as he lumbered about preparing their tea. Late-afternoon sunlight poured in through the two windows in the whitewashed front wall, giving the small room a cheerful appearance. A large, round table filled the center of the room, where a floor cloth of stenciled canvas covered the rough flagstones. A small modern coal grate looked rather lost in the sizable fireplace.

"Can we not help?" asked Falcon, feeling a bit useless as she watched Triss place the kettle over the grate.

The last thing she wanted was to sit and be waited upon. Anticipation made her restless. She had come here not just to see Triss, but to obtain some important information from him. While she did wonder that Triss could possibly have to show her, the other business occupied her attention.

"No, indeed, Miss Falcon," he insisted. "You and Mrs. Meara are my guests. My missus'd 'ave me 'ead if I didn't treat 'ee right and proper."

Falcon knew that Triss's wife had died some years back. She could guess how much he missed her. "Now Triss, how is she going to do that?" she asked gently. "You know Mary's gone."

The Cornishman grinned. "Do 'ee think she'd let a little thing like that stop 'er? You never knew my Mary." He turned away and busied himself with dusting off the teacups from the top shelf of the dresser.

Falcon knew better than to press that topic further. Instead she reached for the basket of paper-wrapped parcels that she and Maggie had carried with them.

"While we wait for the kettle, Triss, perhaps you would open these? We brought something for you."

"Did you, now?" He smiled as he set the cups and plates around the table. Falcon tried not to fidget.

Once his preparations were complete, he sat. He made a great show of inspecting the paper and string which held the parcels together and of feeling the shape of the objects held within them. Comical expressions paraded across his face as he did so, making Falcon laugh. Finally he took pity on her impatience and opened the first one.

"O-ho, oranges!" His delighted chuckle warmed Falcon's heart as thoroughly as Spanish sunshine.

She had brought him almonds and cigars as well as oranges from Seville, all delicacies he had enjoyed in Spain. She and Maggie agreed that he could smoke one of the cigars if he waited until they finished their tea. Falcon watched his face intently as he finally opened the last of the bundles. She had wanted to bring him something truly special, and had gone to considerable trouble to procure this last gift for him.

For a moment he said nothing, staring down into the paper wrappings and fingering what lay there reverently. Then he looked up at Falcon.

"There are several pieces," she said. "It should be enough for a good pair of boots. I would like to have them made for you in London."

"They would be the finest pair o' boots a man such as me ever owned," he said reverently. "Cordovan leather! You shouldn't 'ave done it, missy."

She went to him and kissed his cheek. "Of course I should have. It is the very least I should do, Triss, for a loyal friend who undoubtedly saved my life. If I could have, I would have brought you an entire cask of sherry from Jerez as well. But we would have found it a bit difficult to carry!"

"Now, that's a picture," Maggie said. "Two such Amazons as we are? Sure and he'll be wonderin' why we didn't bring him two."

Their laughter felt easy and comfortable, but then Triss said, "I've something to give 'ee, too, Miss Falcarrah Sophia Colburne—something I've been keeping for 'ee."

Falcon caught her breath sharply, all thoughts of gifts wiped from her mind. She had not heard her real name spoken since the terrible day she had parted from Triss five years ago. The familiar sound of it triggered a rush of agonizing memories that hurt like a knife thrust into a wound that never healed.

"Falcarrah Colburne is dead, Triss. Please do not call me by that name."

"Who is sitting 'ere at me table, then? It honors your dear

mother's memory, you being named for her village in Ireland. Falcarrah's a fine name."

She did not want to explain. She was not even certain that she could, the feelings ran so deep. The years had changed her into someone very different from the innocent girl her parents had loved. She set her jaw stubbornly. "The girl you knew by that name has been officially dead for five years and will be safer if she stays that way, at least for the time being. Please do not use it."

"I know. But just among ourselves . . . ?"

"No." She had buried the past and her name along with it. For five years she had been someone else, as Triss knew well. How else could she have coped with the unbearable pain? All that remained was the business she had come here to finish. "You need to know that I have taken a new identity for this journey. I am using the name Doña Sofia Christina Ynez Alomar de Montero. It simplified matters for traveling to pose as a Spanish widow, and it should protect me and allow me some freedom if I continue the pose until I can resolve things here."

"A Spanish widow," he echoed, shaking his head. "And 'ave you planned what you are going to do?"

"It all depends on what you can tell me and what I learn for myself." She looked at him pointedly.

He heaved a great sigh and got up from his chair with an effort. "First things first."

He rescued the kettle and set the tea to steeping, then left the room, leaving Falcon and Maggie to wonder what he was up to. Maggie made use of his absence to more than make up her missing share of the conversation. When he returned she fell silent once again.

The sergeant was carrying a small leather-bound trunk. He said not a word but stood before Falcon, waiting.

Recognition crept slowly into Falcon's mind, as if it started in her heart and dragged itself painfully to a more useful place. Astonishment came hard on its heels.

"Triss! My father's books! But how—? Where—?"

He set the trunk on the table. As if she were dreaming, she rose and went over to inspect it. She touched the rough leather, remembering all the trials it had suffered. Rain, wind, bitter cold and burning sun, flooded rivers—the trunk had

protected her father's books through it all. She opened the lid
and stared at the books, packed as neatly as if her father had
only put them there this morning.

"Oh," she gasped as twin daggers of grief and joy pierced
her heart at once. What had made her think the past could be
buried? She closed her eyes against a new threat of tears. This
would never do. She was delighted to have the books, was she
not?

She turned to question Triss and discovered him just reen-
tering the room for a second time. She had not even noticed
he was gone. This time he carried something she recognized
instantly. The peculiarly shaped leather carrying case had
been designed for a very particular purpose.

"Oh!" she whispered this time, hardly daring to believe.
"Mama's harp!"

Triss nodded, a huge grin lighting his face.

As precious as her father's books were, this treasure meant
even more to her, almost as if her mother had reached back to
her from the grave. She took the case from him and set it
down, fumbling eagerly with the latch through a haze of joyful tears. When she finally had it open, she lifted out a small,
exquisitely made harp of the old French style, decorated with
carvings of roses and an angel along the scrolled top, with
garlands of roses painted in gilt on the soundboard. She
stroked the strings lightly and did not mind the discordant
sound that came from them.

"It needs new strings, of course. And someone who knows
how to tune and repair it. But I am certain we can find those
in London." She ran her hands along the smooth polished
frame, imagining for a moment that the wood was still warm
from her mother's touch. "Oh, Triss! How did you ever manage to save these?"

He looked at her earnestly, as if measuring how much to divulge. "As 'ee knows, when I caught up to the regiment after
finding 'ee that dreadful day, you and your parents 'ad already been reported dead. I knew your father's equipment
would be auctioned off and your family's valuables shipped
back to your relatives 'ere in England, so I salvaged what I
could. The little things, like your 'orse, I kept with me till I

learned where you were and could send them to 'ee, but these I 'ad shipped back 'ere to Mary for safekeeping."

"I wish I could have met her," Falcon said soberly. "I owe her so much. And you, too. Thank you." Moving the harp aside she jumped up and flung her arms around the sergeant impulsively.

Maggie coughed. "Tch, tch. With all this talk of London this and London that, sure ye had better begin to be practicin' a bit of decorum, young lady. I never saw a Spanish doña who behaved like a hoyden."

"Oh, Maggie, we are not in London yet! Here, now, are you feeling left out?" Falcon came around the table to give her companion a vigorous hug.

"We had best be gettin' back," Maggie reminded her gruffly. "What are ye plannin' to do with them things? Had ye thought about that, now?"

"I can 'ave them sent down to the inn in the early morning," Triss offered. "Young Jebediah Stone comes by 'ere on 'is way to make the milk delivery."

Falcon felt a moment's panic at the thought of ending the visit. "We cannot leave yet! Triss, what about Ensign Sweeney and the other two men I'm seeking? I have come all this way. You wrote that you had information for me. Tell me. Do you know where they are?"

The sergeant turned to Falcon with as stern an expression as his jovial face could produce. "I've not changed my mind about this, Falcon. I want 'ee to go to the authorities with this business. 'Tis no matter for a young woman to be taking the law into 'er own 'ands, as you should well know."

"I must see justice done, Triss. It has been my sustaining thought for these past five years. I cannot and I will not let what happened be forgotten. I know I survived their attack for a reason, and I believe that it is this."

Triss rubbed his nose and looked down at the floor. "I 'aven't 'ad much luck locating Sweeney since 'e sold out and more or less disappeared. I wrote you about that. Pumphrey, too, although I kept track of 'im longer. Drank 'imself right out of the army, 'e did. But Timmins is in London. 'E was wounded at Vitoria and got sent 'ome. Someone fixed him up with a job as a barracks porter 'elping out in the Tower."

Falcon said nothing for a moment, swallowing her disappointment. She had hoped to have more to go on—hoped that Triss would have had more news since she'd last heard from him. Yet at least he had given her a place to start. "Perhaps Timmins knows where the others are," she said thoughtfully.

"If we find the blackguards, I suppose 'tis only right that somethin' be done," Maggie said.

Falcon gave the woman another hug. "Well, we have even more business in London, now. Will you come with us, Triss? You are the only soul I know in England."

"There be plenty o' men left in the Forty-third that would remember 'ee, missy. But I don't see what I 'ave any choice, if I want to keep 'ee from doing something foolish. I'll just need a day or so to sort out my affairs and make arrangements 'ere."

"We will go on ahead. I promise I won't do anything until you join us there. I cannot go prancing into a London barracks unescorted, now, can I?"

"Missy, I wouldn't put it past 'ee to try."

Chapter Three

At the Plough and Hammer, time was running out. Of course it would be, Jeremy thought, now that he was finally getting somewhere. He needed to go through the letters. He had no right to steal from an innocent citizen, if that should indeed prove the case here, but how else was he to discover the truth?

I have no choice, he thought. *I need to read these and I cannot do it now.* He tucked the packet inside his waistcoat and quickly repacked the trunk so it looked undisturbed. Perhaps there would be an opportunity to return the letters later.

He knew he should not leave without checking the items on the maid's bed on his way out. As he turned to go back into the smaller room, however, he noticed in the shadow of the big bed one more piece of luggage that he had not inspected. *Damn!* With a sense of urgency pulsing through him, he crossed to the big leather-covered box and had it open in an instant.

For a moment his breath caught. A long, curved saber in a black leather scabbard lay nestled on top of layers of folded fabric. It was hardly what he'd expected a lady to be carrying in her luggage—a regimental officer's sword.

Beneath the sword he found parts of an officer's uniform— a scarlet pelisse trimmed with gray fur and festooned with silk laces, a corded red sash, and a white leather shoulder belt with the distinctive brass and silver breast plate of the Forty-third Regiment. How had she come to possess them? Could she have been married to an English officer? If so, why would she masquerade as a Spanish doña? Did these belong to the man pictured in the locket?

In a cloth pouch tucked alongside the larger items he found the officer's silver whistle and chain, along with the pair of captain's wings that should have been buttoned onto the shoulders of his missing jacket. If the man had died in battle, how had she come by these things?

There was also a pouch he recognized as one designed to hold a pistol and ammunition. There was shot and a powder flask in it, but no pistol. What had happened to it? Did she have it with her?

The last item in the box was the most incongruous and mystifying of everything that he had seen. It was a toy horse, no more than a dozen inches long, carved out of wood and covered with calfskin dyed to look like dapple gray. It had a black mane and tail of real horsehair. Why did she have it, and why was it in a box with regimental regalia? Did she have a child? The toy was English, he knew well—he had given his own son one almost exactly like it.

Jeremy abruptly replaced everything and closed the box. What in God's name was he doing here? At any moment he was likely to be discovered and hauled before the authorities—that is, if the "Spanish" lady did not run him through with that sword first or shoot him with the missing pistol. How had he been so lucky as to be saddled with this confounded assignment just when he was finally to go home? The sight of the toy horse had unleashed an overpowering craving to see his son. He didn't, at this moment, give a damn if the "Spanish" lady was an agent planning to murder the Prince Regent himself. He wanted to be relieved of this assignment. Unfortunately for him, the surest way to achieve that was to finish it.

His instincts were seldom wrong and at the moment they were fairly screaming that it was time to go. He took a cursory peek at the items on the maid's bed in the other room, but found nothing of further interest there. The packet of letters would have to be the key to this puzzle. If he solved it by the morning it would not be soon enough for him! Feeling the letters secure inside his waistcoat, he cautiously opened the door to the passage, only to close it again quickly.

The sound of voices engaged in a quick exchange of Spanish warned him that his subject's servants were coming up the stairs from the kitchen. *Damn!* He knew he had stayed too long. Which door would they come in? He would only have seconds to make his exit out of the one they did not use.

Wait, he told himself as he stood in the connecting doorway between the two rooms, ready to move. Moving too soon would be as much of a mistake as moving too late. He would be in trouble anyway if the manservant did not come in.

The servants moved to the door that opened into the maid's room and the sound of their excited Spanish told him the exact moment when they discovered that the door was unlocked. As they came inside, Jeremy disappeared silently out the door of the adjoining room. By the time they discovered that that door was also unlocked, Jeremy would be up the service stairs to the next floor. He doubted they would discover anything missing.

Safe in his room, Jeremy pulled out the packet of letters and tossed them onto the bed. He had half expected to find Nicholson waiting for him, but the room was empty. It was not a problem. Nicholson had his own methods of prowling about stables and kitchens, where he learned a great deal. Undoubtedly the man had been a cat in some other lifetime.

Jeremy stripped off his coat and hung it neatly on the only chair before starting to work. He untied the packet and spread the letters out on the bed.

They were all addressed to Señorita Sofia Feliciana Alvez Bonastre. He suspected that Doña Alomar de Montero and the señorita might be the same person, although—or perhaps because—there were no letters at all addressed to the doña. He began to sort them by the senders and to arrange them in chronological order.

They covered a period of almost five years. Most were in Spanish, addressed to two convents in Andalusia, one of which was near Seville. A few of the earlier letters in English were addressed to places farther north. Apparently the señorita had seen a good deal of Spain, despite the war. All of the English letters were from the Cornishman she had gone to see, Sergeant Triss, of the Forty-third Regiment. Were the regimental items in the lady's luggage his? They had belonged to a captain, not a sergeant. But if somehow that were indeed the case, then why had she not taken them along?

There seemed to be only a few other regular correspondents. Once he had established several neat piles, he chose the sergeant's stack and took it over to the chair to begin his reading.

Sometime later, Jeremy was startled when Nicholson approached him.

"Have you eaten?"

"Eaten? What time is it?" Jeremy fished for his watch and quickly consulted it. He could not believe he had become so engrossed in the letters that he had not heard the other man enter the room. He had lost all track of time.

He looked at his assistant sharply. "I take it the ladies have returned? How long ago?"

"Not long. They've sent down for their meal to be taken in their parlor."

"No more expeditions for the moment. Very good." He paused to consider what he should do next. "Would you be kind enough to go down and order some dinner for me? Whatever seems the most edible, given the choices. I shall be along, but not too directly. I think I shall take a small detour on my way down."

Nicholson nodded and departed as silently as he had come. Jeremy was always amazed that a man of Nicholson's size could move so quietly. It was a helpful skill in their business. The fellow was built like an ox, but he was quick and agile as well as powerful, unexpected gifts that had more than once proven extremely useful to both of them. *I hope we'll have no need for those talents this time,* Jeremy thought.

He frowned as he returned the letters he'd been reading to their appropriate spot on the bed. Correspondence was always an intriguing puzzle, like a conversation missing half of its dialogue. The letters revealed more about their senders than the recipient, but even so, he had pieced together something of the señorita's story and her character. She seemed to be a warm, impulsive, headstrong person who had been through some extraordinary experiences and who engendered strong feelings in those who knew her. Just reading the letters had inspired him to feel admiration for her. But was the señorita of the letters the same as his mysterious lady from Spain? He was no longer certain. The letters seemed to suggest that the señorita was quite young. If the two were not the same, why were these letters in his subject's baggage? What was their connection with the British Forty-third? He had even more questions now than before.

He had decided that if he went down to her rooms right now, he might just pick up some conversation that was complete, and possibly even useful. He locked his door carefully and headed along the crooked passageway toward the service stairs.

On the floor below, all things were quiet. No one was in the passage to notice him lurking or applying his ear to the door of the Spanish lady's private parlor.

He listened first for indications that their meal had been delivered, for the last thing he needed was to be caught there. He heard a reassuring rattle of china. He pressed his ear closer, trying to pick up voices. Just as he did, however, the door opened, nearly pitching him headfirst into the room.

Instinctively he sprang backward, but it was not far enough. The Spanish maid, hurrying out with a loaded tray, was looking back over her shoulder to catch her mistress's last remark.

The crash that followed was quite spectacular.

"Madre de Dios!"

"Saints preserve us!"

The opened door blocked Falcon's view of precisely what happened, but she heard the tremendous noise and jumped to her feet even before she heard Benita's and Maggie's exclamations. She came around the door just as the little Spanish maid, kneeling amid a hideous mess of broken crockery in the doorway, burst into tears and put her hands over her face. Beyond stood the lanky form of a brown-haired gentleman surveying his coat and tightly fitted pantaloons, which undoubtedly had been spotless moments earlier. A colorful assortment of stains and crumbs—mustard, honey, bits of ham—adorned his person now.

He made a half gesture as if to brush away the damage, then shrugged and looked up. Falcon's breath caught as she recognized him as the handsome man from the crowd in the parlor that afternoon. She noticed his eyes—slate gray, deep set under thick, dark brows, above a very straight nose. At this moment his lips were set in an unreadable straight line.

Surely he is not about to heap abuse on poor Benita, she

thought. What wretched luck that he must have been passing
by the door at just that moment!

"Good sir," she said, moving forward to claim his attention
and remembering to exaggerate her accent for his benefit.
"What terrible misfortune! *Perdóneme por favor.* You are not
hurt? Please accept my apologies. My maid, of course, had no
idea that anyone was passing by. I am entirely to blame, for I
distracted her just as she started to go out."

His eyes locked with hers, and the intensity of his gaze surprised her. Undoubtedly the glance lasted no more than a second, but it felt longer, as if he were studying her.

"Rest assured that I am perfectly fine, madam," he said,
"although I admit my attire may appear somewhat less than
presentable at this moment." His voice was pleasantly deep
and resonant.

"You must allow me to pay for the damage to your—uh,
your coat," Falcon murmured, realizing suddenly that she
must have been the one staring. Stained or not, his pantaloons
fit his muscled legs exquisitely. She shifted her gaze to the
wreckage on the floor.

"I have other, uh, coats," he said. "Nor need you be overly
concerned with replacing our host's fine China-ware, in my
opinion."

She looked up. "Fine . . . ? Oh." She realized belatedly that
he was speaking in jest, probably in an effort to reassure her.
The inn's dishes were hardly of the best quality. She smiled,
and the answering smile he bestowed upon her was so daz-
zling it nearly took her breath away.

Benita's weeping had meanwhile subsided to sniffles. As
she began to pick up the broken pieces of crockery, the gentleman turned his attention back to her. Astonishingly—and
quite contrary to Falcon's expectation—he sketched a slight
bow to the maid and extended his hand to assist her up.

"Are you quite all right, young woman?" he asked.

"She does not understand English," Falcon explained. "You
are kind to ask, however." She repeated his question in Spanish and was relieved when Benita nodded.

"Sure, the poor girl is frightened, that is all," Maggie said,
efficiently shifting Falcon to one side and setting to the task
of assisting the maid. As she bent down she reverted to speak-

ing Spanish in an unusually formal tone. "Watch your skirts, miss, or they'll get into this mess."

The words were meant to convey a warning, but Falcon chose to ignore it. She did not care at that moment if she was behaving improperly for her role as a Spanish doña. She was quite charmed by the gentleman's unexpected kindness and humor.

You are disobeying every possible rule of propriety, said a little voice that might have been Maggie's but wasn't. *What am I supposed to do?* Falcon argued with herself. *Ignore the entire problem, simply because the gentleman and I have not been introduced?*

The innkeeper himself and one of the maids appeared in the passageway then. Falcon was not the least surprised to see them.

"Here, what's all this?" the man demanded.

Falcon sighed. He had pegged her for trouble, and now here she was. . . .

"I will pay for the damages—" she began, but the unnamed gentleman who had been the victim of the disaster cut her off.

"*I* will pay for the damage," he said. "It was simply an accident—an unfortunate consequence of bad timing."

"I cannot possibly allow you—" Falcon began again, and again he cut her off.

"Please. I insist. You are obviously a visitor to our country. If nothing else, consider it a gesture of hospitality. What happened was no one's fault." He turned to the innkeeper. "I will take care of this matter with you directly. My dinner should already be awaiting me downstairs. At the moment, however, I must repair to my room for obvious reasons."

He bowed to Falcon. As he turned to go, the chambermaid handed him his hat, retrieved from the floor of the passageway. It appeared to be the only item of his clothing which had escaped from the accident quite unscathed.

"Now that was a fine, handsome gentleman," Maggie declared a short while later, after the mess had been cleared away and some sherry and a new pot of tea delivered.

"Handsome and high-handed," Falcon replied with a sniff of disdain, "and that is as much as we know about him. Just another English stranger." If only she truly felt that! Perhaps

if she denied the attraction she'd felt, she would soon forget
him.

"I cannot possibly allow him to pay for the damages, of
course. It is just as well that I had one last word with our
wretched host. Honestly, Maggie, I will be very glad to quit
this place and be on our way to London in the morning." At
least that much was true. She poured a generous amount of
sherry into one teacup and passed it to her companion.

"What you need to do is find a fine young gentleman like
that and settle down," Maggie said, nodding sagely as she accepted the cup.

"Fine young gentleman, indeed. Is that why you were trying to impress him with what a lady I was supposed to be? He
wasn't all that young, and I doubt he understood your Spanish. Please don't start with this again, Maggie! You know we
have had this conversation before." Falcon poured another
portion of sherry, which she handed to Benita. The maid
perched beside Maggie in obvious discomfort on the edge of
the well-worn settee, where Falcon had insisted she join them.
Behind them a fire crackled in the grate.

"I have too much anger bottled up in my heart to make
room for any other emotions," Falcon said, pouring a portion
for herself. "And I haven't even the use of my own name.
How could I marry? What sort of wife could I be to anyone?"

"Once you've settled this business that's brought ye here,
you might feel differently."

"Once I have settled this business, I expect to go back to
Spain. I still won't belong here."

As far as Falcon was concerned, she had no connections in
England other than Triss. Her English relatives had rejected
her father and cut him off over his insistence on an Irish
wife—her mother. She did not know them and did not wish
to.

In Spain she had Carmen Serrano-Bonastre, who had been
like a sister to her, and Carmen's parents, Don Andrés and
Doña Luisa, who had taken responsibility for her at Carmen's
insistence. They had treated her almost like family and Falcon
believed that they had truly become fond of her. But then,
there was the problem of Carmen's brother Ramon Alonso,
who had become too fond of her.

"Why would you go back to Spain after all that you have suffered there?" Maggie asked.

I don't belong in Spain. I don't belong anywhere, Falcon thought, but she did not want to reveal the desperation she felt inside. She sipped her sherry thoughtfully, letting its warmth filter through her. No place had ever been home to her—as a "daughter of the regiment" she had moved with her officer father's battalion wherever they were assigned. "Home" had been embodied in the loving presence of her parents. She had lost it along with them in a few moments of senseless violence.

She shut her mind to the memory of that day, focusing only on the anger that had supplanted her grief. Maggie would never understand. The three men who had killed Falcon's parents had to be found. *I will see them pay or die trying,* she vowed, not for the first time. She would not be distracted by handsome gentlemen strangers or worries about the future.

Maggie's question still hung awkwardly in the silence caused by Falcon's thoughts. "Maybe I'll go to Ireland and see my mother's country, instead," she answered finally, just to say something. "In the meantime, the only place we're going is London. We've a long day of travel ahead of us tomorrow. I suggest we make certain to get a good night's rest."

"Amen to that," Maggie said, holding up her empty cup for a refill.

When they came down to settle their bill after breakfast the next morning, they found the "fine gentleman" waiting for them.

"I did not like to trouble them with too much food in our room this morning, after the problem last night," Falcon was saying to Maggie in Spanish as they descended the steep and poorly lit stairway, "but can you imagine them not having chocolate? I never realized how many habits I developed living in Spain."

"Plenty of rich English take chocolate for breakfast, child. This is a poor excuse for an inn, in an out-of-the-way village . . ."

The conversation halted abruptly as Jeremy appeared at the foot of the stairs.

"Good morning to you, ladies," he said quite soberly. "I hope you will forgive my intrusion—I wanted to be certain that no one had suffered any ill effects after the mishap last evening."

In truth, the lieutenant major had more on his mind than that alone, but it was a good beginning. Certainly the ladies looked none the worse for their upset. His lady from Spain looked more elegant and attractive than ever, although perhaps that was only because he now knew what charms lay hidden beneath her black mantilla. After the disaster in the doorway, he had seen clearly that she was every bit as beautiful as he had guessed she might be, with skin like ivory and glorious hair the reddish color of almost ripe chestnuts. This morning she was dressed in a stylish black pelisse and she did not have the veil covering quite so much of her face.

"Benita is perfectly well this morning, sir," she told him, "thanks to your kindness in not blaming her. I believe that was her greatest fear. But it is we who should be inquiring after you, I am certain, for what happened was my fault, and it was you who suffered grievously. Are you well enough this morning?"

Jeremy flashed his notable grin and held out his arms to display his coat. "As you may see, I am spotless this morning and have suffered not at all. It takes a good deal more than an unfortunate encounter with a dinner tray to ruffle my feathers." He was intrigued that she did not giggle and turn her eyes away from his immodest display.

In truth, his feathers had been considerably ruffled by the disruption of his plans. He had not intended to come face-to-face with the subject of his investigation at such an early stage in the game. Yet, in the end, he thought the mishap had worked to his advantage. He had gotten a good look at the mysterious doña and learned that she was much younger than he had supposed. Certainly that gave weight to the theory that she was the señorita of the letters after all.

Like any good agent, he had readjusted his plans. Now that contact had been made, however inadvertently, he fully intended to pursue it.

"I wanted to warn you not to allow the innkeeper to charge you for the damages from last night," he said, lowering his voice. "I have paid him, but I would not be surprised if he tried to collect twice."

"Twice? Oh, I see. Thank you for the warning," Falcon said in surprise. "I would never have considered that. Impertinent man! I thought I had arranged matters with him that I would pay! I shall demand at once that he refund your money."

"Please do not do that." Extraordinary as her behavior had been at times, he doubted that she would haggle over finances with a stranger in a public inn. He could not allow her to pay, for although he could not say so, the accident had truly been his fault. "Allow me the honor of taking care of it. It is only a trifling matter. I can see that you are ready to make your departure, and this would only delay you."

He hoped that she would happen to confide her destination to him, for although Nicholson had already reported to him earlier that she had hired a carriage for London, Jeremy could not reveal that he knew this. His new plan depended entirely upon furthering their contact in town.

"Yes, we are headed for London," she replied innocently enough, and Jeremy hid his sense of triumph behind what he hoped was a perfectly normal smile. He pushed the nagging thought that this was once again all too easy into the back recesses of his mind.

"Why, I am headed that way myself," he said, feigning surprise at the coincidence. "Would you permit me to present you with my card? If you should find yourself in need of assistance of any kind at all while you are there, I would be honored to be of service."

He fished in his pocket and withdrew the card he had put there earlier, one of the various cards he kept to fit appropriate circumstances. In this instance he planned to take full advantage of the fact that he was well known in London as Lord Danebridge. It was, in fact, his legitimate title, as the rank of baron had been awarded to his great-grandfather by King George II.

The young woman took the card and read it. She looked impressed, as he had hoped she would. "Lord Danebridge? I am certain the honor must be ours. I am Doña Sofia Alomar de Montero. This is my companion, Mrs. Meara."

He decided to see how far he could press his advantage. "A

pleasure, indeed, ladies. Where will you be staying in London?"

"A friend has recommended lodgings."

Her tone left it quite clear that she would not reveal more, and he decided he could not push for more without arousing suspicion. Nicholson would have to take care of that detail by following them to London.

He nodded. "That is always a wise course, rather than taking a chance on some unknown establishment. There are parts of London you should definitely avoid."

She tucked his card into her reticule. "As is the case in any large city. I have heard much of London and I look forward to seeing it. We must be on our way if we wish to do so, however—our carriage is waiting and I still must settle my account."

Impossibly green eyes held his for a moment. "I apologize again for that distressing incident last evening. Thank you for your generosity in that matter and also for offering your assistance if we should need it in London. You are indeed a gentleman."

Did he detect a note of regret in her voice? Or was that merely his male pride influencing his perceptions? She was a very lovely woman. What man would not like to think that she might be a tiny bit sorry at having to part?

He bowed. Acknowledging him with a nod, she disappeared into the inn's parlor to settle with their host, followed by her two women. Once they had gone in, Jeremy donned his tall beaver and ducked out the back door that opened into the stableyard.

Nicholson was relaxing on a bale of straw, chatting amiably with two of the stablehands. Doña Alomar's London carriage stood at the ready, the postboy waiting at the horses' heads and her male servant checking the luggage strapped on behind. Jeremy waited by the door until Nicholson glanced his way. Then he raised his hat in the prearranged signal that told Nicholson what he must do. The husky fellow levered himself up from the bale and moved casually to the back of the stables, where his saddled horse no doubt stood ready, too.

Nicholson would have to be careful not to be seen by the lady's servants, whose acquaintance he had so carefully cultivated. It would be up to him not only to discover where in London the little party was bound, but also to arrange matters so as to make certain that they would need Jeremy's able assistance once they had arrived there.

Jeremy had a good deal to do himself, including writing a letter to his son with some excuse for the delay in his arrival. Still he decided to stay in the yard and see the lady off first. He felt quite confident that this would not be the last she would see of him.

Chapter Four

London loomed mysterious, wreathed in fog. Mist had graced the countryside all day as Falcon and her companions traveled from Wiltshire, but it had been harmless—thin and light, floating above the fields and just softening the edges of the hilltop views. Now it seemed to have collected, concentrated, in the streets and alleyways of the great city, obscuring grand buildings and famous sights along with scenes of squalor as the travelers completed their journey.

"'Tisn't much of an introduction to the grand town, now, is it?" Maggie sniffed in disdain. "We'll be lucky if we can find our way, never mind escape bein' set upon by footpads or brigands."

"I don't mind it," Falcon replied, smiling. "Think of all the times we would have blessed this cool moisture when the summer sun beat down upon us in Spain." She was simply relieved that they had found a hackney to take them and their luggage from the last posting inn to their final destination. "It is already so late, I doubt we would have seen much more of the city than this without the fog. Night will soon be upon us. Perhaps tomorrow we can take in some of the sights."

In truth, the fog struck Falcon as rather appropriate for her arrival in London. It was so utterly English, and it seemed to symbolize her future. The course she must follow now was as uncertain as the road before them or the direction of their lodgings.

The ancient hackney they had hired came to a halt as their coachman sought directions from the driver of a heavily loaded dray. In this street there was barely enough room for the carriage to pass, unlike some of the wider thoroughfares they had already traversed.

"I hope the lodgings Triss recommended are as suitable as

he claimed," Falcon commented, looking about her. "After all, he did admit that he has not been to London in some time."

In the fog it was quite impossible to tell what sort of neighborhood they had entered, but some indeterminate sense had begun to make her feel uneasy. For a fleeting moment she wished they had the company of a capable gentleman like Lord Danebridge along. His handsome image had plagued her thoughts for much of the day, for no particularly good reason. He was attractive; she had liked him. That was all. He was irrelevant to her life and should remain so! *Had she not come this far on her own? Why should she need him, or anyone?*

She tried to tell herself the uneasy feeling was only the natural consequence of her state of mind, anxious as she was over what lay ahead for her in the coming days. But then quite suddenly she realized what was wrong.

"This does not *smell* like a good neighborhood," she stated. *"Esta vecindad no me huele muy bien."*

Benita only nodded, but Maggie took a deep whiff.

"Ugh. 'Tis smellin' like cooked cabbage and filth, now that you mention it, child. But faith, we're not stoppin' here."

Their coachman urged the horses forward and the hackney moved on down the street, turning left at the next corner. Falcon and Maggie's relief was short-lived, however. The smell was no better where their vehicle halted a few blocks further on.

"I do hope this is a mistake," Falcon said, straightening her mantilla and preparing to get out. They had stopped opposite a very tall, narrow, shabby-looking house, so dingy gray that it and its neighbors almost blended entirely with the fog.

Maggie gathered her cloak around her. "Ye'll not be going to that door, young lady. 'Tisn't seemly. I shall go. Carlos can come with me."

Falcon swallowed her protest and watched Maggie bravely march up to the door of the shadowy building with Carlos close behind her. What a pair they made! The tall, lame Irishwoman with wisps of gray hair sticking out from her bonnet, and the short, slightly built Spaniard. What Carlos lacked in stature he more than made up in ferocity, while Maggie was a woman whose determination alone could probably shatter iron. *Anyone with a brain in his head could see that those two are a force to be reckoned with.* Falcon smiled and relaxed a tiny bit at the thought.

The expression on Maggie's face when she returned to the hackney showed that no mistake had been made, however.

"Oh, 'tis the place, no question," she grumbled, signaling that Falcon and Benita should descend from the carriage. "To be sure, the mistake was lettin' that Cornishman of yours be tellin' us where we should stay in London. Hmph! 'Tis nothing like a respectable hotel—'tis naught but a seedy lodgin' house at best, and at this moment I'm having trouble thinkin' that!"

"Maggie, what choice had we?" Falcon shared the Irishwoman's misgivings, but she would not let her blame Triss. "We knew of no other place to stay, and Triss needed to know where to find us when he arrives in the city."

"Aye, more's the pity."

The women moved to the back of the hackney to take what small articles of baggage they could carry. Carlos picked up one of the trunks and followed them up the steps into the building. The hackney driver made no move to assist them.

The house was as dingy inside as it had appeared on the outside. The odor of ale permeated the place, and as Falcon paused in the stair passageway and looked into what she assumed was a ground-floor parlor, she was taken aback to see several gentlemen seated about the small room, drinking and quite apparently waiting for something. They looked at her with interest.

"Maggie," she began, but just then a small, neatly dressed, rather officious blond-haired woman came into the passage from the back of the house. The men in the parlor began to hoot and call to her amid much laughter.

"Annie, oh, Annie! What about us, Annie?"

She ignored them completely. "I just want you to know this is highly irregular," she said in a thin, nasal whine. "We don't usually have any rooms available. I've put you on the third floor, top o' the stairs. Watch the carpet there, it slips. And you have to pay in advance."

With that rather extraordinary speech, she placed one hand on her left hip and held out the other for payment.

"The third floor?" Falcon said in dismay, thinking of Carlos and the heavy luggage. He had deposited the trunk and gone out again to retrieve the rest of their luggage from the hackney. "How much must we pay? We are not certain how many nights we will be here." There was no question it would be as few as possible.

As she fished in her reticule for money, her fingers brushed against Lord Danebridge's card, reminding her of his offer of assistance. *Perhaps I could just ask him to recommend some better accommodations.* She did not think such a request would place her under obligation to him. Obviously, her unfamiliarity with London had already put her little group at a disadvantage, but they could move as soon as Triss joined them.

She paid the landlady for two nights in advance, refusing to pay more, and went back outside to settle her account with their driver. If only Carlos spoke English! He could have handled that transaction himself. A flurry of his excited Spanish was the first thing she heard as she stepped out the door, however.

"Mequetrefe! Imbécil! No oiste nada? Como pudo pasar esto?" Clearly agitated, Carlos was pacing, gesturing frantically with his arms and heaping verbal abuse on the hackney driver, who of course understood nothing.

"Carlos, what has happened?" Falcon asked in Spanish.

"The small trunk, mistress. It has disappeared, and this idiot has been sitting here the whole time!"

A glance behind the carriage confirmed that the trunk was no longer there. Falcon felt a painful twisting sensation in the pit of her stomach. Heavens! The trunk had been there just minutes ago. She could not believe that it was now gone, yet her eyes did not deceive her. She turned to the hackney driver, still sitting on his perch.

"My servant is shouting at you because our trunk has disappeared from behind this vehicle in just these two minutes. Did you see no one? Did you hear nothing? I cannot believe you simply sat there while someone stole our luggage!"

Falcon peered at the man in the deepening gloom, trying to get a good look at his face. To his credit, he looked genuinely surprised.

"What? D'you mean someone's nipped yer trunk while I sat right 'ere waitin'? Impossible!" Nothing for it but the fellow must climb down himself to look, and of course he saw nothing once he had done so.

"It was right there," Falcon said, pointing to the now-empty pavement. "Did you notice no one?"

"There's been people about, gents walking by, a few carts and carriages and such. I didn't notice no one stopping."

"This is terrible." She felt truly shaken. The smaller trunk contained her mother's emeralds and most of the money Don Andrés had given her. Without those, she did not know how she would go on.

"You all right, ma'am?"

She shook her head. A slight trembling was beginning to take hold of her limbs. "I hardly know what to do."

"Y' might try reporting to a constable or the night watch, but in these parts of the city that trunk's likely gone, ma'am, slipped down a side alley quick as a wink. But I swear I never heard a thing. I'm right sorry."

The trunk was gone, she had no doubt. Her fingers shook as she counted out the money to pay the man his fare. He had done nothing to deserve a tip, yet she could not quite bring herself to deny him one. In such a place, perhaps he did not dare to leave his coach unattended long enough to help his passengers!

With a heavy heart, she followed Carlos back into the so-called lodging house. Ignoring comments and verbal invitations from the occupants of the parlor, she made her way up what seemed like an endless, dark stairway. Muffled laughter and indistinct murmurs of conversation emanated from the rooms on the floors she passed. Maggie and Benita were waiting at the top.

"There's two small rooms, both furnished up as bedrooms, and this alcove by the landing," Maggie reported. "No sitting room at all. It has the look of servants' quarters to me." Under her breath she fussed, "Lodging house, my eye! Bawdy house is more the like. Saints preserve us!"

Falcon sighed. "I know, Maggie. Carlos can make a pallet for himself in the alcove using our cloaks and some of the bedclothes once he has finished bringing up the luggage. I do not trust our landlady or any of the other people I've seen in this house. I will sleep better if I know we have a guard at the top of the stairs."

There was no use in delaying the news of what had happened. "One of my trunks has been stolen—right from behind the hackney," she said, repeating the words in Spanish so Benita could understand. "With it we have lost most of our funds! We must be grateful that we at least have a roof over our heads."

Carlos had followed Falcon up the stairs, clutching the remaining trunk as if he feared it, too, would disappear. As Benita and Maggie reacted with shock to her news, Falcon directed him to carry it into the first of the bedrooms.

She closed her eyes for a moment, fighting the fatigue that seemed to have crept unnoticed into every muscle in her body. With the money gone, what should she do? Maggie, Benita and Carlos were dependent upon her, and Triss was in no position to assist her, much as he might wish to.

She would think of something. Had she not learned to rely on herself during her years in Spain? She had also learned not to be too proud to accept help when she needed it. She might have no choice but to seek it from Lord Danebridge, since she knew no one else. Perhaps their meeting had been fortuitous after all. While she could not ask him for money, he might be able to help her to find a teaching position, or at least to send word of her trouble to Don Andrés. Could he be trusted? There was no way to know. However, there was another problem. Lord Danebridge had neglected to say how soon he would be arriving in London, and she had not thought to inquire. . . .

Lieutenant Major Jeremy Hazelton, Lord Danebridge, turned his curricle into Portman Square at an hour close to midnight. The fog had not abated, and its heavy veil confined the light from the streetlamps in pale golden clouds which illuminated nothing beyond their own spheres. Despite this, the streets of the fashionable West End were busy with the social comings and goings of London's Beau Monde. Jeremy was pleased to end his journey without mishap at a modest town house in Fitzharding Street just off the square.

He shook the dampness from the topmost shoulder cape of his greatcoat as he entered and handed a hat beaded with moisture to the waiting footman.

"Good evening, John. It is John, isn't it?"

"Evenin', sir. Yes, indeed, you've a good memory, sir."

The house could only have been opened a few hours earlier, yet there was no sign of it. All the Holland covers had disappeared from the furniture in the front reception room, and a cheerful fire blazed in the hearth. The place was not Jeremy's own, but it would serve. There were definite advantages to being employed by the government.

"Your man Nicholson is awaiting you in the library, sir. Said you'd prefer it to the drawing room."

"Have we someone to take my vehicle 'round to the livery?"

"Oh, yes indeed, sir—you've a full staff at your disposal."

"So soon? Excellent."

In the library he found Nicholson comfortably established in a wing chair with his feet up on a cushioned footstool, a book in one hand and a glass in the other.

"I'm not certain who it is that prefers the library to the drawing room, Nicholson my friend, but I must say you look content."

Nicholson scrambled to his feet instantly, looking somewhat but not by any means completely abashed.

"Uh, sorry, sir. Wasn't sure what time you'd get in, you know."

"At ease, man. I was not voicing a complaint." Jeremy settled himself wearily into the matching partner to the wing chair. "Have we another glass like that one?"

"We do. And some fine brandy to put in it." Putting action to his words, Nicholson moved to the table where the decanter and glasses sat in state and poured Jeremy a drink.

The lieutenant major waited until the other man had delivered the drink and resumed his seat before beginning to question him.

"So, any trouble on your way in today? Fog like this can be a help or a hindrance, but I know you, Nicholson. You always complete your assignments. Your record is unmatched."

"Except by yours, sir."

"Of course. That's because we work together." Jeremy sipped his brandy, savoring the flavor. It was undoubtedly French, very fine, certainly smuggled in. The irony of having it provided by the very government that worked so hard against the smugglers was not lost on him. "I assume you have something to report?"

"Yes, sir."

Silence followed.

"Well, am I to know what it is, man? Tonight?" Jeremy could not understand his assistant's hesitation. "Are you waiting for the clock to strike or the cock to crow?"

He was usually the soul of patience. The only excuse he had for the lack of it now was his own tiredness and his lack of success in convincing his superiors earlier in the evening that this entire business was a waste of his time and their resources. They had insisted that he continue to investigate the mysterious señora. They had reliable information that a foreign agent had been due to enter the country on the date she arrived, and they had only one other suspect under surveillance. The fact that she had aroused the suspicions of the captain on her own ship sufficiently for him to forward a warning counted a great deal in their books.

Jeremy doubted whether they had considered how quick such a captain might have been to see a spy in anyone slightly questionable just to earn the informant's reward. Still, he had no answers to explain the inconsistencies in the lady's behavior or the oddities among her luggage. Something was havey-cavey—he just did not know what.

"The lady and her servants are staying in a fancy-house near Covent Garden," Nicholson said all in a rush.

"What?"

"I knew you would not be pleased."

"Do you mean to say we are going to all this trouble over a common prostitute? I do not believe it!" No prostitute that beautiful would have remained attached to a fancy-house for long. Besides, this woman had just arrived from Spain. Once again Jeremy found himself thrown off balance.

"I couldn't say, sir. But that is where they are staying."

Frowning, Jeremy set down his glass and got up to pace aimlessly on the Turkish carpet, weaving a path around the library table and assorted leather-backed chairs. "This is a turn I certainly did not foresee."

"No, sir."

"Did you take care of the other matter?"

"I believe so. One of her trunks happened to disappear in the fog. It should set her back a bit. We were fortunate enough to get the one containing her money and jewels, just as you described them."

Only now it might be irrelevant. "Hm. No one saw you?"

"No. We used the passing pedestrians trick. Had the cart coming from the other direction just at the right moment—all they had to do was heft the trunk up in and continue on their way, all done in a matter of seconds."

"Nice work. Certainly under our previous assumptions that loss should have created a sufficient problem to make her seek assistance. Now we shall have to see what happens."

Could it be that she was a common light-skirt who had made good in Spain? The country had been crawling with Frenchmen, but the idea seemed preposterous. There was nothing common about her. He had seen for himself that she was exquisite, and she spoke two languages fluently in an educated manner. Had she been a high-priced Incognita, perhaps? Or merely a high-class thief? Both? Perhaps nothing in those trunks was really hers at all. *Perhaps that is how she became a spy.*

He shook his head in frustration. Could he have so misread her character? Their two encounters had been extremely brief, but he was supposed to have some skill in that area. What was she doing in a fancy-house? No, cancel that—he could well imagine, and did not want to imagine, although certain images seemed to come all too easily. Rather, why was she there? He would wager the sum of the highest purse at Newmarket that she was no doxy.

You could make use of her services. The thought came unbidden into his mind despite his instinct that she was not in the trade. Ungentlemanly though it might be, the idea did not displease him. His pulse beat a little faster. Sometimes circumstances victimized a better class of women—where else did all the elegant demireps come from?

He did need another approach to follow if she did not come to him for aid, and in view of Nicholson's information that original plan now seemed unlikely. Jeremy could send a man to keep watch, learn the places she went, and then contrive to run into her quite accidentally. It would not seem unnatural to pursue their acquaintance from there. If she was looking for a new protector, she might be very receptive indeed.

"Have a man assigned to watch her," he said, returning to his seat at last.

"Already done," Nicholson replied. "Figured I'd call him off if that was not what you wanted."

Jeremy raised his eyebrows. "Old fellow, I can't decide if I'm looking forward to recovering my civilian life and being independent from you, or whether I'll feel as though half of my brain has been left behind. Do you already know what I am going to do next?"

Nicholson grinned. "I believe, sir, that you are going to finish your drink and then retire for the night."

Jeremy did. Before he claimed his bed, however, he wrote another letter to his son in Hertfordshire and tried to turn his thoughts to his plans for the future once he was free of this final duty. Part of those plans included looking for a wife. Anne would have wanted him to remarry, and Toby needed a mother. Jeremy's own mother could not take charge of the boy forever.

What Jeremy wanted was someone stable, respectable, and capable of managing his household. Perversely, when he finally lay down his sleep was plagued by dreams of luminous green eyes and a beautiful, mysterious lady who eluded his grasp at every step.

Chapter Five

Falcon arrived at Lord Danebridge's door the following morning with her chin high and her maid hovering in her shadow. Unwilling to leave her two Spanish-speaking servants to the questionable mercy of their landlady, she had convinced Maggie to stay behind with Carlos and had taken Benita with her instead.

The pair had already suffered a humiliating start to their day searching the dismal slum around their lodgings for a hackney or a food vendor, whichever they could find first. The warren of narrow streets and alleys filled with shabby buildings and equally shabby inhabitants yielded nothing to the two well-dressed women except stares and lewd comments. *Certainly Triss could not have known what a place he had sent them to!* Only when they finally reached a main thoroughfare had they discovered a hackney stand at last and escaped from the rudeness they'd met in the streets.

Of course, their driver had nodded his head knowingly when Falcon gave him Lord Danebridge's Mayfair address. When she loftily informed him that she had business to conduct there, he had fixed her with a look that made her cheeks flame.

Still seething at the unspoken insult, Falcon now gathered her remaining dignity about her like a cloak as she seized the polished brass knocker and rapped briskly on the door of number 14 Fitzharding Street. Likely the servant about to answer would think ill of her as well, calling at a gentleman's home and at such an early hour, but at least he would not know what neighborhood she had come from.

The glossy painted door with its gleaming appointments opened at last, revealing a surprised footman. Falcon quickly handed him Lord Danebridge's card, on which she had scribbled her assumed Spanish name.

"I have business with Lord Danebridge," she said, noting that the young man's raised eyebrows remained fixed in their questioning position. "I have come to inquire when you expect him to arrive, for I happen to know he was on his way to London."

The fellow glanced down at the card in his hand. "I'm sorry, madam—uh, señora. I shall inquire." He hesitated, and Falcon knew very well that he was deciding whether to shut the door, leaving her and Benita standing on the steps, or whether to invite her in. She stiffened her spine and attempted to look down her nose at the man.

"I trust you are not contemplating leaving us standing here like common tradesmen while you do so," she said in her most condescending tone.

The door opened wider and she swept in, trailed by her maid. The footman ushered them into the handsomely appointed reception room to the right of the passage and left them.

An elegant pair of settees covered in cream-colored striped silk faced each other in the center of the room. Falcon sat down on one of them for nearly an entire minute. She indicated to Benita that she should sit also and then jumped up again from her own seat. How long could it take for an English servant to learn the answer to a simple question?

She prowled restlessly around the perimeter of the room, looking at porcelain figurines on the tabletops and framed sporting pictures on the walls. They were undoubtedly of fine quality but seemed randomly selected and conveyed no sense of their owner. Was this the English sense of style? She had not forgotten the look of English rooms, with their chimneyed fireplaces and double-hung windows so different from the Spanish, but it surprised her how foreign she felt in this elegant, impersonal room.

After several more minutes passed she began to wonder in earnest what might be keeping the footman from returning. An ominous grumbling from the region of her stomach reminded her that neither she nor Benita had eaten. An equally hungry Maggie and Carlos were waiting for them back at their lodgings. Falcon had promised to bring food when they returned.

There is only enough money for a few days, she reflected, staring at a scene of a swarming pack of hunting dogs without seeing it at all. Last night's wrenching loss of her funds had made her aware of every penny she spent, and the distance to Lord Danebridge's house in the West End had been much farther and more expensive than she'd expected. What would she do if Lord Danebridge could not help her?

With a sigh she turned away from the picture and began to wander about the room again, studying the patterns in the Turkish carpet. She had lost so much more than simply money! She had felt last night as if the last shreds of her heart had been lost with the miniature portraits of her parents and the few of their belongings that had been in that trunk.

Falcon's mother had given her the heirloom pearl and emerald jewelry on her fourteenth birthday and had instructed her to someday give it to a daughter of her own. It was the last time they had celebrated together. The Bible and the rosary had been her mother's, too, and the miniatures had been a gift from her father.

Falcon had let the tears come briefly during the night, but now she could not afford the luxury of grief. She must think!

"Doña Alomar?"

She started at the sound of her borrowed name and looked up. Lord Danebridge himself stood in the doorway.

"Lord Danebridge! ¡Cielos! You must please excuse me. I never expected—that is, I did not think—oh, my. I had no idea that you would be here. So soon, I mean. Already. I would never have called at such an hour—that is to say . . ."

She managed to close her mouth before any more gibberish came out of it. Her pulse was doing a wild dance—no doubt from embarrassment and surprise—while her cheeks burned from blushing. Why had it never occurred to her that he might have already arrived? Just because they had traveled from the same place in Wiltshire on the same day and never once crossed paths or saw each other?

"I must say this is an unexpected pleasure. Unexpected apparently for both of us. You called because you did not think I would be here?" He advanced into the room, sounding more amused than puzzled. "Shall we be seated?"

He moved with the smooth grace and assurance of a fine

athlete, Falcon thought. She nodded and looked nervously behind her for the settee where she had perched so briefly earlier. Seldom had she ever felt quite such a fool. Benita, bless her, had risen upon his entrance and moved to an unobtrusive position near the window.

Lord Danebridge sat upon the settee across from Falcon. For a moment he just studied her. She frantically tried to organize her thoughts.

"I don't know how—" she began.

He started speaking at the same instant. "I don't know—"

They both broke off, and he chuckled, a rich, pleasant sound that was deep, like his voice. Falcon swallowed. Why was she so distracted by him? She tried again.

"I must apologize! I don't quite know how to explain. I never expected that I might need to consider your offer of assistance yesterday morning as anything more than a polite gesture. It was, of course, very polite, and very generous . . ." She was floundering again. She did not want to sound unappreciative. She was afraid she sounded completely rattle-brained.

Jeremy watched her struggle and decided to take pity on her. He gave her an encouraging smile. "But now you find that you are in need of some assistance, is that it?"

She had the grace to color again and look at the floor. If she was not genuinely distressed by all this, she was a consummate actress. But then, of course, a good agent would need to be. He truly was not certain who was duping whom in this game they were playing. If it was a game, of course. He still could not shake off the feeling that she was an innocent caught up in circumstances far beyond her control. Surely the fact that she had come seeking help after all counted for something?

"I began to say that I don't know quite the proper way to handle a business call from a lady so early in the day." *At least, not a respectable lady.* "I think we are both feeling deucedly awkward. As I have not yet breakfasted, what would you say to my having a tray brought in here? Would you partake of some refreshments?"

There was no mistaking the look that clouded her green eyes or the quick glance that darted to her maid. He would wager the crown jewels that they had not eaten. Dear God, had she no money at all? He felt a momentary stab of guilt.

She stood. "I, we, that is, no—we mustn't keep you from your breakfast. This is unforgivable. Truly, we only came by to learn when your staff were expecting you—I never dreamed that you meant to be in London so quickly! Perhaps—perhaps we could call back later. No—I should send round a note, I suppose. Oh, I am so very sorry to be troubling you!"

Jeremy admired the señora's show of pride and apparent concern for propriety, whether or not they were genuine. Although his attention was fixed upon the young woman opposite him, he caught the faintest sound from the maid by the window—a tiny note of disappointment, protest, or frustration—he could not quite tell which. He decided to try a bold move.

"Please, señora, I can see that you are distraught." He had risen when she did, and now he approached her and gently took the hands she had clenched in front of her between his own. "Since you are already here, does it not make more sense to simply proceed with the business that brought you here? I insist that you stay long enough to at least have—let me see, would a cup of chocolate tempt you? You can tell me how I may help you."

Watching her eyes was like looking into her soul. Jeremy did not think any actress could have pretended the conflict he saw there. She was clearly surprised and shocked when he so improperly touched her, yet she did not pull away from him instantly. She seemed to weigh his suggestion. He thought he saw trust battling with suspicion and prudence battling temptation.

He released her hands the moment she did try to reclaim them, and then he tried to pretend that nothing untoward at all had occurred. But it was not true. Something had happened to him the moment he had taken her hands into his, and he felt quite shaken. Something had moved in him, some stone from the walls of his heart, perhaps, and like a hot coal dropped on tinder it had kindled both a feeling of protectiveness and a spark of desire.

Absurd, of course! He did not even know the woman. She might be a spy or she might be seeking a protector of a very different sort. And to feel protective of her went beyond absurd, since he was the one who was investigating her, had ordered her trunk stolen, and yes, was even considering seducing her if it would help him to learn who she was. What a villain he had learned to be!

As she turned away from him he saw the surrender on her face. "I suppose it does make sense, since we are already here." She sat down again upon the settee. "We have already disturbed you."

In more ways than you know, he thought grimly. He stepped to the bellpull and rang for his servants, then resumed his seat across from her.

She raised her chin and looked directly at him. He saw defiance in her green eyes.

"I am sorry to say that since arriving in London we are most unexpectedly in need of assistance. You were generous enough to make your offer to complete strangers, and as I know no one in the city, I am forced to put that generosity to the test."

"My offer was sincerely meant, señora. What kind of people are we if we cannot welcome visitors to our land and offer whatever it is we might hope to receive if our positions were reversed?"

The question was rhetorical, of course. The conversation halted when his butler appeared at the door, but after instructing the fellow to have breakfast served to them in the reception room, Jeremy continued. "How may I be of service to you, Doña Alomar?"

She looked down at her lap. "The lodgings that were recommended to us have proven to be highly unsuitable. For one thing, I was hoping that you might be able to recommend something more, well, appropriate to a modest purse but at least respectable."

She flushed as she uttered the last phrase, and Jeremy found himself admiring her again. She was indeed beautiful. But he must react to her news.

"Where is it that you are currently lodged?" he asked in horrified tones.

"Near Covent Garden. The neighborhood is appalling and the house itself—well, I cannot say." She looked away, as if she could not bear to meet his gaze. Her embarrassment and distress seemed very believable.

He summoned all the indignation he could scrape together. "This was recommended to you by a friend? Certainly you must not stay there another day! I will have you moved out of there in the blink of an eye."

"Oh, no! I'm afraid we must stay until our friend arrives— he expects to find us there. I would not trust the landlady to deliver a message if we should remove before then. And I do not wish to impose upon you any more than I am already. But if you could suggest any more suitable establishment . . . ?"

"There is a house on Charles Street just a few blocks from here. It is run by an elderly widow whose reputation is impeccable."

A rattle of dishes and a discreet knock at the open door announced the arrival of breakfast. A virtual feast was brought in by a procession of several underservants supervised by the butler. Coffee, tea, and chocolate were arranged upon the side table while a card table from the corner was pulled closer to the center of the room and its leaves opened out to support loaded platters of ham, kippers, warm rolls and buttered eggs.

While the servants were at work, Jeremy had a moment to think. He would have to speak with the woman who ran the Charles Street lodging house and make some arrangement to procure "modest" rates. It was fortunate he had had occasion to use her establishment before—she might put a very wrong interpretation on his behavior if he were not known to her. He was also in no position to vouch for the señora's character. But it would be very helpful indeed to have a useful pair of eyes and ears inside the very house where the young lady from Spain would be lodging.

Once the servants had departed, he rose and began to fill a plate for his guest. "You said recommending lodging to you was one thing. Is there something more I can do?" Would she mention the trunk? Ask him for money? She had set him up nicely for that.

As he delivered her plate she looked up at him with eyes clouded by—what? Sorrow? Worry? Both?

"Perhaps you could give me some advice," she said,

scarcely noticing the plate of food. "We suffered another calamity—a part of my luggage was stolen. I must make every possible effort to recover it, but I have no idea how to proceed."

Was this distress genuine, or was she simply far more clever and subtle than he imagined? He played along. "What was lost?"

"A fair-sized trunk. It contained some valuable items. Do I have any recourse at all?"

He thought for a moment. An honest reply would be best. "Bow Street might be able to look into the matter. I doubt the trunk would be recovered, but the individual items might show up if the thieves try to sell them. Another possibility would be to advertise for the return of the trunk with its contents, and offer a sizable reward."

Hope brightened her eyes, but only for a moment. The light went out of them as she shook her head. "Without the trunk I am in no position to offer any reward, I fear. I will have to place my hopes on your Bow Street. What is it? The hackney driver mentioned some sort of patrol."

"It is a magistrate's court with its own force of officers. There are law agents who patrol the streets and runners who are thief-takers and skilled investigators."

"A patrol of such men would have been welcome indeed last night, but we saw no one."

"You will have to call there to fill out a report, and it is no place for an unescorted lady. Perhaps you would allow me to accompany you?"

She sighed. "You are very kind, and far too generous. It is too much to ask."

Not if you knew the truth, he thought guiltily. Aloud he said, "You have had a most unfortunate introduction to our city. You must allow me to do what I can to make amends."

She had not yet so much as touched her food. "Please, eat. I will feel the worst cad to eat in front of you otherwise, and I admit to being famished."

She picked up her fork and looked longingly at the food in front of her, yet still she did not eat.

"Is it not to your liking? I suppose English food is quite different from what you are accustomed to eating."

"It is not that." She appeared to be in an agony of indecision, glancing first at him and then in the direction of her patient maid, standing silently by the window. Finally she said, "Would you be horribly offended if I offered something to my maid? To be perfectly frank, we have neither of us broken our fast yet this morning, and I cannot bear to eat in front of her while she goes hungry."

For a moment he did not know what to say, he was so caught off guard. This woman fascinated him with her talent for doing and saying the unexpected. She was worried about the maid! He set his own plate aside immediately. "I will fix a plate for her myself."

Lord Danebridge not only fed Falcon and Benita but also insisted on transporting them back to their lodgings in his own carriage, by way of Bow Street. This was a great deal more help than Falcon had sought or expected, not to mention a great deal more time spent in the man's company, and she had objected.

She told herself afterward that she should have known better. After all, how well had she managed to prevail over him at the inn in Triss's village? Her determination to refuse was weakened by her awareness of the money he could save her—the considerable fare for a return hackney, after he had already saved her the cost of food for herself and Benita. But she was afraid to be under too great an obligation to him.

He had countered her every argument, agreeing to stop so she could purchase food for Carlos and Maggie and then to stop again at the lodgings to deliver it on their way to the Bow Street offices. She could not disagree when he pointed out that Bow Street had a better chance of helping her if she reported the stolen trunk as soon as possible. When she suggested that he might not wish to be seen in the vicinity of her lodgings, he only called for his carriage.

"You must consider, señora, that no one I know or who knows me is likely to be in that neighborhood, to begin with. Beyond that, I pay no heed to gossip unless it is of the most malicious kind. If that is the case, and I am the subject, I simply take steps to stop it."

"How do you do that?"

"Like most successful campaigns, it requires several methods in combination, both defensive and offensive."

It was not the first time he had made a comment that hinted at a military background. Falcon studied him surreptitiously as they made themselves ready and went out to climb into his carriage. During their meal she had been kept busy deflecting questions subtly designed to draw out information about herself, but a few times during the conversation she had noticed Lord Danebridge's use of terms or a turn of phrase that struck her as odd for a civilian.

Who was he really? What did she know about him? Nothing, in a word. She was supremely uncomfortable trusting him as much as she already had. Yet he had the strangest effect upon her, as if her mind became separated from her will whenever she looked into his gray eyes.

Like now, she thought as he turned to hand her up into the carriage. Their eyes locked momentarily as he took her hand into his.

The warmth of his touch affected her even more strangely, as it had for those moments in the reception room. Such brief, casual contact should not cause her blood to race nor her feelings to eclipse all rational thought! Her only hope was that he might not wish any further contact with her after helping her today.

Of course. That is just the reason he suggested lodgings only two blocks from his home, said the little voice in the back of her mind. Suddenly she wondered if taking up his suggestion would be so wise after all.

Chapter Six

"You and your maid are very much at risk in a neighborhood like this one," Lord Danebridge lectured Falcon when he returned her to her lodgings after their visit to Bow Street. "Are you certain you do not wish me to see you safely to your rooms?"

"It is not necessary, thank you," Falcon replied in a firm voice, appalled at the idea of him coming inside. She gave him her hand. "You have done so much already. You have upheld the honor of your countrymen in assisting a lady in distress! I appreciate it more than you can know."

To her relief, he seemed to recognize her dismissal. "It has been an honor to do so," he said, brushing her gloved fingertips with his lips. "But please, if you should need to venture out again today, promise me you will take your manservant with you, instead of your maid. He would be of far more use in case of trouble."

Falcon smiled politely and nodded, thinking that it was kind of him to care. Only afterward did she wonder how he knew she had a manservant.

The baron bowed and returned to his carriage where he waited, doubtless to see that she went safely inside.

The landlady met her in the passage. "There's a man waiting to see you in your rooms," she announced with an arrogant smirk, making Falcon doubly glad that Lord Danebridge was not still with her.

Falcon ignored the implication. "Triss!" Her visitor could not possibly be anyone else.

Her joy at the news of his arrival must have shown, for the other woman raised an eyebrow and gave her a peculiar look. "This one's nothing so grand as the one you just left, dearie. Now *there's* a fine gentleman—young and handsome, too."

I barely know him, Falcon almost said, but she stopped herself just in time. Such a reply would only seem to confirm what the landlady was already assuming. "It's not what you think," she said instead and hurried up the stairs with Benita behind her. She supposed she should only be grateful that the landlady had not made Triss await her in the seedy parlor with the other "gentlemen callers."

Carlos had stationed himself at the top of the stairs like a military guard and greeted Falcon respectfully. She nodded to Benita to signal her permission for the maid to stay and talk to him. She knew that Benita would regale him with a detailed account of everything that had transpired.

Triss was settled in a chair in the first bedroom, sharing what remained of the meager repast Falcon had delivered earlier and actually indulging in a cup of tea. Where the cups and teapot had come from Falcon did not know, but she guessed that Maggie had bullied the landlady into providing it. From the exaggerated sound of Maggie's lilting brogue and Triss's rumbling Cornish accent, she suspected that they might have "doctored" their tea with something a bit stronger.

Well, at least they have found something in common, she thought with a rush of affection. Such a pair of lovable rogues! She was smiling as she entered the room.

"B'gorra, if it isn't herself returned to us at last," Maggie said. "Greetings, lass. Do ye see who is here?"

Triss lumbered up from his seat to greet Falcon warmly, quite as if a week had passed instead of a day since he'd last seen her. But when he spoke to her his voice was gruff.

"Missy, you promised 'ee wouldn't do anything before I got 'ere—what 'ave 'ee got to say to that? As I understand it, you've been traipsing about the city already, to the West End, to Bow Street and who knows where else? Who is this fellow Lord Danebridge? What do 'ee know about 'im? 'As 'e got a Lady Danebridge?"

Had he? It was a perfectly reasonable question, Falcon realized. *Trust the sergeant to ask it!* She had seen no evidence of a woman's presence at the house in Fitzharding Street, but that did not signify much of anything. Lord Danebridge had not mentioned a wife, but that hardly signified, either. In truth, she did not know.

"He has done us a tremendous service today, for which we must be very grateful," she said. "Nothing else matters. I expect we shall have little contact with him from now on." Why had she not asked Lord Danebridge if he had a wife? She had speculated much about him, but she had not envisioned him with a family.

"He has recommended a respectable lodging house in a better part of the city, and he has helped me to take what steps I could to try to recover my stolen trunk. You did tell Triss what happened, Maggie?" There was no good reason for her to feel so ruffled over the idea of Lord Danebridge having a wife. Surely it meant nothing to her. She tried to put it out of her mind.

"Aye, I told him all about it, child. He's been afther explainin' just how he came to send us to this place, but he might want to try it again now for your benefit." Maggie's previously cordial expression had been replaced by a scowl.

"Now just a minute, woman! 'Tis not as if I 'ad any way of knowing the place 'ad changed so." Triss made a sour face at Maggie and then gave Falcon an apologetic look. "There's no question of 'ee staying 'ere, missy. No, indeed. 'Tis not at all the same as it used to be, not at all. I'd no idea 'twould be like this, despite what *some* people 'ere may think."

He pointed to his vacant chair, offering it to her. She shook her head and instead settled herself most improperly upon the bed.

"I am not blaming you for the loss of my trunk," she said. "We should never have been so foolish as to all go inside at once while there was still anything valuable left in the street. It might have happened anywhere."

"This used to be a respectable house, even though the neighborhood was not the best," Triss said. "Many of the returning soldiers stayed 'ere, and I stayed 'ere when I come on leave. A Scottish woman 'ad the running of it—Mrs. Keirie, and a fine woman she was, too." He cast a resentful glance at Maggie as if to say there was no comparing the two. "The place was clean, and the rates were reasonable. You know I would never 'ave sent 'ee 'ere otherwise, missy. We can't stay, there's no question."

"We'll stay tonight, because we have already paid for it.

We'll make a place for you out by the stairway with Carlos. We stayed here last night and while it was not exactly quiet, at least nothing untoward occurred. Fret over it no more, Triss. Our biggest problem is funds. Without the trunk . . . well, we have very little. I have to hope that somehow it will be recovered, or at least some of the items that were in it will. I could sell my mother's jewelry . . ."

"Now, missy, you don't want to be doing that. I think mayhap there's another way out of this conundrum, not that I'm certain, mind 'ee. You could go to your family's solicitor. 'E 'as offices 'ere in the city, I recollect, and perhaps 'e could 'elp."

"With money, you mean. But I would have to reveal who I am! And he would most certainly want to notify my relatives."

"They are your people," Maggie said. "Would that be such a terrible thing?"

"I want nothing to do with them! If they had not cast my father off, everything might have turned out so differently. As it is, I fear that they would try to stop me from carrying out my mission."

"Perhaps 'e don't 'ave to tell them," Triss suggested. "A solicitor should be able to keep a confidence, being 'ow 'e's in the law. Mayhap there's funds that's rightly yours. 'E might be able to help 'ee with the other matters, too, besides the money."

Falcon shook her head in frustration. "All I want to do is go to the Tower and find Private Timmins."

Triss shrugged. "Seems to me that it'll be 'ard to see the business through if 'ee 'aven't any funds to live on, missy. What'll 'ee do if your trunk isn't found?"

Falcon sighed. Had she not wrestled with that question from the moment the trunk had disappeared? The best solution she had thought of was to hire out as a teacher of Spanish or as a governess, but she had no references or experience and she feared such responsibility might tie her down too much to pursue her real purpose.

"I suppose I have no choice—I shall have to go to this solicitor. I suppose, too, that I should feel grateful that we have even the slightest possibility of obtaining help. But it seems we are grasping at a straw."

She felt anger—a deep, frustrated anger at her lack of control over so many circumstances. But she could not unleash it at the people in this room. None of it was any fault of theirs. "Do you know this solicitor's name or his direction, Triss? How will we find him?"

"I brought with me every piece o' paper I ever 'ad that deals with your father or your family. Somewhere there's instructions your father gave me once in case he was killed in a battle, telling me what to do for 'ee and your mother. I think this fellow's name and direction are in there."

"All right, if you can find it we will call on him tomorrow, before I have time to regret the decision." Exposing herself to the solicitor was a calculated risk; she could only hope that it would prove worthwhile.

In the morning Falcon sent Triss and Carlos to hire a hackney to transport the little party to the lodgings in Charles Street. While the two men were gone, the women gathered together the last of their personal belongings and finished packing the baggage.

"I hope they won't be long," Falcon said, placing her mantilla carefully over her hair and arranging the folds. The small room boasted no such luxury as a cheval glass, but a small looking glass stood in a frame upon the dresser, and she let it guide her efforts as she spoke.

"What will we do if there's no rooms available at this new lodging house?" Maggie asked with a testy edge to her voice. "You haven't been there or sent word ahead of us, child."

"If there are no rooms, I'll simply ask the landlady there to recommend another house to us." Falcon refused to be concerned. There were larger problems to solve than where they would take their next rest.

The thump of footsteps on the stairs outside the room followed quickly by a light knock on the door interrupted them. Maggie opened the door to reveal their current landlady.

"Yer gentleman's below with vehicles to move you out," the woman said. "It's a good thing, too. You haven't paid to be here today and besides, I need the rooms back for my regular, um, residents." She paused with a crafty look on her face. "That is, unless you cared to make a new arrangement?"

"No." Falcon spoke emphatically. "We are leaving as quickly as possible." Then she softened. "Thank you for taking us in unexpectedly. I know it was an inconvenience."

The woman looked surprised. For a fleeting moment a smile that seemed genuine actually crossed her face, softening her features so that she looked rather pretty. "I'll send the gents up," she said, turning to go.

Falcon could hardly believe the speed with which Triss and Carlos had located a hackney. She began to issue instructions to the maid and Maggie, sorting out the bandboxes and parcels that were light and small enough for them to carry. Burdened with the long, leather-covered box that contained her father's precious regalia, she headed out to the stairway, only to stop in surprise at the top.

"You!" she exclaimed in confusion. "I thought . . ." Coming up the stairs was not Triss or Carlos, but Lord Danebridge, followed by two of his servants.

The truth dawned upon her and she closed her mouth. No wonder the landlady had said she would "send the gents up." Triss and Carlos had no need to be sent; they would simply have come up! Apparently they had worked no miracle of speed in obtaining a hackney, either.

"Here, let me take this," Lord Danebridge said, removing the large box from her arms before she could protest or tighten her grip.

"But—"

"Good morning to you, señora. My carriage awaits below along with a good-sized hackney coach to carry your servants and luggage. I spoke with Mrs. Isham at the lodging house in Charles Street after I left you yesterday, and she will have rooms all prepared for you by the time we have you packed up and transported to her door this morning."

"But—"

The baron looked about the dingy passageway and arched an eyebrow significantly. "I trust you have not changed your mind? That is, you have no wish to remain here?"

How could he have any doubt? "No, of course not. 'Tis just that . . . I mean, I was not expecting you to . . ." Falcon sighed. She did not wish to seem ungrateful, but she was rather taken aback by his appearing this morning without so much as a by-your-leave. "Do you always just charge in and take command of everyone?"

He grinned, which only aggravated her more. "Sometimes ladies in distress are too proud to ask."

"And sometimes they can fend for themselves, especially if given a small amount of aid. I believe you already did far more than was necessary yesterday. To do this today certainly exceeds the bounds of what is proper."

He gave her a long and unsettling look. "That depends entirely upon who is defining the boundaries."

Was he challenging her? She could not read the expression in his gray eyes, but she would have sworn there was a light in them. She could not tear her own gaze away. That same inner trembling she had felt with him the day before began to seize her, and he had not so much as touched her. Was this man dangerous? Her instincts told her no, but could she trust them? Lord Danebridge affected her in such odd ways and seemed so easily to rob her of control.

He cannot know that, she reminded herself. She raised her chin just enough to send an answering challenge. "In polite society, I believe it is the lady who establishes boundaries in her dealings with a man. And while I want you to know that I appreciate your thoughtfulness in making arrangements for our lodgings and in placing your carriage at my disposal, I prefer not to be delivered to Charles Street like a plaything in your care. What would the landlady think? I have made my own arrangements for transportation, thank you."

It wastes money to pay for a hackney, chided the annoying voice in the back of her mind. *You are putting pride before practicality.*

I don't care! she almost shouted out loud. *I am not willing to pay the hidden cost of accepting his offer.*

Standing before her with the large box of regalia, Lord Danebridge inclined his head. "As you wish."

A moment of awkward silence followed while she wondered if he would say anything more, whether or not she should take back the box from him, and, if she should, exactly how she might do so gracefully.

"You needn't . . ."

"Allow me to . . ."

He smiled when they both began to speak at once. She found it impossible to resist smiling back.

"Do you go first," he said. "If we are not careful this might become a habit."

Her smile disappeared. "Oh, no. I hardly think so! I merely started to say that you needn't trouble yourself about our luggage." She extended her arms to receive the box.

Instead of returning it to her, the aggravating man turned and handed it to one of his servants standing below him on the stairs. The rest somehow happened all at once—he turned back to her and seized her hand as she was lowering her arms, and Maggie came out of the bedroom behind her just in time to see him press a kiss on the back of her gloved wrist.

"Well!" Maggie was shocked.

"Well!" Falcon was, too, but not for quite the same reasons.

Lord Danebridge appeared to be perfectly comfortable and quite pleased with himself, if anything. "Since we are already here, allow us to assist you in bringing down your baggage," he said calmly.

Whether or not the baron cared to be introduced to her companion, Falcon thought Maggie would expect to be introduced, and Maggie's opinion counted for more at this moment.

"Lord Danebridge, allow me to present Mrs. Meara, my traveling companion. Maggie, this is Lord Danebridge."

He bowed gracefully. "Of course, from the inn in Wiltshire. We did not have the pleasure of a formal introduction, but I have not forgotten."

He smiled so warmly that Maggie's frown wobbled a bit, as if she were having trouble maintaining it. Falcon was relieved to have his attention diverted from herself for at least a moment. His kiss had been a bold, unexpected move, and she was still trying to understand what it had meant and calm her racing pulse. Her entire hand tingled as if she had held it too near to a candle flame.

"If 'tis carrying luggage you've come for, look right in that room where I've just come from, your lordship," Maggie said.

"There's plenty more than the one box." Her tone implied that if he had come for anything else, he had better reconsider.

Of course, there was no room in the passageway for anyone to move. Lord Danebridge took a step closer to Falcon, who backed up abruptly and bumped into Maggie. The Irish-woman, having no place to go, retreated into the bedroom.

Falcon followed her, deep in thought. *Is he only being help-ful,* she wondered, *or does he have the wrong idea about me? Does he think that because I have no protector, I am fair game?*

"What exactly did you tell this Mrs. Isham when you made the arrangements for our lodging?" she asked the baron, who followed her in turn. "I would not want her to misunderstand my situation." *Nor do I wish you to do so, either.*

"Have no fear. I assured her that you are a respectable ac-quaintance of one of my cousins and that I was asked to give you what assistance I could. She was only too happy to oblige."

Falcon hoped it was the truth. She did not know if she could believe him, but she could do very little about it one way or the other.

Lord Danebridge's second servant came into the room and took up the portmanteau, while the lord himself picked up two bandboxes stacked one above the other. As he straightened up, he noticed the harp case sitting with the small leather-covered book trunk. "Is that a harp?" he asked Falcon, his eyes alight with curiosity. "How I should love to hear you play it!"

"That is not likely to happen," she replied ungraciously, still annoyed at his high-handed behavior.

"Do you not play?"

"It is in sad need of strings and probably some other re-pairs." She softened for a moment. "It was my mother's."

Just then Benita came in from the front bedroom. *"Doña, Carlos y el Sargento Triss ya estan abajo con el carruaje."* She had been watching for the others to arrive with the hackney and had spied them below in the street.

"Thank goodness," Falcon said, unable to conceal her re-lief. "Here, let us bring down what we can."

The women followed Lord Danebridge and his other ser-vant down the stairs. When they reached the street, they found that Carlos and Triss had stopped the baron's first servant from loading the leather-covered box onto the lord's carriage.

"See 'ere, we've 'ad one piece o' luggage nipped already," Triss was saying to the fellow quite reasonably. "You just wait with that till I learns what be going on."

Explanations followed quickly and the luggage was stowed precariously aboard the one hackney. Falcon was pleased that Lord Danebridge said nothing but allowed her to arrange matters to her own satisfaction. With the luggage plus the five people who now made up her party, the hackney would be overloaded, but she did not care. They should be all right as long as their driver did not take any corners too quickly.

"Would you allow me the honor of calling upon you this afternoon, after you have had time to get settled?" the baron asked when all the luggage had been brought down and they were finally ready to depart. "I will want to know how you find the accommodations, you know. Perhaps we could take a drive in the park? That is what fashionable people do in London in the afternoons."

"It is no different in Spain, although one waits until after the siesta. But I am sorry. I have business I must attend to this afternoon."

At least he had shown the courtesy of asking her, unlike during this morning's fiasco.

"Have you plans this evening, then? Do you enjoy the theater?"

How tempting that was! Falcon had seen few plays in the course of her rather itinerant past, and those she could count included makeshift productions the soldiers had performed for their own entertainment. She hesitated before she answered, weighing her desire to see a real theater performance against her fear of encouraging the baron in any further acquaintanceship.

She did owe him courtesy in return for his help. To refuse this invitation without a good reason would be extremely rude after refusing his first one, and perhaps her fears were completely unfounded.

"No, I do not have plans this evening, as it happens." How could she, when she knew no one?

She only hoped her decision would not prove to be a mistake. How many errors could one make in the same day?

Chapter Seven

Falcon's doubts redoubled as she and Triss rode in a hackney to the solicitor's office that afternoon. Was she doing the right thing? Never had she expected to find so many ways that she might go wrong.

The accommodations in Mrs. Isham's lodging house were all that could be desired—quiet, clean, attractive and comfortable, but they cost little more than the rooms near Convent Garden, and that made her suspicious. The landlady had betrayed no hint of doubt about Falcon's respectability, but still Falcon wondered—had Lord Danebridge paid a portion of the rent or negotiated a special rate on her behalf? Or had the woman in Convent Garden overcharged her outrageously?

The sooner she solved her financial woes and got on with her business—without Lord Danebridge—the better. The situation made her interview with Mr. Fallesby, her father's solicitor, all the more crucial. She prayed that the man could provide some relief and would not merely remand her into the custody of her relatives.

In contrast to the country people of Wickenham, the clerks in the office of Twyford, Fallesby, Grant and Cox looked everywhere but at Falcon once she went in and stated her need to see Mr. Fallesby. As she sat waiting on an extremely uncomfortable wooden bench, she wondered if they were unaccustomed to women clients or were shocked by the tight fit of her Spanish *basquiña*. Had she made a mistake not to wear her more conventional French-styled pelisse?

She had reasoned that she should wear Spanish dress to support her story and her claim of identity. The best proof she could have offered—the locket with her parents' miniatures and her mother's jewels—was gone with the stolen trunk. All she had brought with her was her father's regimental breast-plate, tucked safely into her reticule.

After an interminable wait a clerk finally informed Falcon that Mr. Fallesby could give her a few moments of his time.

"Your servant may await you here," the man said loftily, inclining his head toward Triss, who stood patiently by the window, looking out at the city traffic.

Falcon felt a momentary urge to change her mind, but she had never retreated from a challenge. She adjusted her mantilla and followed the clerk up a narrow flight of stairs to the far more comfortably furnished office of Mr. Fallesby.

The solicitor did not look up when she entered. Was it only her, or did no one ever meet the eyes of any clients in this place? She settled into a leather-covered wing chair that was large enough to hold two of her and made her feel like a child.

She used the moment to observe the man. If antique meant old, then this man was positively ancient. Balding and bespectacled, he appeared to be as thin and dry as the papers piled upon his desk, quite in danger of blowing away in a fresh breeze. Just as well the one window was closed. She could readily believe that he worked day and night in this tiny room, without sleep or food, for he seemed to have barely enough flesh to cover his bones.

"Señora Alomar de Montero, is it?" The solicitor finally lifted his gaze from the paper in his hand. Behind the small glass lenses the eyes that were fixed upon her now were bright and intelligent, set in a wizened face that seemed almost elfin.

Falcon pushed backed her mantilla and let it drop onto her shoulders so that the man could really see her. "Uh, no, actually, it is not," she admitted. "That is to say, I am not—I mean, I am using that name, but it is not really mine." Suddenly she felt tongue-tied. That was the last thing she had expected. Her palms were sweating. Oh, why could not Triss have been allowed to accompany her? "I'm afraid I hardly know where to begin."

"Try the beginning," Mr. Fallesby suggested dryly.

"Yes. Of course. The beginning." She took a deep breath and pulled herself together. "My name is actually Colburne—Miss Falcarrah Colburne. You represented the interests of my father when he was alive. He died in the Peninsula five years ago."

She saw the solicitor's gaze sharpen as she said the words.

"Captain Myles Anthony Colburne, of the Forty-third," he recited. "A fine man, son and heir to the Earl of Coudray. A tragic loss."

He leaned back in his chair, contemplating Falcon as if he had all the time in the world. His manner belied the interest she could read in his face. "You claim to be his daughter, eh?"

"Yes. I know you are probably thinking that it is not possible. I am supposed to be dead."

"Well, I am listening. The entire family was reportedly killed during Moore's retreat to Corunna. A terrible business." He looked at her expectantly.

At least he has not thrown me out of his office, she thought. "Terrible does not begin to describe it, sir. The retreat itself was an ordeal . . ." Everything she had endured afterward had not erased her memories of it—the roads littered with bodies of the dead and dying, and the fear, exhaustion, cold, and hunger. But ladies were not supposed to talk of such things, and it was beside the point.

"You must be aware from the reports that my parents did not succumb to any of the natural forces which caused the deaths of so many during the retreat, Mr. Fallesby. My parents were murdered, and I was left for dead along with them. It was only by the greatest good fortune that my father's batman found us. There is no question that he saved my life."

The solicitor showed no discernible alteration in his posture or expression. He merely said, "If the batman found you, then how was it that you were reported killed? And pray tell, why have you only appeared now, five years later? You can understand my asking."

"I know it must seem very peculiar," Falcon said. What could she do to convince this man she was telling the truth? Did she need to tell him everything? Was all of this worth the pain and effort when there might be nothing this man could do for her?

"I had to be left behind—I was too badly injured to travel," she said woodenly. "Triss—that is, Corporal Triss, took me to the priest in that village and asked him to help me. The

French were not far behind us. Triss, of course, could not stay—he would have been accounted a deserter. I—well, I have spent the last five years in Spain, what with the war going on."

"You were captured?"

"No. I managed to avoid that fate, but the telling is a very long story. I was a fourteen-year-old girl, brutally robbed of my parents and very nearly of my life as well. Suffice it to say that many people helped me."

"And now you have come to me for help, I assume. What exactly did you hope I might do for you?"

Had she really dared to hope? For the moment Falcon was simply relieved that the man did not press her with more questions about the murders or her time in Spain. Recalling the details would only stir up nightmares and bitterness. Besides, she was certain he would not approve of her mission of vengeance, and she feared that he would refuse to help her if he guessed her true business here.

"The batman—Sergeant Triss, as he became afterward—is with me now. In fact, he is waiting in your clerks' office below. It was he who knew of your existence and suggested I come to see you. I have run into difficulties here in London. One of my trunks was stolen as soon as we arrived here—it contained nearly all of the money I had been given by Spanish friends to cover my expenses." She could not say, *while I am here.* He would only ask more questions. She hurried on, so as not to afford him the opportunity.

"Triss thought there might have been some provision made for me—that is, did my father leave a will? Are there any funds to which I might have a claim?" She was keeping her emotions tightly reined in, but nevertheless a hint of her desperation escaped. "If only there were! It would make such a difference!"

Mr. Fallesby tented his fingers and tapped them thoughtfully against his small chin. "Ah, it always comes down to the money."

Falcon feared that she had failed to convince him. She opened the strings of her reticule and withdrew her father's breastplate. "This is the only small item I could bring with me as proof of who I am." Her hands were shaking. "Triss removed what he could of my father's regalia so that it would not become the property of looters. I had some items of my mother's—a locket with their portraits and some heirloom jewelry, a set of pearls with emeralds—that were lost with my stolen trunk."

She handed the badge across the desk. The solicitor took it from her and studied it for several long moments before handing it back. Then, still without a word, he reached behind him and pulled on the bellpull that hung behind him on the wall.

That is it, then, Falcon thought. *He is going to have me escorted out.* Hoping that she was wrong, she bit her lip and said nothing.

One of the clerks appeared in the doorway, and Mr. Fallesby turned to him. "Fetch me the file on Captain Myles Colburne. Our last use of it would have been about two years ago."

Two years ago? Falcon was puzzled, but she remained quiet. This was no time to allow her natural impulsiveness to rule her behavior, no matter how hard that might be to control. At least it appeared that Mr. Fallesby might believe her story after all.

"I believe you have omitted a great deal of your story, Miss Colburne," the man said, returning his attention to her. "However, I imagine it is painful for you to dwell on the past, so I will not pursue my questions for now. I will say you have the look of your mother—you have her striking eyes and coloring. She was a very beautiful woman, and both strong and charming besides. Few who met her wondered that your father would give up his birthright for such a woman."

He must have believed her all along! "You met my mother? You remember her? Then you must know that my father's family . . ."

He nodded. "Your father always felt that if your grandfather had only met her, he would not have cast them off, but the earl would not receive her. He was a very stubborn man, your grandfather."

"As was my father."

"Yes. Yes, he was. He would marry your mother, no matter what the consequences. And your mother was no better, for she would not be separated from him. Cared nothing for convention, either of them. And so you were raised in the regiment, eh?"

"Yes, sir, I was."

"Hmph. Not a fit life for a gently bred woman and child. A tragedy all around—a tragedy and a terrible waste." He stared off into space and for a moment he seemed to forget that she was there.

"It was the only life I knew," she said softly. "I did not mind it."

"Hmph." He seemed to come back to himself. "The old earl is more to blame than anyone. He let your father go on believing that he had disinherited him, and that the army was the only life open to him. It was only when your grandfather died that we learned he had never changed his will."

Falcon was stunned. "Do you mean to say that my father was never disinherited?"

"Yes, that was the case. The earl died about two years after your family's tragedy. He took it very hard."

Falcon could not find it in her heart to feel sympathy for an old man who had caused so much pain and trouble, but she thought no one could be more to blame for her parents' deaths than the men she had come seeking. "My father always believed that he had been cut off with nothing. No one ever let him know otherwise. He devoted his life to his military career, because he believed that was all he had, besides us, that is—my mother and me. It is too sad to contemplate."

"Your father's cousin is the seventh of Earl of Coudray now," Mr. Fallesby was saying. "Everything went to him, of course, since your father was gone. But I'm sure there were provisions for you in your father's will—your marriage portion and other matters. Since we thought you dead, they were null. To have you now appear very much alive five years after the fact makes matters complicated indeed, but I feel certain that we can sort them out."

He folded his hands in front of him on the desk. "Of course, it may take some time, and there will certainly be some questions. I believe an affidavit from you and probably one from your Sergeant Triss would be helpful. I'm afraid you will have to provide more details of where you have been and what you have been doing during these last five years."

"I can do that if I must," she said. "If it would help matters at all, I have some very respectable connections in Spain who could vouch for me, although of course it will take time to contact them." *What of the present?* she wanted to ask. *How will I feed and house five of us? How will I have the money to go wherever I need to go?*

She may have betrayed her thoughts by some flicker of worry or dismay, for although she said nothing, the solicitor's next remarks spoke exactly to her concern.

"As for the present, I believe I could give you a small amount as a loan against the time this is all sorted out. I will contact a friend in Doctors' Commons who can help us with the will. I assume that we will also be contacting his lordship. You are not yet twenty-one, Miss Colburne?"

She shook her head, dreading where this was leading even as she rejoiced at the prospect of some financial relief.

"You must have a legal guardian, and the earl is the logical choice, as he is your closest relative and the head of the Colburne family now. I am certain that he will not hesitate to take responsibility for you as soon as we have made this extraordinary situation known to him."

"My relatives are more likely to have as little interest in my existence as I have in theirs," Falcon said with some spirit. "You must remember how they failed to receive my mother, sir. I am, after all, that objectionable Irishwoman's daughter. They probably blamed the two of us for the loss of my father as much as I blame them."

Mr. Fallesby smiled. "I am certain the earl will see his responsibility in the matter, Miss Colburne. You must remember that he is not your grandfather. I will write to him immediately. Why, where else would you expect to turn, now that you have returned to England?"

Where else, indeed? Falcon thought that if the man knew the truth, the very idea of what she intended would knock him over like a stiff wind. But she was not well and truly trapped, not yet.

"He is bound to be shaken by the news of my survival," she said carefully. "It is not every day that a relative suddenly returns from the dead. Perhaps it would be best if I wrote to him myself? I could explain what happened to me, and answer some of the questions he is bound to have, as you pointed out yourself, sir. I could say I am writing at your suggestion."

As she hoped, he agreed, clearly not suspecting for the world that she might have any other plan in mind. "Perhaps you are right, young lady. You are certainly better qualified to explain what has happened than I. He is probably at the family seat in Kent; as soon as my clerk finds the file, I will have him give you the direction."

He reached behind him and pulled the bellpull a second time. "I will advance you some funds—would twenty pounds be sufficient for now? I can always advance you more if necessary, but I am certain the earl will make sure you have pin money."

He considered this pin money? Her family must be wealthy indeed. Twenty pounds equaled a lieutenant's pay for two months, or as much as an upper servant might earn in a year. *The earl will never know I was here,* thought Falcon, *but that should not matter.* Twenty pounds might carry her until she could get word to Don Andrés or at least find some other solution to her problems.

Chapter Eight

Jeremy stood absolutely still in the dressing room of the Fitzharding Street town house while his valet put the finishing touches on a masterfully tied cravat. The lieutenant major could not turn his head for the moment, but he could see Nicholson's reflection in the looking glass placed at an angle beside him.

"So, Nicholson. Tell me where she went this afternoon."

"Twyford, Fallesby, Grant and Cox—a solicitor's office," the big man answered, consulting a folded piece of paper upon which he had obviously made notations. "She was there for close to an hour. The Cornishman, Sergeant Triss, went with her, but he did not see the attorney—he remained waiting in the front office, visible through the windows. Afterwards, they returned directly to the lodging house in Charles Street."

"Do we know which solicitor she saw there?"

"Had to be Fallesby, sir. Twyford's been dead for ten years, Grant is retired, and Cox is not in town at present."

"How fortunate for us." Jeremy continued to stare thoughtfully into the looking glass for a moment, seeing nothing. What business could his "Spanish" lady have with a solicitor? Finding out could be a sticky problem—most attorneys did honor their clients' privacy. Perhaps in the relaxed atmosphere of the theater this evening he could get her to confide in him.

He had behaved rashly in offering that invitation for this evening—it was most unlike him. He not stopped to consider the consequences. He could not even excuse himself on the basis that he was impatient to be finished with this assignment, for that had been no part of his thoughts at the time.

He was, in effect, about to publicly introduce into London

society a young woman whose name and character were completely unknown to him. His presence as her escort would be seen as proof of her acceptability, for he was not the kind of man who paraded his mistresses in public. How in thunder was he going to explain who she was? And suppose he ultimately learned that she was indeed a spy? What a devilish stir-up that would cause!

That prospect, however, bothered him less than his impulsive, unprofessional behavior. What *had* he been thinking of? Green eyes, inviting lips, a smile that did strange things to him?

Too late to ponder these things now. He was not cowardly enough to send a note canceling their evening. But he had better watch himself very carefully, lest he make any more such imprudent decisions.

Jeremy's valet finished arranging the intricate folds of the baron's cravat and stepped back to survey his handiwork. Jeremy faced the looking glass and realized that Nicholson was patiently waiting.

"My apologies, Nicholson. What else?"

"After a short while, she went out again with the Irish woman. They went to a dressmaker's shop in Oxford Street, and made some purchases. Nothing else, sir."

But that last piece of news was significant. Somewhere, the "señora" had acquired some money or credit. *Where, or how? The solicitor?*

"Any instructions for this evening, sir?"

"Keep one man watching the lodging house and take the night off for yourself. You've earned it." Jeremy did not relish the idea of sharing his evening with any unseen assistants. He brushed an imaginary speck from his elegant white silk waistcoat and held out his arms ready to receive his coat. "I will handle this evening myself."

Falcon had been in a quandary about going to the theater. She had never intended to make any truly public appearances—she just wanted to tend to her business and be gone. Somehow she had lost her focus in a moment of weakness. It was a mistake—a big mistake. She should have realized it, she told herself, but it was too late to change the plans now.

Maggie had brought up another aspect of the problem by asking Falcon what she intended to wear. Falcon's better dresses were in the trunk that had been stolen.

"Oh, Maggie, I don't know!" she had snapped. "If I had thought, I might have worn my *basquiña,* but now I have already worn it today. I have nothing suitable. What about you? Have you something to wear? For of course you must come. How could I ever have accepted his invitation? The last thing I want is more of his company!"

Unabashed, Maggie had simply smiled. "Perhaps because ye'd like for once to live life the way ye deserve to! Where's the harm in a night at the theater? 'Twill be a treat. As for me, I've me best dress to wear, so that's all right. But you? It could not hurt to spend a little of the ready ye've received on a gown or two. Ye have to have clothing!"

She suggested they consult with their landlady Mrs. Isham, who promptly packed them off to her own dressmaker in Oxford Street.

The modiste had two suitable dresses on hand, one that had been refused by a client and another that had been made up as a sample. After a hasty fitting and some expert alterations, Falcon and Maggie had returned to the lodging house with a confection of ribbon-trimmed green gauze suitable to be worn in the evening and a promise of a deep burgundy-colored walking dress to be delivered in the morning. Falcon had to confess that her spirits were remarkably improved.

"What do you think?" she asked now, twirling around in front of Maggie and Benita.

"I'm thinking it's a shame to cover yourself up with a mantilla, ye look so fine, child. Ye'd catch any man's eye, ye would."

"*That* is not the point at all," Falcon said, failing completely to look as severe as she wished. "It is a pretty gown, is it not? I hope we will not later regret spending the money."

A discreet knock announced the footman at the door, who informed them that Lord Danebridge awaited below.

"Oh, ¡cielos! Is it time already? Surely he is early!" Flustered, Falcon hurried over to the dressing table and reached for the ornately carved tortoise shell comb that was not yet anchored in her upswept hair. Jamming it in at an angle, she swept the lace mantilla off the chair upon which it had been carefully laid out and held it out, saying, "Maggie, Benita, help me—*ayúdame con este, por favor*."

A few minutes later Falcon and Maggie descended to find Lord Danebridge awaiting them in the reception parlor. As he rose to greet them, Falcon thought he looked taller and more handsome than ever in his elegant evening attire. The crisp, stark contrast of his black coat and snowy white linen seemed to emphasize the touch of color in his face and the sun-bleached highlights in his hair. He looked like a man unused to indoor confinement, yet he seemed perfectly at ease in these formal clothes. His eyes lit in unmistakable appreciation as he greeted the women.

"What a privilege to be escorting two such lovely ladies, this evening," he said, politely including Maggie even though his gray eyes never left Falcon for a moment. "I fear my humble company cannot do you justice."

Falcon could not resist his infectious good humor. "What, should we wait here for a better offer?"

"You might, but my footman is holding some excellent box seats for us," he replied, his warm smile expanding into the breathtaking grin Falcon had first noticed in Wickenham. "Besides, you'd risk missing the first part of tonight's program."

As Maggie began to help Falcon with her cloak, he stepped in and took it from her. "Allow me."

Falcon's smile disappeared. She tried to ignore the warm flush that crept up her neck and into her face as he arranged the cloak around her shoulders. What a presumptuous thing for him to do! Surely it was improper—it seemed to her a very intimate and familiar gesture. And not a word of protest from Maggie! A fine *duenna* she was turning out to be! Falcon resolved to have a word of her own with the Irishwoman later.

"What are we seeing tonight?" she asked, trying to keep her voice steady as she was forced to hold the mantilla up and out of the way of Lord Danebridge's ministrations.

"Kean is performing *Richard the Third* at Drury Lane. I will be interested to see what you think of him—he has become quite the rage, and his style of acting is quite unique."

The baron's voice was warm and vibrant close to her ear, and his fingers brushed her neck.

Falcon stepped away, hurrying to fasten the front of her cloak herself. By heaven, she was *not* going to show that he disturbed her in any way! Wretched man!

"Surely if this Mr. Kean is so popular it is a testament to his skill," she replied. "I have so little experience with the art of acting, I should be the last person to make any judgment."

He offered his arm. As he did, she barely made out the words he uttered under his breath, "I believe that remains to be proven."

The overstated opulence of the Drury Lane Theatre impressed Falcon beyond all comparison. She could not stop looking—first at the gilded ornamentation around the proscenium, then at the splendid decorations adorning the boxes and the ceiling overhead. Handsome figures of Comedy and Tragedy graced the boxes on either side of the stage. Brilliant lamps with multiple wicks illuminated the entire front of the theater, including the pit, although some other portions of the audience areas were cast in shadow. It was only when Falcon realized that most people in the theater were busily engaged in ogling each other that she realized she was drawing her share of curious looks and thought of withdrawing to a less noticeable seat in the box Lord Danebridge had procured for them.

"Are you not comfortable?" the baron asked, rising with her as she stood up. "Perhaps a different chair?"

Falcon sat again abruptly, realizing that she was only drawing more attention to herself. "I, uh—no, this is perfectly acceptable." She took a deep breath. "I just—I did not realize that the audience would be on display fully as much as the players will be."

Lord Danebridge smiled, but she thought there was a curious look in his eyes. "Why, that is all part of the entertainment, my dear lady. To admire and be admired. What do you think of the theater?"

At least she could answer that quite honestly. "Oh, it is splendid, there is no question. I have never seen anything like it!"

"I hope you will enjoy the performances as much."

He had not taken his eyes off her once. She could not help wondering if he was going to watch the players on the stage half so much as he was watching her.

From Kean's opening lines, however, Falcon was drawn into the story of Richard III, fascinated with a kind of underlying horror at how close the matter struck to her heart. The Lady Anne's dramatic curses and appeals for revenge as she was confronted by the villainous character of Richard seemed an echo of Falcon's own anger over the murder of her parents. She almost cheered aloud when Anne took up the sword against Richard, and could not help but feel dismay when that lady gave up the effort.

"Oh, why ever did she not run him through!" she exclaimed, quite forgetting herself.

Lord Danebridge laughed. "For one reason, the course of history would have been considerably altered, and for another, this would prove to be Shakespeare's shortest play."

Kean's portrayal of Richard captured a sly depravity and outrageous evil that infuriated Falcon. She felt ready to climb onto the stage herself to put a stop to his endless machinations and growing list of murder victims as the play progressed. It was only at occasional moments that she was suddenly and rudely jolted back into the present by the response of the audience to what was happening on the stage.

The reactions of the audience to the players surprised her. The people in the pit hooted and answered back, and the entire theater would burst into applause after what was judged a particularly fine speech or action. While each interruption startled her, she found it almost a relief to be rescued from the intensity of the emotions the play aroused in her.

She could not help looking down into the pit at those who were the loudest in their replies. At just such a moment near the end of the play she saw something that shocked her more than the audience's noise or the horror of the story. Amongst the crowd in the standing space behind the benches in the pit a man waved his hat in derision at Richard's poignant fear and guilt at dreaming of the ghosts of his eleven victims.

"Sweeney," breathed Falcon, hardly daring to believe it. Could she possibly have found him here, at such a moment?

She stood up. She must not lose him now. But she had quite forgotten Lord Danebridge sitting quietly beside her.

"What is it," he asked in alarm, rising also. "Are you ill?"

Falcon felt as if her head was spinning. "No—no. It's just—I thought I saw—oh, dear. There's no time to explain." She began to move hurriedly toward the back of the box. "I must go downstairs. There's someone in the pit—I thought I saw someone."

Maggie had arisen from her chair, her face etched with concern, but Falcon hurried past her.

The baron was at Falcon's elbow. "Of course, I'll take you down, if that is your wish." She could hear the puzzlement in his voice. "Do you not wish to wait for the interval? It is customary for everyone in the theater to mingle then. They are preparing for the final scenes! The sword fight is said to be Kean's finest moment."

Falcon shook her head. She might never find the man she thought was Sweeney once the entire audience began to mill about in the theater. Lord Danebridge's words only pressed her to move faster. She wrenched open the door to their box and nearly ran down the passageway to the stairs. She had to slow then lest she miss her footing.

Lord Danebridge touched her arm. "Don't leave me behind, fair one. You might get lost."

She did not care if he was behind her or not. Only one thought filled her mind—Triss had not been able to locate Sweeney, and now she thought she had found the man. She could not let him get away. She had to know if it was really him.

Words from the stage rang in her ears as she opened the door into the lower theater and began to search among the standing crowd for the man she thought she had seen. "A bloody tyrant and a homicide; one raised in blood and one in blood established . . ."—so Richmond exhorted his soldiers to rise against Richard. As far as Falcon was concerned, he might just as well have been describing Sweeney, the man most responsible for her parents' deaths.

She found her task less easy than she expected—amongst the crowd she could not get her bearings or make out the man she sought. In distress she turned to ask Lord Danebridge to point out as a reference which box they had been sitting in, only to find he was no longer behind her. Well, she could not wait for him to catch up. Determinedly, she plunged on, squeezing through the press of bodies. If she worked her way through the standing crowd from one end to the other, surely she would come upon the man.

And then what? If he was Sweeney, what would she do? She had not planned so far as that. It would be too dangerous to reveal who she was, but she had to make contact, create some connection. *Señor Sweeney, is it you? A friend bid me to seek you out. What good fortune to run into you here!* All she needed was an address, a place where he was staying, a way to find him again, if she could but find him this once.

A firm hand clasping her arm halted her urgent progress. "What is your hurry, señorita? If you are late for a meeting, perhaps I can help you find a better use for your time."

She turned to see what stranger had addressed her. "Please," she said, carefully accenting her words, "do not detain me."

Unfortunately, the rude fellow found this humorous. When he began to laugh, she jammed her elbow into his rib cage and as he reacted she kneed him as hard as she could in the groin. She apologized to those she jostled and then hurried on through the crowd. Being raised among soldiers had its own rewards.

She reached the opposite side of the theater without finding anyone who resembled Sweeney. Had she really seen him? Or had she conjured him up out of her own distraught state of mind? No longer certain, she paused to let her racing heart slow to a normal pace, finding welcome support against the wall. She continued to scan the faces of those on benches within the pit, allowing that Sweeney, if she had indeed seen him, could well have found himself a seat. Lord Danebridge found her there a few moments later.

"I did not know I had brought a madwoman to the theater," he said, standing disconcertingly close to her and staring down at her with an odd expression on his face. "Do you know what havoc you have left in your wake? They are taking bets on who you are, and have already dubbed you the Spanish Spitfire. Kean is warming up to his final death scene, and you have effectively stolen his thunder. Tomorrow I have no doubt that the papers will have as much gossip about the mysterious Spanish lady who caused turmoil at the show tonight as there will be commentary on the performance."

He paused for breath, his eyes as dark as smoke and locked with hers. For a long moment it seemed to Falcon that they just stood there staring at each other, and then the baron reached out and put his hands on her shoulders. He turned her toward the stage, saying, "Look. They are fighting—now Richard meets his end."

If she had not found Lord Danebridge so distracting Falcon would no doubt have admired Kean at that moment—his fall in death seemed so real, it riveted the attention of every pair of eyes in the theater. How much easier to watch him than to consider her own thoughtless actions! But the baron had not removed his hands from her shoulders and his touch was causing strange tremors to run through her veins.

"Come, now is my best chance to slip you back upstairs unnoticed. Richmond has still one long speech before the play is done," he whispered.

His hands slid from her shoulders but one hand remained at the small of her back, guiding her toward a small doorway nearby that opened into narrow, winding stairs. Falcon took one last despairing look behind her, but still saw no trace of Sweeney.

"We must hurry," Lord Danebridge urged.

The stairs opened into the upper level passage on the opposite side of the theater from his rented box. Taking her by the hand, he led her quickly past the doors of the private boxes on that side, through the upper lobby, and finally regained his own box on the other side. Just as the theater erupted in wild applause for the finished play, he closed the door and pushed Falcon into a chair in the shadows at the very back of the box.

"What happened, child?" Maggie asked, her eyes as round as marbles. She looked as if she had aged a year in the few minutes Falcon had been gone.

"Nothing, Maggie," Falcon replied with a deep sigh of frustration. "Absolutely nothing."

"Except, of course, for the small matter of her having bodily assaulted a rude fellow who accosted her as she pushed her way through the entire standing gallery and her having drawn the curious attention of half the people in this theater by so doing," Lord Danebridge amended.

"I hope you are planning to explain what that was all about," he continued. "But in the meantime, I must warn you that we are likely to have visitors now, during the interval. I know a number of my friends saw us sitting here during the performance, and they will want to be introduced."

He touched the black lace that covered Falcon's head and shoulders. "Would you consider removing the mantilla? If they meet you without it perhaps they will not later connect you with the gossip in the papers."

"Too late for that," Falcon said tartly. "Since they have already seen me, what is to be gained?" She could not risk removing the veil. What if there were other people who had known her mother? It was clear from her visit with Mr. Fallesby that the resemblance was striking and her mother was well remembered.

The baron sighed. "Somehow I was under the impression that you were uncomfortable about attracting attention. Apparently I am mistaken about that—and perhaps other things as well."

He paused, perhaps to see if she would correct him. Falcon decided to say nothing, wondering what "other things" he meant.

"I realize that I do not even know what to say when I introduce you, señora. It is customary to give more than a name— do I say that you are here on business, or a visit? Your husband does not travel with you—do I make a right guess that he was killed in the war?"

"I lost my entire family in the war, Lord Danebridge." She gave him a long, level look that she hoped would discourage him from further questions. "You may say that, and that I am here on business related to that loss."

The footman who had dutifully held the box seats for them before the play had disappeared during the performance, but he silently reappeared during this conversation. When the first knock sounded on the door to the baron's box, the young man opened the door to admit the first visitors.

"Danebridge, you rascal!" exclaimed a short, plump fellow

who bustled in energetically without further ado. "When did you get into town, and how could you have failed to send round your card to let us know? Thought you were still overseas! You are in deep trouble with my mother now." He jerked his head toward the older woman who had trailed in behind him. Plump and short to match her son, she was tastefully gowned and plumed in pale amethyst.

"Giddings! And Lady Giddings. You must accept my apologies," the baron said. "I was brought into town unexpectedly on business, and did not expect to be here long. I had hoped to be on my way home to see Tobey by now, in fact, but I find I am detained. I have been here only a matter of days, truly!"

"I'm certain your son must miss you a great deal," allowed Lady Giddings sympathetically. "I will forgive you as long as you introduce us to your charming companion!" She wiggled her gloved fingers at Falcon in a friendly fashion.

Lord Danebridge opened his mouth to reply but before he could do so another knock sounded on the door of the box, and the footman admitted yet more visitors. The conversation was repeated in a similar vein, more visitors arrived, and suddenly the box was quite crowded beyond capacity. If such a crush was normal, Falcon wondered if anyone was ever accidentally pushed out over the rail of the balcony.

"I will introduce all of you to my guests, Doña Sofia Alomar de Montero from Spain and her companion, Mrs. Meara. The señora lost all of her family in the recent war. She is here visiting London on business."

Lady Giddings was all sympathy for Falcon now. "You poor dear! And so young, too," she said, inspecting Falcon curiously through her quizzing glass as if to determine if her assessment was correct. "Well! I am certain now that we know you are amongst us, Lord Danebridge, we must have you join us for an evening. Won't you take dinner with us on Saturday? And señora, please, you must join us as well! We will make a charming party out of it."

Falcon looked helplessly at Lord Danebridge, hoping he would find her some way out of accepting the woman's invitation. She was in no position to begin socializing with people in London!

"I'm sorry, Lady—Giddings, is it?" she started to say, but Lord Danebridge spoke up at the same moment.

"That is very kind of you, Lady Giddings." He shot a wicked smile at Falcon. "Doña Alomar knows hardly anyone in London. I'm sure she would be delighted. And you know I cannot possibly turn down a chance to enjoy the superb offerings of that fine cook of yours."

Not to be outdone, the other visitors, too, offered invitations to various entertainments and events, including a ball on the following Wednesday. Lord Danebridge accepted all of them. Falcon thought perhaps she should give up on Sweeney, Timmins, and Pumphrey, and just wreak vengeance on Lord Danebridge instead. *At least I know where he is,* she thought ruefully.

A bell rang to signal the end of the interval, and the visitors departed, although a few left slowly, perhaps hoping to be invited to stay and share the box. Lord Danebridge was charming and cordial but did not go so far as that, to Falcon's great relief.

Once the crowd had departed, she chose her words carefully. "Lord Danebridge, I must protest. I have no wish to socialize with anyone in London. I know you meant well, but—"

"Of course, you must trust me. I have your best interests at heart. You are well on your way now to becoming a Toast of the Town, a very enviable thing to be. No door will be closed to you—you'll see! I am so delighted to be able to help you in this way." He grinned.

Exasperation was pushing the edge of Falcon's temper. On the stage below the farce had begun, and the bursts of laughter from the audience could hardly have been more opposite to her mood. "This—this is not the sort of help I need, Lord Danebridge! I would more than appreciate it if you would refrain from making decisions for me, with or without so much as a 'by your leave'!" If looks could kill, the one she gave him should have struck him down on the spot.

The baron, however, replied with an expression that was all innocence. "My only wish is to assist you. I admit I would find the task easier if you would only confide in me. I do apologize if I have erred."

Falcon could not help feeling that somehow Lord Danebridge knew exactly what he was doing. What could she say?
What did he really want?

"Will you not at least explain now what that earlier fiasco
was all about?" he prompted. "I do not truly believe you are a
madwoman—there must be some reason why you would suddenly dash into the lower regions of this theater and disturb
all those people in the standing area."

Angry as she might be, she did at least owe him an explanation. "I—I thought I saw someone I knew—someone I am
seeking. But when I got down there I could not find him. I am
not certain now that I saw him at all."

"This person is named Sweeney?"

Falcon realized that she must have failed to hide her surprise, for he explained at once, "You said his name when you
jumped up from your seat."

"Oh." Truly, the play must have unnerved her more than
she realized. She was reading far too much into Lord Danebridge's behavior. Not everyone had secrets to hide and con-
spiracies to put in motion. "Yes, Sweeney."

"Is a theater a likely place to find this person?"

In fact, it was. Falcon remembered that Sweeney had been
quite interested in theater and that he had at times encouraged
the soldiers in the Forty-third to take part in their own small
productions. She nodded.

"Well, you see? There is something right there that I can
help you with." He looked immensely pleased with himself.
"A man, you know, has many greater resources at his disposal
than a woman, especially in a great city like London. I will be
happy to make a circuit of the various theaters and inquire if
your friend is in the regular habit of purchasing tickets. I
might even be lucky enough to procure an address. Knowing
the interests of a person can be a great help if you are trying to
locate him."

Falcon resented his patronizing tone, but she admitted she
might never have thought of checking with the theaters. Why
should she not allow Lord Danebridge to help her with this
one problem? Triss had not been able to find Sweeney—perhaps Lord Danebridge could.

Chapter Nine

On the morning following the Drury Lane performance Falcon paced the carpet in her room impatiently, waiting for the arrival of her new walking dress. She looked at Maggie and sighed. "I suppose the modiste did not expect that we would plan to go anywhere before noon. I had hoped for an earlier start to the day."

"Child, the Tower of London has stood for centuries—how much difference in the scheme of things would it make to be gettin' off to see it an hour sooner?"

"None, I suppose, Maggie. If only we could be certain the difference will be only an hour or so! I am determined not to let another day go by without an attempt to see Timmins."

"As ye've no other suitable clothes, there is not a thing ye can do but wait. The woman said mornin', and mornin' it still is. Have patience, lass."

Falcon rolled her eyes and went to the window. Patience was not and never had been one of her strong suits, despite her mother's many efforts to teach her.

She had intended to ask Lord Danebridge about posting a reward for the return of her trunk, hoping that she could afford to pay a suitable sum now that her finances were somewhat improved. She held little hope that her valuables would still be in the trunk, but surely the reward would be less costly than purchasing more clothes! Yet every day that passed with no word of her trunk made her less hopeful of its recovery.

So much else had seemed to happen at the theater last night, she had quite forgotten to inquire about the reward. She had failed to ask other planned questions, too—about his wife, for instance.

She thought over what she had learned about Lord Danebridge from his friends at the theater.

He had a son whom he obviously loved. That had only surprised her a little. It helped to explain the absence of his wife—she assumed that Lady Danebridge must have stayed in the country with the son. But one thing was still puzzling about that—no one, not even the baron himself, had so much as mentioned her.

His friend Giddings had clearly been genuinely surprised to see him, and had mentioned that he'd thought the baron was still "overseas." That puzzled Falcon, too. If Lord Danebridge had only just returned from there, as he claimed, what had he been doing in Wickenham? The small Wiltshire village was not directly on any route leading from any major port on the English coast.

Finally, Falcon wondered, if the baron had been unexpectedly called to London on business and was in such a hurry to go home, why on earth was he spending so much of his time with her? For the past two days he had given the impression of having nothing better to do at all.

She turned back from the window and began pacing again. The man was going to drive her mad. On the one hand he had been and was continuing to be extremely helpful. On the other, he was overbearing and presumptuous—imagine committing her to all those social engagements without so much as consulting her? And when he knew perfectly well the constraints on her purse strings! Or at least, thought he did.

Falcon stopped cold in the middle of the room. His intentions might not be perfectly clear, but she thought they were becoming more so by the minute. He was slowly, cleverly, insidiously manipulating her into a growing dependence upon him. But to what end? She could only think of one, and it was certainly not honorable.

While she pondered the best way to find answers to her questions, her dress arrived. Maggie went down to retrieve it and came bustling back up the stairs with the large parcel in her arms.

"Here 'tis—I can hardly wait to see ye in it!"

Falcon hurried to unwrap the package and lifted out the heavy silk dress whose rich color had attracted her yesterday.

"While Benita helps me to dress, Maggie, would you please

find Carlos? Send him to Triss to let him know I will be ready to go in a very few minutes."

In his study in Fitzharding Street, Jeremy, too, had been pondering questions that he had failed to ask and information that he had managed to glean during the previous evening.

He had been surprisingly content to simply watch the señora during the first half of the program. She had become so thoroughly engrossed in the Shakespeare, he did not believe that the emotions that flickered across her face could have been anything but genuine. She seemed to have forgotten everything but the action on the stage and was truly startled each time a major response came from the audience to break the spell. He had found ample opportunity to study the perfection of her skin, the curl of her eyelashes and the expressive curve of her lips—and the true distress the matter of the play seemed to bring out in her.

The business about Sweeney had sent him scurrying back through Señorita Alvez Bonastre's letters from Corporal Triss as soon as he had returned home last night. He thought he remembered some reference to Sweeney, and some other names as well, and was gratified when he found it. In many of the letters, Corporal Triss had reported on Sweeney and two other men. In the later letters, after he had become sergeant, he expressed increasing difficulty in keeping track of the men.

Who were they? Lovers who had left her behind? Had she followed them to England to try to gain their protection again? The thought, along with something that might have been a twinge of jealousy, had crossed his mind when she rushed off in search of Sweeney in the theater last night. Or were they contacts, involved in some intrigue that might threaten the nation, or the fragile peace in Europe, as his superiors feared? The Treaty of Paris was not yet signed, although Louis XVIII was back in Paris and Napoleon was in exile on Elba.

Jeremy was convinced now beyond doubt that the señorita and the señora were the same person. How many more names did she use? And why? Perhaps if he could find Sweeney, he would find some answers as well.

He had attempted several times during the previous evening to steer the conversation around to how Doña Alomar de

Montero had spent her afternoon, but each time she had
seemed to find a way to circumvent him. She had not mentioned any change in her financial state or given any hint of
what had occupied her time. He had no better idea now than
before of her reason for visiting the solicitor.

In truth, he was making very little headway on this case at
all. A growing urge to spend time in the woman's company
was the only result he had to show for several days' effort,
and he was not particularly pleased about that. She was already too much in his mind. To form any personal feelings
about a case was dangerous in his work.

Patience, he reminded himself. Her show of temper last
night was a sign of progress, was it not? He was slowly,
steadily attempting to maneuver her into an impossible situation, hoping she would be forced into revealing the truth or at
least into making an error that would give away her game.
How long could she carry on the masquerade? There was
some time pressure on her now, with a round of social engagements on the horizon. And Jeremy had yet some cards to
play.

In an improved state of mind, he put on his hat and gloves
and headed for the door. Too bad Mr. Fallesby's office was
not on the way to Charles Street. He would have to stop in
later today to make an appointment with the solicitor.

Falcon was waiting for Triss to return with a hackney when
Lord Danebridge arrived at Mrs. Isham's.

"I have a certain feeling of *déjà vu* about this," she said,
greeting the baron with a frown.

He grinned. "Why, whatever do you mean? Is that any way
to greet one's friends?"

"I believe it was only yesterday morning that you arrived at
the Covent Garden lodgings while I was waiting for Sergeant
Triss to come 'round with a hackney, and here we are again."

"*Au contraire,* my dear. Today I am here at a very respectable few minutes after the noon hour. It is not morning at
all."

"I'm afraid I am just on my way out."

"What?" His disbelief was terribly exaggerated. "Surely
you cannot mean to say you are engaged again for the after-

noon—two days in a row! I must have been mistaken when I thought you had few acquaintances in London! And here you are, seeking out even more—your Mr. Sweeney. Perhaps you have changed your mind about looking for him?"

"Oh, no!" Falcon assured him. "That is, I am not so busy socially. Business, you know. It can be tedious."

He nodded vigorously. "Oh, yes, indeed—how well I know that. Perhaps you would allow me to accompany you—I could endeavor to keep you amused."

His look was innocence itself, but Falcon did not trust whatever he meant by that last remark. "I do not think so," she said coldly.

"You don't think I could amuse you? I am crushed!" He feigned a wounded look that was so ridiculous she was hard-pressed not to smile. Then he exchanged it for a smoldering, seductive look that triggered a response in her pulse despite her intended resistance. "There are ladies who would disagree with you quite heartily, I want you to know."

What was it that fascinated her so about his eyes? She knew it was a mistake to look into them, yet she never seemed able to stop herself. How quickly they changed! A moment ago they had been as light as silver, and now they had darkened to the deep gray of steel. They made her forget what she was going to say next.

Fortunately, at that moment Triss arrived to announce that he had procured a hackney.

"Good day, your lordship!" he began jovially. "Saw your rig outside. Shall I 'ave the 'ackney wait, señora?"

"Yes."

"No," said the baron at the same time. "No need. I am happy to make my vehicle available for the señora's use."

Falcon finally found a smile for Lord Danebridge. Surely she had him this time! "Unless you came in something other than your curricle, sir, I'm afraid we cannot avail ourselves of your offer." She made little effort to disguise her satisfaction. "Sergeant Triss needs must accompany me this afternoon, and you cannot possibly accommodate all three of us."

The baron only laughed. "Well, then, let us all three go in your hackney! I am not above using a public vehicle when I must!"

Triss turned a puzzled face to Falcon. "'E's coming with us to the Tower?"

She sighed. So much for concealing her destination. "I believe not. You cannot possibly wish to join us, Lord Danebridge—my business takes us to the Tower of London this afternoon. I am certain you must have been there countless times. You would find the excursion utterly boring."

"Not at all! I find the Tower fascinating—such a sense of history and all. I do hope you plan to take in the Royal Menagerie, and the Jewel Office. Oh, and the Church of St. Peter ad Vincula. You must not miss those, while you are there on your business. Allow me to act as your personal guide and escort."

Was he unstoppable? "You mustn't feel obligated. I already have an escort in the sergeant. It is not at all necessary."

Apparently he was.

"It will be my pleasure. Let us proceed!"

Jeremy was quite pleased with the level of chagrin he had inspired in his mysterious lady from Spain. He thought she looked particularly fine today—her deep red walking dress was of the first stare, and its black ribbon trimmings echoed the color of her ever-present lace mantilla. For the first several minutes of their journey to the Tower, she would not speak to him at all and kept her head turned away toward the carriage window. He pretended not to notice, making small talk and idle comments about the sights of London they passed along the way.

Eventually, however, she sighed and turned back to him.

"Something puzzles me, Lord Danebridge. Perhaps you would be kind enough to enlighten me?"

"Anything, dear lady."

"I understand that you have a doting family at your country seat eagerly awaiting your return while you are detained here in London on urgent business. Yet you seem to have ample time to escort me to the theater and to the Tower, and you have made social commitments that extend through the next fortnight. Is this the way all Englishmen conduct urgent business?"

He could tell by the light of battle in her green eyes that she thought she had issued a challenge he could not meet. He was so charmed by the way that light seemed to enliven her entire face, he almost hated to disappoint her.

"My business unfortunately depends upon the actions of other people, over whom I have very little control," he said with a perfectly serious face. "I have no choice but to wait upon them, and I must admit they are moving far more slowly than I could wish."

"How old is your son?"

Jeremy smiled, thinking of Tobey. "He is a precocious seven-year-old, as interested in frogs as Latin."

She looked surprised. "Why, he is nearly of an age to be sent away to school! I thought he must be younger. Why does your wife not join you in the city?"

This time she had caught him by surprise. "My wife?"

"Yes. You never mention her. Last night I had thought perhaps she might be joining us at the theater." She glanced at Sergeant Triss and then back at Jeremy. "To be perfectly frank, sir, I wonder at the propriety of being so much in your company in her absence."

"Allow me to set your mind at ease if that is all that is troubling you," Jeremy said soberly. "My wife Anne died two years ago."

"Oh! I am sorry. I had no idea."

Was it true that he never mentioned Anne anymore? There had been a time when he could hardly converse without doing so, and an even longer time when he still constantly thought of her. Yet it was true, he realized, that he had hardly thought of Anne at all these last few days.

"I can assure you that my friends would not be so ready to embrace you, señora, if they thought there was any question about our behavior." Secretly, he was pleased that the matter had crossed her mind at all. Perhaps it meant she was not as indifferent to his charms as she pretended. Now that she knew he was a respectable widower, would her attitude toward him change?

"Well, I suppose I am glad to hear that, at any rate," she said and lapsed back into silence.

The imposing White Tower at the heart of the complex that made up the Tower of London was visible to the passengers

in the hackney long before it dropped them off near the foot
of Tower Hill. Falcon had seen some spectacular fortresses
and castles in Spain, but nothing she had seen prepared her for
this.

She suppressed a shiver as she and the two men approached
the entrance. The foreboding outer walls rose above the moat,
gloomy even on such a sunny spring afternoon.

The menagerie was situated just to the right of the west entrance before the bridge that crossed the moat. The animals
were housed in the crescent-shaped remains of the Lion
Tower, a medieval relic with two connected sections. Large
but ill-lit dens with iron gratings in the openings displayed the
occupants to anyone who rang the bell for admittance and
paid the keeper's fee. Reluctantly Falcon allowed Lord Danebridge and Sergeant Triss to persuade her to view it.

She had to admit afterward that the big cats—lions, tigers,
panthers, and leopards—had impressed her with both their
size and grace, although few had been inclined to move about.
The "ant bear" and the intriguing raccoons from America had
been more active and entertaining. But nothing could distract
her for long from her main purpose in coming.

The little party crossed the moat and entered the outer ward
of the fortress through the Byward Tower, where they were
joined by one of the splendidly costumed yeoman warders as
their guide. Falcon had no wish for an immediate tour and
would have asked the way directly to the garrison barracks,
but the warder had so much information to impart that he
hardly paused for breath. It was nigh to impossible to inter-
rupt him. By the time he came to pointing out the barracks,
the visitors had heard the history of most of the thirteen inner
ward towers and numerous other buildings as well.

"Sergeant Triss and I have business at the barracks," Falcon
said quietly to Lord Danebridge. "You must excuse us for a
few minutes. Perhaps you can even keep our devoted tour
guide occupied—ask him some questions about the Roman
walls, or find out who feeds the ravens. I'm sure he has plenty
of stories to tell."

The baron thought he could do better than that. It was of utmost importance to him to learn the lady's business here, but
discretion was required.

"You know I am happy to assist," he said, wondering how much it was going to cost him to be rid of the warder and how quickly he could convince the fellow to disappear. The warders served under the Constable of the Royal Palace, an officer of the army. Perhaps the style of one military man to another would be the best approach.

"I doubt that you will be allowed inside the barracks," he warned as the señora turned to head across the parade ground toward the large, colorless building with Sergeant Triss. Not that Jeremy saw that as a problem, of course.

The warder was fascinated by the tale of military intrigue that the baron told him, and with a suitable reward for his services went off in search of new visitors to guide. Jeremy had carefully walked in the direction of the adjacent St. Peter's while they were talking, in hopes that the lady from Spain would pay him no further heed. If he pretended to be occupied with studying the exterior of the church, he thought he might still be able to hear whatever went on in front of the barracks entrance.

Sergeant Triss went inside the barracks and returned a few minutes later to confer with the señora. Jeremy heard enough to realize that they had come seeking someone and that the person had been sent for. The name Timmins leapt out at him as one he recognized from the señorita's letters.

What was she doing? Rounding up a reunion? He still had no inkling of what her connection was to the three men.

When Timmins arrived, Jeremy was bold enough to stop dissembling and simply stand and watch.

Falcon had not realized how difficult it would be to hide the shock of recognition she felt when Timmins finally stepped outside of the barracks. Five years had changed her, and dressed as she was and partially hidden by her mantilla, she was confident that he would not recognize her. But her shock at seeing him came in part from the changes he had himself undergone—in her mind's eye he had remained frozen exactly as he had been on that awful day during the retreat to Corunna.

Triss's words came back to her—"'E was wounded at Vittoria and got sent 'ome. Someone took pity and got 'im a job at the Tower barracks . . ." Timmins had been a young private with much to learn, but he had been a strong, sturdy fellow with a strong survival instinct. His loyalty to Sweeney had been his first mistake. But the man Falcon found before her now bore little resemblance to the one who had murdered her mother a thousand times in as many nightmares.

His once-youthful face was marred by a long scar that ran from his left eyebrow to his jaw, deeply furrowing his cheek. The eye on that side was covered by a patch. He walked unevenly, like Triss, and seemed unable to stand straight. Falcon looked at the bare, plain building where he spent his days and the even more forbidding surroundings and thought that if he were actually a prisoner his life would be little different from what it was now. The Tower was a prison. He had already paid a high price for his service.

Forget him, her first instinct told her. *Just say you've made a mistake and leave!* But she reminded herself that Timmins might be the only link to finding the other two men. She had to carry out her plan.

"Señor Timmins," she said in thickly accented English. "I bring a message for you from a friend in Spain."

He looked puzzled and a little pale, but it was nothing compared to the color he turned when she delivered the rest. "The message is, 'Remember *Astorga*? Someone else does, too. There was a witness. Be on your guard.'"

All remaining color drained from his face and for a moment Falcon thought he would faint. In a voice that was barely audible he asked, "Who sent you? Who sent this message?" Then with growing vehemence he continued, "Who is in Spain? Who is the witness? Who are you?"

He took a step toward her, but Sergeant Triss moved between them. Timmins took a good look at him then, and began to shake. "I know you! Martin Triss! The Forty-third! What does this mean? Who is she?"

Falcon kept a safe distance between herself and the distraught man, but moved out from behind Triss where he could see her. In a remarkably calm voice she managed to say, "I am only a messenger. Do you know a man named Pumphrey? I have the same message to give to him."

The man stared at her. Falcon began to fear that he would recognize her after all. It was a risk she had felt she must take.

"Best place to find Pumphrey's in a gutter somewhere," Timmins mumbled. "Near St. Paul's, likely. S'pposed to live in the Aldersgate Almshouse, but he's never there."

Signaling to Triss to follow, Falcon turned on her heel and began to walk away.

"Leave Pumphrey alone!" Timmins suddenly shouted after her. "He's got devils enough without bringing back the past! And I don't know where Sweeney is, if you want to know that!"

He was screaming now, his pale, scarred face distorted with fear and anger. "Go to the devil, and take your countrymen with you! Wish I'd never set foot in that accursed place! 'Be on guard.' What does that mean? What in hell am I supposed to do? Spanish witch! Go back to the devil! That's who sent you! Go to the devil! Go to the devil!"

When Falcon looked back, Timmins had collapsed, sobbing and chanting his last words over and over again. Two guards from the barracks had come out and were half carrying him back inside.

Chapter Ten

The following morning brought gray skies and a threat of rain. At Fitzharding Street Jeremy, feeling as bleak as the weather, set aside a note from his son with the pile of other mail beside his empty breakfast plate. Tobey missed him. The lad's laborious effort to set those sentiments on paper in a letter included with his grandmother's told volumes more about how much than the actual words he had chosen.

Jeremy missed Tobey, too. He had tried to send a letter each day since he had arrived back in England, but the night before last he had been so busy digging through the señorita's letters looking for Sweeney's name, he had neglected his parental duty. He pictured Tobey, dark head bent over the task of writing, or eagerly watching for mail from the village. He knew that what seemed a small oversight at this end would create a large, disappointing hole in his son's day at the other end.

Shaking his head, Jeremy gathered up the mail and rose to go upstairs and dress. He had an appointment at ten o'clock with Mr. Fallesby, and he did not want to be late. Working on this case had turned his normally well-ordered priorities topsy-turvy. It was all the fault of a certain green-eyed lady whose real name he did not even know.

He should have taken advantage of her distressed state yesterday to pursue a line of questions, but he had not been able to make himself do so. She had been too shaken by the incident at the Tower to stay there after meeting Timmins. The trio had left immediately, searching out another hackney to convey them back to Charles Street. She had offered no explanations, even though it was obvious that Jeremy and half the people in the Tower could not have helped hearing Timmins' shouted comments.

Her conversation with Timmins had given Jeremy an important new clue—Astorga. Something had happened there. It was obviously the link between the three men she was seeking, and apparently connected her and the sergeant to them as well. He should have at least found out if she intended to look for the third man, Pumphrey, but all he had managed was a suggestion that St. Paul's was worth seeing. He had not even been able to bring himself to mention the speculations about "the Spanish Spitfire" that had appeared in *The Morning Chronicle* yesterday after her performance at Drury Lane. He had been too concerned for her emotional state and distracted by his own irrational urges. He had felt an overwhelming desire to knock Timmins flat and whisk the señora out of harm's way when the man began to rail at her. Jeremy had wanted to protect and comfort her. This, when he did not even know what game she was playing or whose side she might be on!

At least the puzzle pieces were beginning to come together. He wanted one more piece—some clue to her real identity—before he reported to his superiors. He had hopes that his interview with the solicitor this morning would give him that piece—if he played his cards cleverly enough. He had also put a man onto the task of checking the theater ticket offices in case that might help to locate the mysterious Sweeney. Perhaps this case would be closed soon, after all. The sooner, the better, before he began to feel any more inappropriate urges.

The grayness of the day reflected Falcon's state of mind that morning, also. Ever restless, she roamed through her sitting room in the lodging house, distraught and disconcerted. Her meeting with Timmins had rocked the foundations of everything she believed. During the five years she had spent waiting for it, she had imagined many scenarios and many ways to seek her revenge, but the reality had been nothing like any of her visions.

Yes, she had wanted to instill fear when she met the three men again, if such a thing were possible. She had wanted to stir the ghosts of the past against them, and had hoped they would suffer nightmares and sleepless nights while visions of Astorga visited them. She had wanted them to wonder how their crime could come back to haunt them now—after five

years of freedom, and in a place so far away. The beginning
of her revenge was to have been watching them live in fear of
they knew not what or who, never knowing if or when they
would be called to pay for what they'd done. If that had not
proven enough to unravel and destroy them, she would have
pushed the stakes higher.

It had seemed only a fitting retribution for the murder of
her parents and the nightmare her own life had become ever
since that day. But she had never imagined Timmins as such a
sad shadow of the man he had been, half destroyed already.
Oh, she had succeeded in her aim admirably, but she had
never imagined how such success would make her feel. As
she had watched him disintegrate and be led away, it felt as
though she had thrust a knife into her own heart.

Why did she feel so pained by what she had done? These
men had murdered two loving, innocent people and left a
young girl to die. Fully believing they had committed three
murders, they had lied to cover up their crime and had gone
on to live out their lives. They deserved to be punished, did
they not? What the law had failed to do could still be achieved
in other ways! Falcon was the only witness to their deed. Why
else had she survived but to accomplish this? Her own reaction confused her profoundly.

Seeking consolation, she opened the leather case that contained her mother's harp and took out the instrument. As a
child, she had always imagined that the angel carved on it was
a special guardian. She ran her hands over the wooden frame,
tracing the carved decorations. How much she had hoped to
see the harp repaired and restrung. But for the loss of her
trunk, she might have been playing this now, finding solace in
its music instead of the object itself. She stroked a finger
across the strings, releasing the discordant sound into the
room. When she closed her eyes, she could still see the look
of astonishment on her father's face as the life went out of
him. She could still hear her mother's anguished cries cut
short in an instant, as if it had only happened yesterday.

She remembered little else of that day, but she remembered
the looks on the faces of the three soldiers whose actions they
had never expected. Timmins and Pumphrey had looked
scared. She had never felt that excused them—she had

scorned them as too weak to resist evil and had hated them for their weakness. Sweeney was the one who had looked absolutely unperturbed. She remembered watching him wipe her father's blood off his sword.

Falcon let the tears come, sitting down and cradling her mother's harp against her. She would get herself in hand in a moment. Action was the only answer to this emotional pummeling. She had things to do.

Jeremy sat on the bench in the outer office of Twyford, Fallesby, Grant and Cox, watching the clerks go about their business while they studiously ignored him. They had developed the art of being unimpressed to a fine degree, and it rather amused him. *I'd wager that they would ignore Prinny himself once he stated his business,* Jeremy thought.

Eventually he was escorted up the stairs to Mr. Fallesby's small, dark office and was seated in the large wing chair.

"I salute your taste in furnishings, Mr. Fallesby. A man can actually be comfortable in a chair that offers so much space."

The venerable Mr. Fallesby merely looked up from the piece of paper he was studying. "And how may I help you today, Lord Danebridge?"

Jeremy had no objection at all to coming straight to the point. "I've come on a matter concerning a young woman who met with you two days ago. She was attired in Spanish style clothing at the time—I'm certain you know who I mean." He gave the elderly attorney a knowing look, as if they were fellow conspirators sharing a secret.

Now, if only the fellow would have leaned back in his chair and said, "Ah, yes, Miss So-and-so," Jeremy would have had what he was after and he could have simply made up something appropriate to fill up the rest of the interview.

However, Mr. Fallesby merely nodded in acknowledgment and waited for Jeremy to go on. The old man was nobody's fool.

"I have actually come today in an effort to do a service to you, or perhaps I should say, to your firm, Mr. Fallesby. The young lady in question here is currently under investigation by our government—the Home Office has reason to believe that she is an impostor."

It was not exactly true, but Jeremy settled back to see what effect this pronouncement would have on the solicitor.

The old man appeared to be genuinely surprised. "An impostor! Well, humph, harumph. Is that right? Don't know about that," he sputtered. "I found her convincing. I met her mother, you know. She looks remarkably like the woman, I have to say." He rubbed his chin, regarding Jeremy thoughtfully. "And I thought she showed her mother's pluck to march in here with no appointment and such an extraordinary story!"

Jeremy would have given almost anything to know that story, but he had to maintain the pretence that he already knew it all. He could guess now why the señora wore her mantilla everywhere, at all times. He waited, watching while Mr. Fallesby weighed this new "information."

"If she's not the real girl, she should be on the stage," the lawyer continued. "Wasn't her idea to come at all. Said her father's batman put her up to it. She didn't so much as blink when I told her she might need to return to give a deposition."

He gave Jeremy a shrewd look. "She made no bones about the fact that she was after money. I suppose that is always what it's about. But she seemed reluctant, and she was very hesitant to have me contact her relatives."

The lawyer tented his fingers and gazed down at them thoughtfully. "Perhaps now you have given me the explanation for it! She was quite definite about contacting her cousin herself. Thank God I only gave her a small advance."

Aha! So she did get money, thought Jeremy.

But Mr. Fallesby was not finished. "Now I suppose I must write to Lord Coudray right away and warn him, before this girl takes him in."

Lord Coudray. Finally, a clue.

The solicitor looked up sharply at Jeremy. "She did know her father was supposed to have been disinherited. And other things, too. You are certain about this?"

"No, sir. As I said, we only suspect this to be the case. The matter is under investigation." Jeremy did not want to make matters any worse than need be. Suppose his lady proved quite innocent? Armed now with the name of her cousin he thought he could learn her identity quickly.

"Then what is it you think I should do?" Mr. Fallesby asked.

"You must do as you see fit," Jeremy replied evenly. "When it came to our attention that she had been to see you, we thought it only fair that you be warned." He stood up. There was no reason to prolong the interview, now that he had something to work with.

"Perhaps the earl is the best judge of whether the girl is an impostor or not," the ancient fellow said softly, almost to himself. He stood up, too, to ring for a clerk to see Jeremy out. The last thing Jeremy heard him say was, "I must say it did seem rather remarkable that she could have survived." The tone in his voice sounded almost wistful.

Quite unaware that she was a topic of discussion elsewhere in the city, Falcon sent for Triss and Maggie and gathered them into her sitting room in Charles Street.

"We are going to go out and try to find Corporal Pumphrey," she announced.

Maggie and Triss exchanged a dubious look. "Are ye sure 'tis what's best, child? Ye have been more than a little upset since ye found the first of the villains yesterday."

"'Ow do 'ee expect to find the man, missy?"

Falcon nodded. "I am not surprised that you have questions, but I have given this a good deal of thought. We will pay a visit to the almshouses where he is supposed to live, and see if we can gain any information. And we will visit St. Paul's Cathedral, which is a wonder to be seen at any rate, I am told by Lord Danebridge. While we are there we will look around us and ask questions. We have more clues to find Pumphrey than we have for Ensign Sweeney. Perhaps Lord Danebridge will have some luck with that."

She frowned, noting how Lord Danebridge kept creeping into her conversations lately. "On the way to Aldersgate I wish to stop at a musical instrument makers in Cheapside that Mrs. Isham has recommended to me. I am going to have my mother's harp repaired and restrung. I only wish we had the funds to have your boots made, Triss. But if we recover my trunk . . ."

She was determined to speak to Lord Danebridge today about posting a reward for her trunk. What was the point of

having the money from Mr. Fallesby if she was too cautious
to use it? If she could recover the trunk with at least something of value still in it, it might solve the whole problem. If
not, she would find another way to get more. Perhaps the
lawyer would advance her additional funds if she asked for
them. Or perhaps she would advertise her services as a Spanish teacher, after all. Surely someone would hire her even
without references. Maybe Lord Danebridge would provide
her with a reference.

Falcon knew that she should actually be more wary than
ever of her involvement with the baron, now that she understood he had no wife. She was still distrustful of his intentions, but the slight prospect that he would be interested in her
for legitimate purposes seemed the height of all folly. She was
no candidate to be anyone's wife!

I should only need his help for a short while longer, she
consoled herself. *Just until I can find Sweeney and see this
through.*

She smiled at Triss and Maggie. "Everything is going to be
all right, truly. Let us be on our way, and pray that it does not
rain. I believe our stops are all in the same part of the city, but
we may still need most of the day to accomplish this list!"

St. Paul's at the top of Ludgate Hill dominated the section
of London where it stood, its great dome visible from every
direction. They had to pass it on the way to deliver the harp,
and Falcon had to admit the cathedral was both handsome and
impressive. She was glad now that Lord Danebridge had suggested she visit it if she went looking for Pumphrey. She
would make certain she toured the inside when they returned
to it. Unbelievably, she almost felt sorry that today the baron
was not with her. He was undoubtedly a fount of information.

The harp was duly delivered to Rudkin and Bowles, pur-
veyor of fine instruments, in a small warehouse in Cheapside
that had splendid instruments in the showroom. Falcon was
easily distracted by a dainty pianoforte whose satinwood ve-
neer was inlaid with a delicate design of flowers. Mr. Rudkin
waited on her personally, admiring her mother's harp and exclaiming over its fine quality. He spoke of Spanish harps with

enthusiasm, but Falcon assumed he did so primarily to flatter her and ensure himself of her patronage.

Back outside, Falcon directed the hackney driver to take them to the Aldersgate Almshouses. She was nonplussed when the man informed her that there was no such place.

Had Timmins lied? He had seemed to her too distraught to intentionally mislead her.

"All right, then, what is there near here that might be called such a thing in error? There must be some kind of almshouses in Aldersgate, are there not?"

The driver removed his hat to scratch his head. She hoped he did not have lice.

"There's almshouses near the City Chapel. Mayhap that's it. Or there's the St. Giles Workhouse—that's only a block away from the other." He paused, looking at her skeptically. "You certain you wish to go there? Risky business—cost you extra."

Falcon nodded. "We will try both places," she said, her resolve unwavering.

The chapel almshouses were tiny, set in a dismal row in an alley beside the City Chapel itself. Falcon decided the safest place to inquire about the residents was inside the chapel, where she discovered no one who had heard of an ex-soldier named Pumphrey. Dirty, ragged people in the street outside eyed her with suspicion and skulked in the shadows as she and Triss hurriedly returned to the waiting hackney. This was very clearly not a safe part of the city.

The carriage could not fit through the narrow alleys that laced through the intervening block to the workhouse, so they were forced to go around to reach Moor Street. The St. Giles Workhouse was disguised by small, shabby buildings that stood in front of it, but the main building itself was large, with a vast complex of small alleys and additional buildings connected to it at the sides and back. Falcon again instructed Maggie to wait in the carriage while she and Triss went inside. She did not think thieves would dare attack a hackney waiting in front of the workhouse.

Corporal Pumphrey had indeed been a resident of the workhouse for a time, the records showed. "Says here he was dismissed for drunkenness—that's no surprise," said the woman in the overseer's office. "You have to understand, we have rules. They can't stay if they can't follow the rules." She sounded almost apologetic.

"Have you any idea where he might be found?" Falcon asked.

"St. Paul's," the woman replied. "They go there to beg, to get drinking money. There's three services a day at the cathedral, so there's more people to take pity on them."

In the dark hallway, Falcon caught a glimpse of women and young girls in drab gray dresses filing into one of the workhouse rooms. The place was undoubtedly depressing, but she noted that at least it seemed clean. *No doubt the inmates scrub the floors,* she thought. *What a terrible way to have to live— without hope!* But at least these people had some shelter, food and clothing. It sounded like Pumphrey had not even these.

"We must go to St. Paul's," she announced once she and Triss were settled in the hackney again.

She agreed to tour the inside of the church before they searched for Pumphrey. "Ye might be too upset to do it afterwards if ye find the man," Maggie counseled, "and Lord Danebridge said ye must be sure to see it."

As far as Falcon was concerned, Maggie ascribed far too much importance to what Lord Danebridge thought.

The cathedral was vast and beautiful inside, well designed by Wren to inspire. It took some time to view the monuments and tour the side chapels and climb the stairs to the Whispering Gallery. The contrast between the splendor of the cathedral and the poverty of the workhouse was almost dizzying in such close proximity. Finally, Falcon drew the others outside.

"Let us walk about, and see if we come across anyone who might be Pumphrey."

There were many people strolling the open pavements around the great cathedral, including some legitimate vendors and a number of beggars. Falcon bought an apple she did not especially want to eat and matches for which she had no need. But finally she saw a beggar in the rags of an old soldier's uniform, and insisted on speaking to him.

"Do you know another fellow, like yourself, who often comes here? He served his country, too, as I can see that you did."

At her reference to his uniform, the man stood up a little straighter. "Twelve years I put in," he said with some pride, but then bitterness crept into his voice. "You can see where it's got me." He looked at her suspiciously then. "It might be I knows of another feller. What's the gain for me?"

Falcon sighed and fished two precious shillings from her reticule. She knew the man would likely spend it all on drink, but perhaps there would be enough to buy some food, too. It amazed her to see how his entire face brightened.

"I can show you him," he whispered, as if imparting a great secret. Falcon took hold of Triss's protective elbow and nodded, ready to follow. But they only went a little way around the building to a sheltered angle of the protruding walls. There, curled up in sleep, was another ragged, unshaven man who reeked of gin—a crumpled caricature of the man she had known.

"Is his name Pumphrey?" Falcon asked, and received an affirmative answer.

She went to the sleeping figure and tried to rouse him, even calling him by name. But the drink-induced stupor was too strong, and he slept on, another sad, useless soul whose life had become punishment enough.

"Does he have any friends? Anyone who cares where he is?" she asked the other fellow.

He shrugged. "Who does?"

She thought she ought to simply walk away. Pumphrey was dying a slow, miserable death. Was that not justice? But she could not do it. She was learning that her compassion outweighed her hatred.

"I am going to have him taken to hospital," she said. "I just wondered if there was anyone I ought to notify."

Jeremy could not resist the impulse to stop by Mrs. Isham's house in Charles Street after his interview with the solicitor. He had not abandoned all hope of taking the señora for a carriage drive in the park. As he stopped his curricle in front of the house, he noticed no one on watch. That was why when he inquired for Doña Alomar de Montero he was not surprised to learn that she had gone out.

"Out? Gone out? And here I thought I was calling at an indecently early hour—it is not yet even noon." He winked at Mrs. Isham. "So, where has she gone?"

The landlady dutifully reported what she knew of her lodgers' itinerary.

Jeremy sighed. He was better off if he did not pursue such ideas as carriage rides in the park with mysterious ladies from Spain. What he needed in his life was a nice, biddable respectable young woman who loved children and would make a good mother for Tobey. Someone utterly dependable and stable, from an unexceptional background. No matter who his lady from Spain turned out to be, she would never fit that description.

He climbed back into his curricle and pointed his cattle back along Piccadilly, trying to focus his thoughts on Tobey. *Soon, soon, I'll be home. I am almost finished with this case, I am certain.* He would try to write an encouraging letter to his son tonight.

In the meantime, he would head for the offices of his superiors, to make his report.

"Ah, Lieutenant Major! Come in, sir, come in. Just the man I need to see. Was going to write you a note this afternoon, but here you are," said the elderly gentleman to whom Jeremy made his reports. Even on such a dark day, his office was light, with large windows and white painted paneling. A series of portraits of the gentleman's predecessors hung on the inside wall.

"Still working on that agent case that was assigned to you in Portsmouth, are you not?"

"Yes, sir. You know that I am." Jeremy had worked for the man too many years to be taken in by his casual approach. His superior kept track of everything in surprising detail. "In fact, I stopped in to make a report. I've collected an assortment of information that I would like some help connecting. I think once we do that, we'll have a clear picture of the lady, past and present."

"And future? It seems to me that interests us the most. What have we got, then?"

Jeremy proceeded to tell him. He explained how the lady only practiced her Spanish act diligently in public and when engaged in her efforts to find the three mystery men, whom he named. He described how she seemed reluctant to let anyone see her, wearing her mantilla everywhere, and added that after talking with the solicitor, he did not know if she was hiding a resemblance to someone or the lack of one. Or, simply hiding her appearance altogether.

He mentioned the letters and named not only the señorita, but the other correspondents in addition to Sergeant Triss. One never knew which details might prove significant. Finally, he brought up the Forty-third Regiment, Astorga, and the Earl of Coudray, possibly the lady's cousin. Or not.

When Jeremy was finished, his superior rose and held out his hand in dismissal. "All right. That's quite a bit to go on. I'll look into the records for you, and get back to you as soon as we learn something."

Jeremy shook hands and left, hoping that he would hear very soon. In the meantime, he had his own leads to follow. He had men tracking down Sweeney and keeping track of the señora. His next stop would be his club. Someone there was bound to know about Lord Coudray and his family—maybe even the name of the lady from Spain. If nothing else, Jeremy was bound to find a few friends there who would sympathize with him that green-eyed women were nothing but trouble.

Chapter Eleven

The cost of putting Pumphrey into St. Bartholomew's Hospital bit deeply into Falcon's funds. As they had no letter of recommendation from a hospital governor, she was required to pay a deposit to have the man admitted, and she had to leave money to pay for new clothes, since Pumphrey's ragged ones were to be burned. She spread shillings liberally all over the hospital ward, or so it felt by the time she had paid fees to the nurses, the steward, the woman who changed the bed linens, and even more people she could hardly remember.

Nevertheless, she was still determined to put up a reward for the return of her trunk. To that end, she set off again for Lord Danebridge's establishment in Fitzharding Street once she had returned from the afternoon's expedition. Thank goodness she still had hackney fare. She did not care about the propriety of the visit—she had business with the man, and if any of his busybody neighbors formed opinions about it, they were welcome to them. She took Benita with her so Maggie could rest.

To Falcon's surprise, the baron already had visitors awaiting him when she arrived at his residence.

"Lord Danebridge is not in," the footman informed her at the door, but she noted that his attitude was a good deal more cordial than the first time she had called there.

"Might I wait?"

"His lordship's son and mother are already awaiting him in the front reception room. Do you care to join them?"

Falcon simply could not resist an offer like that. She smiled. "That would be utterly delightful. Thank you!"

She gave her light cloak to the footman. As she entered the room, she thought of the last time she had been here, hungry and worried about the theft of her trunk, only three days ago. So much had happened since then!

Seated on one of the cream-colored settees were a little boy dressed in dark blue and an elegant lady in a pale rose-colored gown. The lady's dark hair was streaked with gray, much the same as Lord Danebridge's was streaked with blond. *So, he takes after his mother,* Falcon thought with a smile. She wondered if the lady's eyes were gray like his.

The two looked up as Falcon and Benita entered, and Falcon saw the anticipation on their faces. It vanished quickly, to be replaced by disappointment and then curiosity.

"I am sorry," she said, "I am not Lord Danebridge. Only another visitor who had hoped he might be here." She smiled warmly, hoping to be friends and feeling somehow that it was of utmost importance. She hoped they were not shocked that she should be calling on the baron. "I hope I am not intruding? I had a small business matter to discuss with Lord Danebridge and thought I might wait in case he should return sometime soon."

She supposed the expected thing would be to introduce herself, but she hesitated, suddenly uncomfortable in her role of the Spanish doña. She realized that she cared what these two people thought of her, and she hated to deceive them. This once, Falcon wished she could use her real name. It was the first time she had felt that way in a long time. But it was too soon—her business was not finished. She could not yet give up the masquerade.

"In his absence, would you permit me to introduce myself? I am called Doña Sofia Alomar de Montero." Phrased with those words, it seemed less of a lie.

"Are you really from Spain?" Lord Danebridge's son asked, hopping up and coming over to her to make a very proper bow. How could she not be charmed? He gazed at her with an expression of interest and smoke-gray eyes exactly like his father's.

"I have just arrived from there," she said carefully. "My ship came into Portsmouth six days ago." Amazing how it seemed so much longer!

"Say something in Spanish!"

"*Encantada de conocerte. Como te llamas?* That means, 'I am pleased to meet you, what is your name?'."

"Oh!" He stopped, suddenly abashed, as if he realized then that perhaps he was being impertinent.

His grandmother rose and approached Falcon with gracious dignity. "I am Mary, Lady Danebridge, and this is my grandson, Tobias. Please forgive him—he is exceptionally curious."

"That is a wonderful quality to have at his age," Falcon said, flashing the child a reassuring smile. "I do not mind in the least. I am honored to meet both of you."

"A shared pleasure," Lady Danebridge said. "I am always pleased to meet acquaintances of my son. It happens so seldom. Please, we may as well sit," she added, gesturing toward the settees. She and her grandson returned to their previous stations, and Falcon followed them, settling on the settee opposite them. Benita went to the seat by the window that she had used on their last visit.

Empty cups and plates that held only crumbs stood on the side table. "Have you been waiting long?"

Lady Danebridge consulted a small pendant watch that hung from her belt. "Hm. An hour, at this point. They said he has been out since this morning."

"Goodness." His business matter must have finally come to fruition, Falcon thought. Would that mean he would be leaving London? But now his son had come to the city!

"Do they have frogs in Spain?" Tobias asked.

"Oh, yes," Falcon answered honestly. "And the luckiest ones have a fishpond or a fountain to live in. There are many fountains in Spain."

"Have you ever been to a bullfight?"

Falcon laughed. "Yes, I have done that. Many fiestas include a bullfight as part of the celebrations, and I have seen one or two."

"What is a fiesta?"

"It is like a great citywide party, with music and dancing and all sorts of entertainment for special holidays."

"Sort of like a fair?"

"Well, yes, rather like that, only held in the city streets."

"I'd like to see that! Did you ever see any fighting? I'll bet everyone is glad now that Napoleon's gone to Elba."

Lady Danebridge stopped him there. "That is more than enough, Tobias. Poor Doña—I'm sorry, what was it?"

"Doña Alomar de Montero. Really, it is all right. I know he means no harm. Yes, Tobias, everyone in Spain is glad now that Napoleon is gone, the same as people here." Falcon did not want a young child to hear what she had seen of the fighting.

With a rattle of china, a footman appeared in the doorway with a new tea tray and additional refreshments. It looked as though they might have a long wait.

Jeremy waited on the steps of Brookes's while a groom fetched his curricle from the livery stable in the next block. Vaguely he noted that the street pavements were wet—it must have rained at some point. The fresh air seemed particularly bracing and the clatter of traffic in the street seemed more than usually loud. Perhaps he should have waited inside to be called, after all, or more likely, perhaps he should not have indulged in that one last glass of port. Wine and cards and companionship had seemed like a very good idea while he was at it, until it occurred to him that he should head home. He had not planned on dining at the club.

Lucky that it wasn't raining now. He swayed as he climbed into the driver's seat and claimed the reins from the groom. Oops. Definitely one glass too many. Well, he had driven home in worse states than this many a time. Fortunately he did not have a long way to go. But he had not learned much about Lord Coudray.

"You have visitors waiting in the front reception room," the footman informed him as soon as he had handed over his hat and gloves inside the door at Fitzharding Street.

"Visitors!" *Confound it, who? At this hour?* It was very late in the day indeed for social calls. If it was any of his men reporting in, they would not be lording it in the reception room.

"Your mother and son," pronounced the footman in sober tones. "They, and the Spanish lady, Doña Alomar de Montero."

"The devil be blasted, all at once?" Did he really deserve to have all of the problems plaguing his life converge like this? What in God's name were his mother and Tobey doing here? He scowled, and the footman backed up a step. Jeremy was not in the best shape to deal with this right now. "How long have they been here, John?"

"Your family, not quite two hours. The Spanish lady, less—perhaps three quarters of an hour."

He really should not keep them waiting longer. Damn! But then an intriguing thought brightened his mood. *I wonder what they've talked about all this time.* Perhaps his mother and Tobey had learned something useful about Doña Alomar. He wondered how well she had managed to keep up her pretence, especially in light of Tobey's endless questions. The thought actually made him smile.

He allowed the footman to precede him and open the door, lest his own coordination betray him. Taking a deep breath, he walked straight in and bowed.

"Ladies, Tobey. I do apologize for keeping you waiting. Of course, I had no idea that you were here." *That came out all right, didn't it?* He hoped the smile on his face didn't look as idiotic as it felt.

Lady Danebridge rose and went to kiss her son. "Oof, Jeremy. You've been at your club, I can guess. You smell like a bottle of port." She wafted her hand in front of her, as if to ward off the fumes.

"Oh, come, Mama. Not that bad." He laughed. "And Tobey! Have you no hug for your lonely papa?"

Tobey needed no further prompting. He flung himself at his father, almost knocking him over. "Then you don't mind that we've come, Papa? May we stay? Please? Grandmama thought we should keep on waiting and she said you might not have enough room in this house, since it isn't ours. But I thought it sounded like you would still be here *weeks* from now. I just couldn't bear it."

Jeremy managed to keep his balance and hugged his son tightly, so full of love at that moment he could hardly bear it himself. This child, this bundle of questions and energy and joy, was the center of his life, or would be, from now on. But as he glanced up he saw Doña Alomar sitting with quiet grace on the settee, watching him greet his family.

What was going through her mind? The expression on her face was almost wistful, he thought. She was so very lovely. How would it feel to hold her in his arms?

Jeremy's mind was only too quick to fill in that picture, but then he shook his head. Too much port—that must explain it. How could he be thinking about her when he was holding his son? He pulled his mind back to Tobey.

"Son, I am thoroughly delighted that you're here. Yes, you may stay. We will find room to put you here somewhere."

But not for long, he promised himself. Today he had made real progress toward solving the mystery of the lady from Spain. Perhaps once he knew her whole story, she would cease to fascinate him so. Perhaps then he would not feel as torn apart as he felt right this minute, as if two great forces were pulling him in opposite directions. He knew he would find it easier to put her behind him in Hertfordshire than here.

"Mama, how long will you stay?"

"Until you are able to escort us home, dear boy. There are plenty of amusements to keep us occupied in London!"

"I hope so, for I shall still be busy."

Jeremy turned his attention to the señora. "I hope you have had a pleasant coze with my mother and son in my absence?" Somehow, the question came out sounding a bit accusatory, which he had not meant.

She stood up. "I am certain you have a number of things to do to see your family settled in. I should not be bothering you at all. I had just hoped for one moment of your time."

"And you shall have it. Mama, you will excuse us? I will return to you and Tobey in just a moment. I have been helping Doña Alomar to deal with some problems since her arrival in the city."

"I see," said Lady Danebridge in a tone that told Jeremy she was seeing far too much. *Damnation!* Well, he would have to put her straight about that right away. In the meantime, he asked the señora to step into his study.

"My maid?"

"She is comfortable—leave her. You said this would only require a moment."

As they left the reception room, he heard Tobey say, "But, Grandmama! She never did tell me if she saw any of the fighting."

Jeremy ushered the señora into the study ahead of him. It was one of his favorite rooms in this rather impersonal house—

someone had painted the paneled walls a deep slate blue and thereon displayed a collection of tasteful English landscapes. "And did you?" he asked, carefully leaving the door to the study open behind him.

"What?"

"Ever see any of the fighting. In Spain. During the war."

He could see by the sudden lift of her head that he had surprised her.

"It did not seem a fit topic to discuss with a child," she answered.

"But I am not a child." He stepped close to her. "I am a man. As I hoped you'd noticed."

She wouldn't look at him. In fact, she was looking everywhere but at him—she was nervous. That pleased him. He knew he was behaving abominably, but he could not seem to stop himself. He wanted so badly to shatter her mask, to make the woman she really was step out and let him see her.

Avoiding a desk, she edged sideways away from him. "Indeed. Well, it does not seem a fit topic for any *polite* company." Her emphasis made "polite" feel like a glove thrown in his face.

He moved after her and stopped even closer than before, his voice low. "What if the company is not so polite?"

"Then I don't believe any conversation is appropriate at all."

Oh, how he would like to prove her right about that! Perhaps if he went ahead and kissed her, he would stop thinking about it and wondering what it would be like. But the drink slowed him—she moved away again. They might as well have been in a ballroom, engaged in a dance of advance and retreat.

"I had no idea that your family would be here," she said. "I think I was wrong to wait and take up your time. But I came to ask you about posting a reward for my trunk. You do recall telling me that sometimes stolen property could be recovered by advertising, offering a reward? I was not in a position to do that a few days ago, but I would like to do so now. Can you tell me what I must do?"

Ah. He had known that sooner or later she would be bound to ask about the trunk.

"Yes. You must thank me as nicely as you know how, for I have already taken care of it all. The notices are out and the reward is posted." He was lying, of course, but she would never know it. "Ten pounds. I hope you will feel that is sufficient?"

"Ten pounds!" He could hear in her voice that it was more than she expected, more than she could have paid. "I suppose that is wonderful! I cannot help wondering if it is so generous that you will be encouraging more thieves to indulge in stealing luggage."

"Ah, there are already more than enough of them." Although he did not usually count himself among them. "But I understand there are items of great sentimental value to you in this trunk."

"Sentimental and monetary. I suppose I should be expecting too much to hope those will still be in it if we get it back." She finally looked at him. "Do you think it is already too late? Is there a chance it will be returned?"

The note of anguish in her voice betrayed the strong feelings reflected in her eyes. Like a prod it drove him to step closer—he wanted to comfort her. But if he came too near, she would only draw away again. "It means a great deal to you, I can see. I can tell you that I think there is a good chance we will get it back—in fact, I am certain of it. The reward is generous."

How grateful she would be when he returned it to her! That was a cheering thought, even if his guilt shadowed its edges.

"I am grateful to you," she said. "You have done a great deal to help me. I hesitate to even ask, but there is one more thing . . ."

She looked down at her hands and he took advantage of the moment to take another step closer. "Anything, dear lady."

She did not appear to notice his movement but began to pace rather distractedly about the small room. "I had thought— it seems wise, that is—I would like to advertise my services as a Spanish teacher. But I have no references. I thought perhaps—"

"That I could be your first student?"

"Well, no. I thought perhaps a letter . . ."

"Teach me some Spanish, then. How do I say, 'Who is that pretty lady'?" That stopped her.

"There are more useful phrases we could begin with . . ."

"Teach me, then." She had walked herself into a corner blocked by furniture and this time there was nowhere for her to go when he moved in on her. He positioned himself directly in front of her and lowered his voice. "How do I say, 'I think you are as beautiful as flowers in a meadow or stars in the sky'?"

"Lord Danebridge, please."

"That doesn't sound like Spanish." He grinned wickedly. "How do I say, 'I want you to kiss me'?"

Would the Spanish Spitfire meet his challenge with an elbow to his ribs and a knee to his groin as she had the rude fellow at Drury Lane? Undoubtedly he deserved it, but he would not stop now. "Spanish is said to be the language of lovers. How do I say, 'I want to make love to you'? Teach me!"

She just stood very still, staring at him with those huge green eyes. Her skin smelled faintly of jasmine. He wanted to taste it.

"You want to thank me, do you not? You want a recommendation, do you not?" His voice was husky. "All I want is one kiss."

"That is blackmail," she protested.

"Perhaps. I was thinking of it as more of an exchange. You see how desperate you have made me! I am an unprincipled rogue, you now discover. I am not the honorable nobleman you took me for at all. I am a villain."

"All right."

Her sudden capitulation caught him by surprise. What had caused her to change her mind? She stood stiffly, her eyes closed, waiting.

"No, no, no," he whispered, a soft chuckle lurking beneath his words. "I can see now that it is I who must teach you, *querida*."

Chapter Twelve

Falcon opened her eyes in surprise when she heard the baron's Spanish endearment, and at that precise moment he kissed her. He had slipped his arms around her waist and as he touched her lips gently with his own, he pulled her firmly against his body. Hard and soft at once—the erotic and unexpected combination triggered an onslaught of answering sensations rippling through Falcon's own body, overwhelming her judgment. As the man's lips moved on hers, gently nudging, exploring, she could not maintain her rigid posture but melted against him.

"Papa?"

The voice in the passageway outside struck them like a dousing of ice water. Lord Danebridge almost leaped away in his haste to have half a room between them by the time Tobey reached the doorway.

"Papa, you said you would only be a minute. I came to find you." Tobey looked from one to the other of them, clearly seeking some explanation.

"It turned out that the señora and I had, uh, a bit more business to discuss than we thought," the baron said, recovering himself first. "We are nearly finished. Run along back to grandmama in the other room, and we will be right along. Truly."

Falcon felt as if his kiss had drugged her. She struggled to gather her wits. "I believe we *are* finished," she said firmly as soon as the boy had left.

"Pity. That felt like the beginning of something extraordinarily nice."

Nice? Was that what he thought? What had happened just then? He could not have meant to seduce her—not in an open room with his family and her maid two rooms away. What had he thought he was doing, then? His behavior had shocked her less than it left her puzzled and annoyed. What had truly shocked her was her own physical response.

"Lady Danebridge is right, you are foxed." She had tasted the wine on his lips, but she was not about to admit that she had found it seductive.

"Are you all right? Should I apologize?" He looked like a little boy himself at that moment, pretending to be contrite.

She put her hands over her ears in exasperation. "You should just stop saying anything! An insincere apology would be no better than none. Just go and deal with your family. I will collect Benita and show myself out."

"Very well," he said, bowing without ever taking his gaze from her. "I shall obey. But I must remind you that we are engaged for the Giddings' dinner tomorrow night."

"*You* may be engaged for dinner. What makes you think I will attend?"

"I believe you could not stand to be thought a coward." He grinned like a devil.

The worst of it was, he was right. For that reason she would go, despite her meager wardrobe and missing trunk.

"In the meantime, I shall endeavor to put together some sort of letter for you, but I must say I cannot yet speak for your ability to teach languages."

She debated throwing something at him. "Sir, it appears to me that you already know far more than is good for you."

Jeremy had never meant to kiss the woman. At least, not then, not there. Dear God, what was the matter with him? He put on a cheerful face for the length of dinner with his family that evening, but despite his joy in seeing them, he was glad when they retired early. He followed soon after, only to spend much of the night in a restless wrestling match with himself.

After so many years, he was breaking all his own rules in this one last case. Never before now had he ever mixed his private life and personal affairs with his work. Never had he embarked on a plan without thinking it through quite thoroughly first. Yet suddenly, here he was, allowing his family under the same roof where he was working and taking the subject of his case in his arms!

Oh, he could blame his overindulgence in port at his club, but that would be no more than a convenient excuse. He was in trouble with this assignment. The signs were obvious.

He had assumed that he could learn more about the señora simply by being with her. To that end he had made deliberate efforts to be in her company as much as possible. He had also thought that forcing her to maintain her masquerade in difficult situations would ultimately yield useful results. Did that explain why he had kissed her? No. What of the social engagements he had accepted for both her and himself? He could not deny that he was looking forward to seeing her in a glittering social setting, and to escorting her.

The fact was, he craved her company, and now he was starting to want even more. Far from satisfying him, the kiss had opened the doors to desires he thought he had locked away for all time—desires that went beyond the mere physical craving of a man for a woman. *Oh, Anne, can you forgive me?* He had never thought his heart could be vulnerable again.

Jeremy received reports from two of his men at Fitzharding Street the following morning. As he closed the door behind the second one of them, he shook his head.

According to the first man, Sweeney had purchased tickets at the Covent Garden theater for Tuesday evening. This was good news, but Jeremy's first response to it had been all wrong. Accompanied by a joyful sense of anticipation, his first thought had been that now he had a reason to take Doña Alomar to the theater again.

The second man's report had caused quite a different but no less emotional response. This morning the señora had gone back to the solicitor's office and had not been received. Jeremy thought he knew whose fault that was. When she had returned to Charles Street, she had sent the Cornishman off somewhere with a package. Jeremy told his man to track it down. He suspected that she needed more funds, and he felt guilty as well as concerned.

How did he expect to continue his investigation when he could no longer think objectively—or think at all? In simple terms, his assignment was to learn if the lady was a spy. So far, he had found absolutely no evidence to support that idea.

If she was using an assumed identity, a theory which he had yet to prove, the reason appeared to have no relation to politics, international or otherwise. The people with whom she had connected since her arrival all appeared to be harmless nobodies, with the exception of the Earl of Coudray, if she had indeed contacted him. If the earl were somehow involved in the military, or in the negotiations for the Treaty of Paris, or even if he were remotely related to someone else who was, that might have been different. But what little information Jeremy had gleaned at his club about the man pointed to someone utterly apolitical and very much caught up in his own world of expensive pleasures—horse racing, gaming and hunting, like so many others with similar wealth or rank.

Was the señora truly the earl's cousin? Or was she involved in some fraudulent scheme? Jeremy knew that he was treading a fine line along the boundary of where this case became someone else's responsibility. But he could not let it go.

If I could just find out a little more. He had learned that the earl's family name was Colburne. A perusal of the man's family tree should reveal how the señora was supposedly related and who she was or at least was supposed to be. If he could just learn Sweeney's role in all this! Perhaps all he would need were these few more days.

Lost in such thoughts, he was startled when Tobey knocked on his door.

"Papa?"

"Yes, Tobey. Come in."

"Who were those men?"

How the devil was he supposed to do his work with a curious seven-year-old around? Nevertheless, seeing his son seemed to make the whole morning brighter.

"Those were just some business acquaintances involved in my work," Jeremy said, smiling.

"Like the Spanish lady?"

"The—well, somewhat like that."

"Will she be coming again today?"

"No, no. Although I will be seeing her later. She and I have a dinner to attend tonight."

If Tobey was disappointed to learn his father would not be

at home for dinner, he did not show it. "I liked her. When will she come again? She taught me some Spanish."

"Did she now?" *That's more than I achieved.* "What did you learn to say?"

"*Encantada de . . .* something. Aw, I forget the rest. Something about a llama. Isn't a llama a kind of animal, Papa?"

Jeremy laughed. "Now how do you know about llamas, my son?"

Tobey looked at him as if he should know better. "From that book you sent home to me last year, *Voyages*. Grandmama read me all the stories."

"Ah, yes, Hakluyt. Well now, I think what the señora may have said was, *'Como te llama?'*. Does that sound right? It means 'What is your name?'"

"You speak Spanish, Papa!"

"Only a little—*un peu*, as they say in French." Jeremy looked at his son thoughtfully. "Are you interested in learning Spanish, Tobey? The señora is seeking students—she might be willing to teach you."

He had second thoughts as soon as the words came out of his mouth. What was he doing, involving his own son in a case? Another plan with no forethought at all. But it was already too late. Tobey's face lit up with delight at the prospect he had offered. Apparently Doña Alomar had quite captivated his son.

"Oh, could she? Would she come here?"

Well, it was one way to help her with her finances, Jeremy thought defensively. And it would give him yet another way to stay in close contact with her. *For the sake of the case.*

"Suppose I stop in to ask her this afternoon while I am out?" He needed to tell her the news about Sweeney, anyway, and there might not be a good opportunity tonight at the Giddings'.

"Do I still have to do my Latin study?" Clearly in Tobey's mind the new lessons were already confirmed.

"We'll see, we'll see," Jeremy answered just as his mother came in.

"What is it we're going to see? I thought I would take Tobey out to Greenwich, it is such a fine day."

"Oh, Grandmama! Papa says I'm to have Spanish lessons and that nice lady is going to teach me!"

"The señora?" Lady Danebridge gave Jeremy another look like the one she had used the previous day. "Well, I must say I quite liked her. Very elegant and gracious. Yes, I was considering that I might host a small soirée in her honor. What do you think, my son?"

Jeremy thought that his ordered universe was beginning to spin out of control. He was determined to try to grab it back.

Like Jeremy, Falcon, too, had spent a restless night pondering what had happened between them. How could something so wrong have felt so wonderful, so utterly right? In that fleeting moment it had felt like a reunion of two lost souls. But it had been horribly wrong, and the baron's behavior had renewed all her concerns about his motives in helping her.

Quite possibly he was a villain. When he had warned her of it, she, foolish woman, had thought only of the warmth, kindness and humor that she knew lurked behind his gray eyes. She thought she had known villains enough—men like Sweeney, capable of horrors she doubted the baron could even imagine, like turning suddenly on someone they knew and viciously murdering them without reason or warning! The idea that Lord Danebridge should label himself one of them seemed almost laughable. Almost.

But then he had kissed her, and Falcon had discovered the truth. His kind of villainy was subtle. With one kiss he had almost turned her into a weapon against herself, too weak to resist the pure pleasure she had found in his embrace.

A man with such power was dangerous indeed! How easily he might draw her from her current path into another path of his own choosing! Lord Danebridge had been generous in all that he had done for her and was continuing to do for her, but she wished now that she had never asked for his help.

Was it too late to disentangle herself from his involvement in her affairs? Finding Sweeney, recovering her trunk, even the precious letter of reference were all in his hands at the moment, but surely she could undertake some of this herself. Perhaps Mrs. Isham would write her a reference—a letter from a lodging house owner would be less helpful than one from a peer, but it would be better than none at all. Perhaps she could discover where Lord Danebridge had posted the notices for her trunk and see to its recovery herself. And why should a woman not haunt the theater offices seeking information on Sweeney? She would not make the mistake of going to them alone. Her biggest handicap was a lack of funds—newspaper circulars and hackney fares would eat up her meager balance in no time.

Determined to rectify that matter, she had set off this morning to call on Mr. Fallesby at his office, never dreaming that she would be turned away. She had hated the need to ask for more money, yet the man had indicated that the funds would by rights be hers once the legal matters were settled. She did not know how long it would take her to find students ready to pay to learn Spanish.

She had been informed that Mr. Fallesby could not see her, and she had not been allowed to make an appointment. Be patient, she was told. He would contact her soon. She had left wondering if the man had changed his mind about believing her story. But if so, why? And what recourse was left to her now?

Sometimes she just felt tired of struggling. However, she had known when she vowed vengeance for her parents' deaths that her course would be difficult, even dangerous. She would never give up. With a heavy heart she had decided to sell the silver-framed hand mirror that had been a gift from Carmen. It might not fetch much, but any amount would help fill the gap until she could earn some teaching income or her trunk was recovered. As much as she hated to part with one of the few treasures she had left, she refused to think that she could do nothing without Lord Danebridge's assistance. She had dispatched Triss to a pawnbroker Mrs. Isham recommended.

Now Falcon stood by a window overlooking Charles Street, watching the flow of pedestrians and vehicles below her as if she could make sense of it all. She was struggling hard to keep her spirits up and feeling very much alone in a universe that had become a thoroughly perplexing puzzle. Triss, Maggie, Carlos, and Benita were all a comfort to her, but they were as much outsiders here in London as she was. She no

longer knew what to think about the only two allies she
thought she had found since coming here, Lord Danebridge
and Mr. Fallesby.

Almost as if she had conjured him by her thoughts, Falcon
saw Lord Danebridge appear in the street below, slowing his
curricle in front of the house. Oh Lord. What was he doing
here? She had not expected to have to deal with him until the
dinner this evening.

"I'm sorry, your lordship, the señora says—that is to say,
the señora is not in," Mrs. Isham's footman informed Jeremy
not two minutes later.

"Yes, I know," he replied with a resigned sigh. "She seldom seems to be, this time of the day. This is the fourth time I
have tried to take her for a carriage drive in the park. However, you may tell her that I have some news I must discuss
with her."

"But . . ."

Jeremy had seen his man watching the house from the entrance to the mews across the street. Certainly the señora was
not out. "I apologize for putting you in an awkward position. I
realize that she may not be 'at home,' but I am perfectly well
aware that she is 'in.' Tell her that I insist upon having a word
with her. It is in her own interest."

A few minutes later the footman returned. Doña Alomar
followed him closely down the stairs to the entry passage
where Jeremy stood waiting. She was dressed in a day gown
of white sprigged muslin that he had seen during his explo-
rations through her luggage. He recognized the pink silk
shawl around her shoulders, as well, and it gave him an odd
feeling of intimacy to be so familiar with her clothing.

For once she wore no mantilla, since he had caught her unexpectedly. Her splendid chestnut hair was swept up into a
knot of ringlets at the back of her head. Soft curls framed her
face, and a pink ribbon had been threaded through the whole
for a simple but charming effect. She looked beautiful, yet ordinary, with no air of exotic mystery about her. She might
have been anyone. And still he wanted her so much that for a
moment he was speechless.

"You wanted a word with me, sir?"

So much more than just a word! But he must not say that. "Yes, I have news. And as it is such a beautiful day, I thought the most pleasant place to discuss it would be driving through the park."

"I see no advantage in discussing it elsewhere than here."

"Oh, but there is! Two distinct advantages—fresh air, and privacy." He stepped closer, lowering his voice. "I have some information about your Mr. Sweeney, and also about your trunk."

He thought that perhaps, after yesterday, she would not feel privacy was to her advantage at all. He was happily surprised when after a moment's hesitation she relented.

"I will just need a few minutes to get ready."

He fully expected to wait half an hour, so he was surprised when she came down again ten minutes later. She had donned the black pelisse he had first seen on her in Wickenham, and was draped once again in black lace that concealed her hair and part of her features.

"Ah, once again the mysterious señora," he could not resist saying, which caused her to look at him sharply. As they went out to the street he added so that only she could hear, "You do yourself an injustice not to let the world see your beauty. They would fall at your feet."

"That is precisely what Napoleon thought when he invaded Spain, Lord Danebridge. It is my experience that the world does that for no one."

How prickly she was today! He could guess the reason—he should never have attempted to kiss her yesterday. And yet, and yet. It had not seemed as though she found him repulsive when she was in his arms. More the opposite, he would have said.

"Napoleon vastly overrated his own charms. You do not. I rather suspect you underrate yours," he replied, helping her up into the carriage.

He took his seat beside her and they drove the short distance to Hyde Park in silence.

"This is the best place to have a private conversation in all of London, if you don't mind occasional interruptions," he told her as they entered the park by the Cumberland Gate. He guided his matched bays carefully into the flowing current of vehicles making the circuit of the park. "While we are most certainly not alone, we will not be overheard, and may say quite anything we please. I am afraid there is no remedy for being stopped by acquaintances, however—it is all part of the ritual."

The señora was gazing at the park with interest. "It goes on for miles! I had no idea London had any parks this large. I must say I am impressed. As for the ritual, it is no different in Spain. In Madrid they drive along the Calle de Alcalá and in the Prado, and socialize in just the same way. But, you were saying that you had news for me?"

"I have learned that your Mr. Sweeney has tickets for Covent Garden on Tuesday night. I assume that you will wish to attend?"

"I . . . yes. That is . . ."

"Good. I have made arrangements to procure a box for that night, if possible." She looked uncomfortable, but he decided to ignore it.

"Have you . . . rather, did the theater by any chance provide an address for this Mr. Sweeney? Suppose he is the wrong one—some other man by the same name?"

"How would you tell? I thought you did not know his address," he said quickly. What deep game was she playing?

"Well. I just thought . . . it might be a way to tell—afterwards, I mean."

He thought he knew exactly what she meant. She meant that what she really wanted was this fellow's address, and if she could get it without actually having to go to the theater, so much the better. Who was this fellow? What had happened at Astorga?

Jeremy decided to try to make a game of it. "Why are you seeking this fellow, after all?"

She shook her head.

"Let me guess—he was your lover in Spain and you have followed him here."

He knew that was outrageous, but even so he was not prepared for the look of sheer horror that came over her face.

"A former friend of your husband?"

"Please! He is not any kind of a friend."

"Ah. A business acquaintance, then."

"No. Please, he is just someone I need to find. Thank you so much for discovering that he will be at the theater on Tuesday."

"There is no guarantee that he will actually appear. Suppose he bought the tickets for a friend?"

"Then I will have to keep trying. Did you not say you had news of my trunk, as well?"

He let it go, for now. That she was so reluctant to talk about whatever it was seemed significant in itself. Before he could tell her his scheme to return her trunk, however, they were hailed by a couple in an elegant high-wheeled phaeton that had drawn abreast of them.

"Yoo-hoo, Lord Danebridge!" It was Lady Varnham and her husband, the earl, who were clearly as surprised to see him in London as Lord Giddings and his mother had been.

Jeremy had no choice but to introduce the señora to them, more aware than ever that each time he performed this act the social repercussions spread a little further, like the ripples on a pond after a stone has been cast. He had seen the entries about the Spanish Spitfire in the betting book at his club, speculating on how soon the mysterious newcomer's identity would be discovered. By the time this day ended, he had no doubt that her name would be in full circulation among the elite members of the *ton*.

Once Lord and Lady Varnham moved on, Jeremy picked up the thread of conversation with his companion. He was about to spin an entire web of lies in order to return her trunk. Acting a part, lying, dissembling—these were necessary tools of his trade. He had fallen into his profession almost unintentionally, first as a result of military need and then out of a sense of duty to his country. But how much he looked forward to quitting it! He had sacrificed too much and stayed in it too long. *And I should never have accepted this last case.*

"I received an anonymous message about your trunk," he began. "Someone interested in the reward claims to have your trunk and will return it tomorrow. There is always the danger of paying the reward for the wrong item, however. I was hoping you would agree to accompany me, to identify it and the contents."

"What must I do?"

"Attend Sunday service at St. George's Hanover Square with me." If she was indeed Catholic, would she object? But she simply waited for him to go on.

"I suspect our thief will be there at a very early hour. I have been instructed to go there and look for the trunk. I am to leave the reward money under the cushion of a particular pew."

"Does it not seem very peculiar?"

"There will be few witnesses at a church in the wee hours to see someone leave off a trunk there. Yet later, particularly on a Sunday, there will be many people about, insuring anonymity for the thief who returns to gather the reward. It is actually rather ingenious."

"It seems fraught with risk for the thief, to me. What is to stop us from catching him when he leaves off the trunk? Or to prevent us from retrieving the trunk without bothering to leave the reward? Or for that matter, from watching that pew to see who collects the money and catching him then?"

She was too clever, by half. "I suppose he, if it is a 'he,' imagines that we are not interested in catching him, since he is returning our goods to us. I thought your chief concern was the recovery of the trunk?"

"Yes, it is. But it seems so wrong to allow someone to succeed at this."

"It seems dishonorable to advertise a reward and then withhold it. Suppose the person returning the trunk is not the one who originally stole it?"

"Oh. I had not considered that."

"Imagine, too, how desperate someone's circumstances must be to push them to such measures. In a city the size of London, there are many destitute souls. I do not begrudge them the money since our anonymous person is at least returning what was taken."

"Yes, I suppose you are right, of course . . ."

They had come to the place where the carriageway paralleled the shore of the Serpentine for a distance. Jeremy slowed his cattle, allowing other vehicles and riders to pass them. The view framed by the trees that edged the road was admirable, particularly on such a fine day. The feathery spring foliage was a brilliant green. The sun sparkled on the water, and a flotilla of ducks and swans dotted the swath of blue. Doña Alomar had grown quiet and stared out at it all thoughtfully.

"Penny for your thoughts, or should I make it a pound?" He would have gladly paid any price to know what went on in her mind.

She shook her head, but at least she smiled. Suddenly he felt as if the sun was truly shining for the first time since his arrival at her house this day.

"Then you will go with me in the morning?"

"Yes. Oh, you cannot imagine what it will mean to me to have my things back, if indeed it is not a trick being played upon us. I must have hope."

"'Shall I live in hope? All men, I hope, live so . . .'" he quoted. It was a line from *Richard III*.

She laughed. Actually laughed! The musical sound filled him with joy. He had no idea such a small victory would affect him so much.

She said, "I do hope my affairs shall turn out better than did Anne's in the play. Oh, there I go—more hope!"

He laughed with her, and it felt like freedom. He could not remember being as happy and in charity with a woman as he was at this moment since before he had lost his own Anne. Perhaps it was only the combination of the warm sun and the sparkling view that caused the feeling—but no, he knew it was the radiance of this beautiful woman's own warmth as she sat beside him.

The moment felt like a gift. He wanted to savor it, prolong it, but he did not know how. What would he not give for them to be ordinary people, on an ordinary carriage drive! But he could not change who they were—a woman who was a mystery and a man who must unmask her. No matter who she turned out to be, no matter what reason was behind her masquerade, still his own deceptions would always stand as a barrier between them. They came to the grove that marked the end of the Serpentine and continued along the carriageway.

"I believe I may have found a student for you to teach, if that would add to your hopes," he said. "My own son wishes to learn Spanish."

Chapter Thirteen

"I am not invited for any merit of my own, Maggie, but merely because I am connected with Lord Danebridge and am someone new and different—in short, a novelty," Falcon said late that afternoon as she prepared herself for the Gidding's dinner party.

She peered into the small looking glass that stood on the dressing table in her bedchamber and applied one last stroke of burnt cork to darken her eyebrows. A box of Chinese colors borrowed from Mrs. Isham sat on the table before her along with a small pot of rouge, both of which had contributed to the deepened color of her skin and lashes.

"How unfortunate that I cannot change the color of my eyes. Black would be so much more the thing!"

She had chosen to wear her traditional close-fitting black *basquiña* with rows of fringe, but instead of pairing it with her modest, long-sleeved bodice she had decided that the more daring, V-necked bodice with short sleeves seemed appropriate for evening wear.

"They want a Spanish woman, and that is exactly what they shall have," she proclaimed.

She only wished that she felt as confident as she sounded. Why had she allowed Lord Danebridge to bully her into this situation? The evening had every prospect of being an ordeal. What if the other guests asked her personal questions she could not answer? What if she made some sort of mistake that would betray her identity as a false one? She was not at all certain she could carry off this masquerade.

"Time?" she asked, getting up and taking one final, critical turn before the tall cheval glass near the window.

"'Tis that close to seven, child," Maggie answered. "You look as fine as fivepence."

"Do you think they will believe that it is the Spanish fashion to forego jewelry?" Falcon felt naked with nothing to adorn the length of her throat exposed by the neckline of her bodice. She would not be able to keep her mantilla wrapped about her neck and face for the entire evening if she hoped to eat. At least no one would know that the small jet earrings on her earlobes were the same ones she had been wearing every day since the theft of her trunk.

Lord Danebridge arrived no more than two minutes later. Falcon went down to meet him since she was ready; she felt a great reluctance to have him in her private rooms, as if somehow such admittance symbolized a breach in the barrier she wished to keep between them. She could not afford an involvement with this man, no matter how much she might be tempted.

She had tried to make the adjustments to her appearance subtle. Would he notice any difference? He raised an eyebrow as he smiled and complimented her, but he made no direct comment.

The carriage awaiting them outside was not his curricle but an elegant, glossy, dark maroon closed coach with heraldic arms emblazoned on the doors. She could not help expressing her surprise.

"Your equipage, Lord Danebridge? How beautiful!"

"My mother and son came up in it from my estate in Hertfordshire," he answered, handing her up the steps.

The interior was as luxurious as the rest, with thickly cushioned seats upholstered in brown velvet and walls covered with butter-soft leather. The discomforts of travel would surely be minimized in such a vehicle! Falcon's admiration was only distracted when the baron climbed in and settled himself beside her.

It did not matter that he left a respectable space between them, just as he had done earlier in the day in the park, or even that he made no attempt to touch her. He might just as well have climbed in and pulled her into his arms. His close presence charged the air between them and in the small enclosed space Falcon felt nearly overwhelmed by it.

¡Cielos! Surely she could do this. She had resisted his attraction well enough this afternoon. She was quite certain he

did not know the power of his effect upon her. Steel could resist a magnet if held away with sufficient force.

The carriage lurched forward and she gave up any idea of
switching to the seat opposite him. Changing seats would not
allow her to escape from her own feelings, at any rate.

Apparently quite unaffected, Lord Danebridge reached into
the pocket of his coat and brought out a small box. "I hope
this will not seem presumptuous on my part. I mentioned to
my mother that your luggage had been stolen, and she has offered to loan you a piece of her own jewelry to wear at the
dinner tonight."

Falcon felt the heat rise into her cheeks. How carefully he
must have been observing her, studying her—when? It had to
have been the night they had gone to the theater, for surely in
the daytime her lack of jewelry would not have drawn notice.

He opened the box, revealing an exquisite necklace of gold
filigree and black jet beads. "You did not say so, I know, but I
guessed that your jewelry was among the items lost with your
trunk. Would you not wear this as a token of friendship, just
for tonight? My mother would be most pleased to think she
had done something to help you."

He set the box on his lap while he stripped off his gloves
and then he lifted the necklace out of its velvet nest, holding
the piece gently between his fingers. It looked very delicate
indeed in his strong, masculine hands.

He sounded so sincere. Should she accept? Just when she
had resolved to disentangle herself from him, she seemed to
be getting more deeply involved than ever. Yet, to refuse
would seem ungrateful and she might offend Lady Danebridge, who surely meant nothing by the gesture but kindness.
If the necklace were a gift offered by the baron that would be
quite a different story.

"Your mother is thoughtful and generous, indeed," she answered slowly. "I had thought that perhaps no one would notice . . ."

She had carefully kept her eyes on the necklace, but now
she looked at him, meeting his gray eyes almost reluctantly.
"Thank you."

The warmth of his smile reflected in his eyes and very
nearly undid all of her resolutions to resist him. If he had tried

to kiss her at that moment, certainly she could not have pretended any kind of indifference. But he did not. He simply held out the necklace. "May I help you with it? If you hold your mantilla out of the way, I think I can see well enough to fasten the catch."

Falcon gathered up the lace veil and raised it. She closed her eyes, trying not to notice the warmth of his fingers at the back of her neck. She tensed at his touch, but he was done in an instant. *He must have great experience at this sort of thing,* she thought.

Until they were finally set down in front of the Giddings town house, Lord Danebridge chatted amiably about the various people he thought were likely to be at the party, and a little bit about Lord Giddings and how he had come to know him. He also instructed her in the peculiar British custom of "taking wine," which was sure to be observed at the dinner. *Only the English would take something as natural as drinking wine during one's meal and turn it into an elaborately structured social ritual,* she reflected. The thought brought a wry smile to her face.

She suspected that Lord Danebridge's intention was to help her relax. He truly was a kind and generous man. It was a shame that she was not some other person, one who could make him a suitable wife.

Lord Giddings's mother took charge of Falcon once they arrived, ushering her about to meet the other guests. Lord Danebridge was never far away; he seemed to be hovering almost protectively. Falcon found this surprisingly reassuring, although she was too busy to give it much thought. It was only when they went in to dinner that she felt suddenly quite lost without him, for they were each partnered with other guests and he was not seated close to her.

The party seemed to Falcon excessively glittering for something that had been termed a small gathering. In the Giddings dining room a long table robed in spotless white linen was set for a dozen couples and boasted a vast, impressive assortment of gleaming silver and sparkling crystal. Here before her was the very model of cultured civilization that the officers' wives had struggled so often to emulate both at home and on campaign, to their own frustration. But Falcon pushed such thoughts aside. The food was plentiful and excellent. The conversation at the table was lively and frequently turned toward her.

"And where were you during the war, Doña Alomar?" asked an older gentleman who had been introduced as General Crouchley. "It would seem that there was no safe place to be in all of Spain from what we hear."

"Ah, I take it then that you yourself were spared from having to serve in the Peninsula, General?" Falcon thought she might deflect the question by turning the conversation in another direction.

"I don't believe that the señora enjoys discussing the war," Lord Danebridge interjected from his place farther up the table.

Was he trying to rescue her? But it was his fault that she was here in the first place. Almost to spite him she decided to answer the general.

"I was forced to change my location several times," she said, glossing over months of hard, dangerous travel and experiences that had changed her forever. "For much of the time, however, I was in relative safety in convents, one in the Andalusian mountains and later in another nearer to Sevilla." With a smile she added, "We spent many hours making bandages and bullets, and many more helping Wellington—by praying for the deliverance of Spain, of course."

Chuckles and approving smiles met this sally, and Falcon began to feel more at ease.

"Do you find our English houses strange?" a lady asked, peering down the table at Falcon through a quizzing glass. "I recall that Lady Holland said the Spanish houses have no fireplaces! Lady Holland was there ten years ago—I don't suppose you met her."

"I did not have that pleasure," Falcon responded politely. "In Spain we do not have chimneys in our houses such as one sees here. We heat our rooms with the *brasero,* a kind of basin made of copper or brass. It is filled with coals and set on a wooden base in the middle of a room."

The company had many such questions, which Falcon answered as best she could. She tried to keep away from any discussion of religion, even though that appeared to her to be the biggest difference of all between England and Spain. In Spain, religious devotion was as much a part of living as breathing, pervading every detail of daily activity from the greeting given to people who knocked on one's door to praying in the streets when the Angelus bell rang. Here in England, she had formed the impression that practicing religion was observed merely as an afterthought, tacked on at the end of a week, but she did not think such a comment would be appreciated.

Her considered replies seemed to please the company, who continued to seek her out in conversation. To her intense relief, no one asked anything terribly personal. She nodded and smiled, even laughed a little, and the stiffness began to ease out of her shoulders. She could do this.

Jeremy was not enjoying his dinner. The food tasted flat and he could not seem to pay attention to the conversational offerings of his dinner partner, an attractive young lady who was exhibiting considerable patience with him. She was no doubt quite charming, if he would only notice. But he was too busy watching the señora and listening with great trepidation to what he could hear of her conversations.

This is exactly what you intended when you accepted this invitation, he reminded himself. *You have only yourself to blame.* Indeed, he had wanted her to be thrust into a situation where she would have to reveal something of her past in Spain and perhaps would even by some blunder reveal the truth or at least offer up some new clue about her identity. But how could he have predicted that instead of listening with rapt attention to glean information, he would instead feel protective of her? He was listening for trouble, ready to head off any situation or line of questions that might be difficult for her, no matter how helpful to him.

Even more reprehensible was that he felt jealous. He resented the other men who were taking delight in the señora's company, and when the ladies withdrew from the dining room after the dessert course, he was keenly aware of which gentlemen did not stay behind but went with them. He very quickly excused himself to join them.

"There is an art to bullfighting that you might find similar to your art of fencing," Doña Alomar was saying to a group of admirers gathered around her. She was like a queen holding court. Jeremy could not even get close.

Later, after several of the ladies had entertained the company by singing or playing the pianoforte, someone pressed the señora to take a turn.

"I am so sorry," she said with a regretful smile, "I do not sing or play at all well." She hesitated, and then she looked straight at Jeremy. Her smile turned devilish, looking just like Tobey's when he hit upon some mischief. "If you wish, perhaps I could demonstrate a Spanish dance!"

This offer, of course, was greeted with great enthusiasm. Jeremy was forced to watch while Doña Alomar taught a lively clapping rhythm to the group and proceeded to dance a variation of the fandango. She moved with remarkable grace and speed, but in her rather revealing Spanish dress, the performance was also a bit scandalous. Jeremy knew she had done it just to spite him.

"You have utterly charmed them all," he said to her later when he finally found a chance to catch her alone. He could not seem to keep the irritability out of his voice. "Have you been enjoying yourself?"

"Why, yes. Much more than I expected to," she answered, offering him a heartwarmingly innocent smile.

"I noticed that Lord Fulford was particularly attentive."

"Yes, he has been very kind. He asked me to drive in the park with him tomorrow afternoon, but of course I had to refuse, since that is when I promised to give your son his first lesson. He also invited me to go to the theater with him on Tuesday. Poor fellow, I had to explain that I was already engaged to go that night with you."

Jeremy did not feel any sympathy for the "poor fellow" at all. In fact, he secretly felt rather pleased.

"No doubt you will find this disappointing, but I must insist that we be among the first guests to leave tonight. If you recall, we have some business to attend in the morning and have not the option of sleeping till noon like most of these others."

His tone was unduly harsh, and he could see the look of surprise that passed through her eyes. But there was something else there, too. Was it disappointment? Or relief?

"Yes, of course, you are right. I'll just get my shawl."

He accompanied her, unwilling to share her company with anyone else any longer. Knowing that his feelings were utterly irrational did not improve his mood.

In the carriage, he put as much distance between them as possible and spoke not at all. He could not seem to get rid of the idea that kissing her would make him feel better.

"Did I do something wrong?" she finally asked him. "If somehow I have offended you or your friends, I must apologize. But I am at a loss to know—"

"You did nothing wrong."

"I must return your mother's necklace. It was very kind of her—"

"Not now." If he had to touch her now, he knew he would lose his battle for control.

"But . . . ?"

"No." Of course she did not understand. But then he made the mistake of looking at her, and the mixture of puzzlement, hurt, and concern in her eyes touched him as surely as an outreached hand. "God help me, do you not realize I cannot resist you?"

In an instant he closed the gap between them and took her into his arms, pouring into his kiss all of the passion long buried within him. At first she seemed passive, accepting but not returning his ardor. Still he could not stop himself. Then, slowly, miraculously, he felt the response build within her. Her hands came up, not to push him away, but to encircle his neck, and her soft lips began to answer his movements.

Oh God! How much he wanted this woman. She had completely addled his brains, and he did not even care. It was a total shock to him when the carriage shuddered to a halt moments later in front of her lodgings. The drive, which only a few minutes earlier had seemed endless to him, had suddenly become accursedly short.

He released her, thinking how beautiful she looked with the heightened color and dazed expression of a woman just roused from passion. "I should apologize, but I do not want to," he said, his voice husky. "Must I?"

She looked away, so he could not read her thoughts in her eyes. But slowly she shook her head. "I am as much at fault as you," she replied, her voice barely a whisper.

* * *

Jeremy felt better when his footman awoke him in the early hours of the following morning. Last night he had been at odds with himself and out of control. He could hardly explain what had happened. Today, at least, he felt quite clear about what he was doing. When the señora identified the contents of her trunk, he fully expected to learn something useful.

He had arranged for his men to take away the trunk yesterday afternoon while his mother and son were not in the house. The last thing he needed was for Tobey to start asking questions of him! He was counting on the lad to direct questions to the señora during their lessons and hoped that she might be less guarded in her answers to a child.

Meanwhile, his men should have secreted the trunk in a corner of St. George's within the past hour, and he was expecting them to come by soon to report. He dressed with care, patiently waiting while his valet fixed his cravat, and then went down to take an early breakfast.

Nicholson knocked on the door so discreetly that Jeremy had no idea the man had arrived until the footman brought him into the dining room where Jeremy sat at table. After observing the way the fellow eyed the aromatic spread on the side table, Jeremy took pity on him and invited him to help himself.

Munching a warm, buttered muffin, Jeremy waited.

" 'Twasn't much choice of where to leave the trunk, sir," Nicholson said after wolfing down toast and a boiled egg in herbed cream sauce. Forking a slice of cold ham onto his plate he added, "We've left it behind the stairs that lead up to the north gallery. 'Twas there or in the chapel, and we didn't fancy carrying it in through the church, or you having to carry it out again."

"That sounds perfect, Nicholson. Thank you. The chapel would definitely have drawn too much attention to us all, coming or going." Jeremy nodded, satisfied that his plan was well under way.

He had explained to his mother and son yesterday about the hope of recovering the stolen trunk—there was no avoiding including them in the lie, since they insisted that they would accompany him to church. Having to do so had left a bitter taste in his mouth, however. Lying to his own family! Was there no end to the deceptions his duty required of him? In order to finally quit this business, must he sacrifice the last remaining vestiges of honor and decency that he hoped he still possessed?

The cost was exorbitant, the irony too cruel—especially now, when he was no longer certain that his assignment had merit. He had found no proof that the señora was a foreign agent. Without that justification, the mere fact that this was his job did little to soothe his conscience. How he wished that he could enjoy Tobey's delight at the simple prospect of "something interesting" going on!

A good hour after Nicholson had left, Lady Danebridge and Tobey came down to breakfast.

"Are you going to try to catch the thief?" was the first thing out of Tobey's mouth after he greeted his father.

"Thief?" said Lady Danebridge.

"You know, Grandmama. The trunk thief."

The baron thought there was a familiar ring to this conversation. "Well now, Tobey, all we would have is a person who returned the trunk to its rightful owner, don't you see? We would have no proof that the person was the same one who stole it."

"Oh." The boy's disappointment was obvious.

"Doña Alomar will be very happy to get her trunk back, I think, even without catching anyone."

The mention of the señora brightened Tobey right up again. "Will she come in our carriage, Papa? When will we go to meet her? Can we take a drive with her after church?"

"We will go to fetch her in our carriage soon after you finish your meal, lad. We would like to be early enough to look for the trunk before the church is full of people and the service begins. Therefore, you would be well advised to forego asking questions in favor of eating. Unless, of course, you have changed your mind about coming along?"

Jeremy had to chuckle when he saw how fast the food began to disappear from Tobey's plate.

A short while later they were en route to Charles Street.

"I know you would like to take the señora for a drive after church, son," the baron said as their coach turned the corner of Manchester Square, "but remember that she will want to take her trunk back to her lodgings right away. I realize that weather is no doubt irrelevant to someone of your age, but even so I would point out to you in addition that it is cool and gray this morning, with a threat of rain in the air. Will you settle for a Spanish lesson? She has promised to give you one later this afternoon."

"Oh yes, Papa!"

That issue settled, Tobey moved on to other questions, such as whether Doña Alomar lived where she did because the street around the corner was called Spanish Place. Moments later the coach turned into Charles Street and drew up in front of Mrs. Isham's lodging house.

Falcon was ready when the baron and his family arrived to escort her to church. She had resolved to put the events of the previous evening behind her, as if they had never happened. She would pretend that it meant nothing. Certainly Lord Danebridge would behave with decorum in front of his family. And so would she.

She had, in fact, been waiting for quite some minutes, so eager was she to go to the church and find her trunk. She had convinced herself that her mother's jewelry would be gone, but she held great hope that the other keepsakes would not have appeared to be valuable to anyone else. Perhaps even the banknotes, drawn on a foreign bank as they were, might have presented too much of a problem for a common thief to bother with.

She had decided that her mantilla would only single her out for attention among the Sunday churchgoers. Accordingly, she had borrowed Maggie's best black silk bonnet, which was trimmed with fabric flowers and a small plume of the same color and which had an admirably deep, concealing brim. The effect, combined with her burgundy-colored walking dress and a large black silk shawl, was utterly sober and discreet. She hoped that Lord Danebridge would not see anyone with whom he would be expected to exchange greetings or introductions.

His expression was inscrutable when she came down to

meet him. "You are looking, uh, very respectable this morn-ing, señora," he said, offering his arm.

As she took it he turned to her with a quick grin and peered playfully under the brim of her bonnet. "I do have the right woman, do I not?"

She pulled back instinctively, and he chuckled, patting her hand, still in the crook of his elbow. "Just checking, you know." As the door closed behind them and they descended the steps to the sidewalk, he added in a low voice, "I admit I can think of ways I might enjoy testing that."

He deserved a slap for that impertinence, but she could not do it in front of his family, who were sitting in the waiting carriage. She was spared the necessity of replying as he opened the door of the coach and assisted her up the steps.

She settled beside Lady Danebridge, relieved to sit any-where that was not beside the baron. She did not even have to look at him after he seated himself opposite her, for Tobey was well pleased to have her attention. It felt very odd to Fal-con to be riding in their carriage so much like a little family group; it called up memories of a past lost forever and con-jured up images of a future that could never be.

"You look sad," Tobey remarked, honest and observant like most children his age.

"I was just remembering days long since gone by. Forgive me?" She smiled. "In Spanish we say, *'perdone'*."

Tobey grinned and in that moment resembled his father so greatly that she had to look away. She found herself wonder-ing what the baron's wife had been like.

They reached St. George's a few minutes later. The mas-sive, stone-columned portico impressed Falcon as the little group hurried up the steps and went inside.

"The trunk is supposed to be behind the stairs," Lord Dane-bridge whispered, taking possession of her arm and steering her past the stairway to the north gallery. Back in the shad-ows, it seemed to Falcon that he kept hold of her a bit longer than necessary. But sure enough, tucked back against the wall was a trunk. It looked like hers.

"Is it locked? I must check the contents to be certain . . ."

"I do not think we can take the time just now. People are beginning to come in for the service. We'll have to wait."

Jeremy had no more wish to wait than the señora did, he was certain, but the risk of attracting attention had become too great. He could just imagine the curious looks and indignant reactions they would receive if people arriving for church were met by the sight of a young woman rifling through the contents of a trunk and displaying her personal items for all to see.

"Come, let us deposit the reward money and take seats. I am sure the trunk will still be here when the service is over. We will just have to wait until everyone leaves."

Jeremy had prearranged for one of his men to bring his own family and sit in the pew where the reward money was to be left. He experienced a few anxious moments between the time he left the reward and the moment when the man and his wife appeared—what if someone else filled all the seats in that pew? But it seemed to work out perfectly; the man and his wife arrived early enough to be sure they got the pew, and a short while later their eldest daughter came in with two younger children, who sat quite innocently where the money was hidden.

Never had a church service seemed to pass so slowly. Jeremy was as fidgety as Tobey by the time the sermon was over. He glanced at the señora frequently, trying to determine if she was uncomfortable in a Protestant setting, but she did not seem to be. Perhaps he had been mistaken when he thought she must be Catholic.

Suppose he was mistaken about her in everything? Could she not be both the cousin of the Earl of Coudray *and* the widow of a Spanish lord? Had she ever claimed to be Spanish born? She had never made any claims at all, and he had never been in a position to confront her. He had lied to, stolen from, and spied upon her. And he very much feared he was in love with her.

Chapter Fourteen

Jeremy studied the señora's face as she watched the congregation of St. George's slowly and sociably make their way up the aisles after the service ended. He had no doubt that she was looking at each person, wondering who among them had returned—and quite possibly previously stolen—her trunk.

Did she seek to know the thief out of righteous anger or compassion? Since so many of the people gathered there for worship were well-heeled residents of the most fashionable West End addresses, there was an element of the ridiculous to it all that tugged at his sense of humor along with his sense of guilt. But how shocked and angry she would be if she knew that the true culprit was sitting right beside her!

Meanwhile, Jeremy's mother smiled and nodded happily at various acquaintances, occasionally pointing out certain people to Jeremy. "You see?" she would say, tugging his sleeve. "There's Lady So-and-so. I had no idea that she attended St. George's! I'm so glad we came."

For the life of him Jeremy could not see why which church Lady So-and-so attended and whether or not his mother knew about it should make any difference in anything. But at least she was happy and occupied for the moment. Tobey, on the other hand, begged to be released from captivity.

"Can I go up in the pulpit, Papa? Do you mind if I go see the chapel? What about the gallery? I want to go up and see the great organ and look down upon all the people."

Jeremy thought the church could not empty out soon enough. However, Tobey's curiosity did provide a good excuse for their little group's staying behind when the last stragglers finally paid their respects to the minister and went out. The good reverend had no problem with visitors who wished to admire his beautiful church and left them to it. While

Tobey climbed the stairs to explore the upper regions and Lady Danebridge went to examine the painting of the Last Supper behind the altar, Jeremy and Doña Alomar pulled her trunk out into the light. As Jeremy knew perfectly well, it was not locked.

"Yes, this is my trunk—it truly is," she whispered excitedly as she knelt down beside it and opened it. "My clothes . . ."

But Jeremy, squatting beside her, noticed that she gave the clothing only a cursory glance, delving quickly to the bottom of the trunk. *Yes,* he thought, *that is where the important items are. Tell me your secrets, lady from Spain.*

She leaned over the trunk, feeling for the items underneath the clothes, her face a mixed study in anticipation and concentration. Then with a sudden cry of "oh, botheration!" she gathered a huge armful of clothing and dumped it unceremoniously onto the floor. The items at the bottom of the trunk lay revealed.

Jeremy knew that she would find everything there. Which item would she seek out first? The purse of banknotes? The Bible? Which item meant the most to her? She seemed to have forgotten that he was there with her, which suited him very well for the moment.

"Yes," she whispered, "Oh, yes." She touched the Bible, the box of rosary beads, even the packet of letters he had so carefully replaced. But it was the other box, the one with the jewels, that she lifted out reverently. "Oh, I cannot believe that they left me this!" She hugged the box, then set it down and opened it. "There they are."

The pearl and emerald jewelry lay nestled in the box, but it was the miniatures she took out, cradling them in her hand. The look of longing and loss on her face moved him profoundly.

"My parents," she said so softly that he almost didn't catch her words.

Her parents. Her father was the British officer. Not her husband, or anyone else. And the woman who looked so much like her was not her at all, but her mother. It made so much sense. But what small sense of triumph he might have felt at beginning to learn some answers was completely overwhelmed by his realization of the heartache he had caused her by stealing the trunk.

"What about the other items?" he asked gently. He wanted answers now more for himself than for his job, simply for the sake of knowing her. He looked at her closely and saw the unshed tears lurking in those beautiful green eyes.

"My mother's Bible, my mother's rosaries, my letters, my purse, thanks to God," she recited. She replaced the portraits of her parents in the wooden box and touched the pearls. "My father bought these for my mother when they married. She always hoped I would someday pass them along to a daughter."

The tears spilled over, but Jeremy was ready. Standing up, he raised her by the hand and then took her into his arms. He did nothing but hold her, wishing for once only to offer comfort. He pressed his handkerchief into her hand.

"It is all right now," he said, relishing the feel of her in his arms. "You have them all back. Someday you can give those to a daughter after all."

He was surprised when she shook her head vehemently. He held her a little tighter, inhaling her faint scent of jasmine. "Now, no one can know what the future holds. For the immediate future at hand, I suggest we pack this back up and have it taken to your lodgings. St. George's Church seems a very unlikely place for a lady to be unpacking her luggage!"

He released her and stepped back, studying her as she dried her eyes. He was gratified when she answered his slight attempt at humor with a small, brave smile. "I will summon the others and go outside to find our coachman," he said hurriedly, before the urge to take her back into his arms could become too strong.

It was only later, after he had delivered her and her trunk to Charles Street, that he thought any more about what she had said. Her mother's Bible and rosaries—her mother had been the Catholic. But she had claimed the letters as her own. That did not begin to explain why they were all addressed to Señorita Alvez Bonastre.

"'*Buenos días*' means 'good morning or good day,'" Falcon instructed Tobey several hours later. Lord Danebridge had set them up comfortably in his study at Fitzharding Street, and she and the boy were proceeding with his first lesson. "*'Buenas tardes'* means 'good afternoon or good evening.'"

"*Buenas tardes, señora,*" Tobey said dutifully, looking at the beginning phrases Falcon had inscribed on paper for him. "But why aren't the '*buenos*-es' the same? One has an 'o' and one has an 'a.'"

"That is right, Tobey, they are different, and you are very smart to notice it. It is the same as in Latin—certain words, the nouns, are masculine or feminine. The other words that describe them, the adjectives, have to match."

The child seemed to positively glow whenever she praised him, and he seemed eager for her attention and company. *He is lonely,* she realized. Perhaps Lord Danebridge had shown greater wisdom than she had credited to him when he had asked her to undertake this task. Teaching his son gave her experience, possibly a good reference, and at the same time it provided Tobey with both diversion and social contact. Now that she had recovered the banknotes Don Andrés had given her, she should not need to pursue this course, but she had not wanted to disappoint the boy.

"Do you remember which one of those means, 'pleased to meet you'? It is what I said to you the other day when we first met."

Tobey found it almost immediately. "*Encantada de conocerte.*"

She laughed delightedly. "Excellent! Oh, I can see that you have a natural talent for languages, young sir! No wonder your father wished you to have lessons."

They were interrupted by the arrival of tea, which included a platter of tempting small pastries among the delicate cups, pots, and silver canisters. Falcon indicated that the lesson could be stopped while they refreshed themselves. She poured the tea while Tobey helped himself to a plate of tempting tidbits. In between mouthfuls, he plied Falcon with questions.

"Are you going to make your home in London now, señora?"

"Well, no. I came here on some business, and when it is finished I shall have no reason to stay."

"But London is so jolly! Do you not like it?"

"London is without question a splendid city. Certainly I

like many things about it." Sitting, she sipped her tea but found it too hot. Quite improperly, she fanned it with her hand.

"Will you stay in England when your business is done? What kind of business is it?"

She tried to respond very casually. "Oh, I came here to find some people. Once I have done that, I expect I shall return to Spain, even though it can be very hot there in summer. Tell me what *you* like about London."

This prompting released a flood of information about Mrs. Salmon's Waxworks and Burford's Panorama and Mr. Bullock's incredible Egyptian Hall in Piccadilly. Falcon was grateful that her effort to change the direction of the conversation had worked so well.

"Grandmama has promised to take me to Astley's to see the horses perform—have you ever been there? Perhaps you could go with us!"

Tobey was truly an endearing child. Something about the eagerness in those gray eyes so like his father's touched her deeply. What would it be like to be the mother of such a child? What had Tobey's mother been like? Thinking of the late Lady Danebridge led Falcon further, to thoughts of the baron and forbidden imaginings of what it might be like to have a child with him.

"Perhaps Papa could come with us, too."

"I beg your pardon? Where?" Falcon was embarrassed by her momentary lapse of attention and grateful to be brought back to reality.

"To Astley's," Tobey said with admirable patience.

"Of course. I am sorry."

"How did your husband die?"

Falcon took a deep breath. Ah, the dangers of changing direction with a child! One never knew where they might go next. She knew Tobey was merely curious and meant no harm.

She tried to avoid lying to him. "My family were all killed very early in the war. In wartime, things can become very confused—things happen that are hard to explain or understand. I miss them very much, as you must miss your mother."

"My mother is with the angels, Papa says."

"I am certain that he is right." *He must have loved her,* she thought, pleased by the idea. Sometimes love seemed a very rare and precious gift in the world. Her parents had had that gift. "Your papa must have loved your mother very much, as he loves you."

"And I love Papa. Do you love him, too?"

¡Cielos! What a question! Falcon realized that she did not even know the answer. But at Tobey's age, innocence was blinding. As she searched her mind for a suitable reply, Falcon also realized that just as he saw nothing wrong in the question he posed to her, Tobey would see nothing wrong in anything she might ask him. She smiled. Turnabout could be fair play.

Listening in the next room, Jeremy was as startled by Tobey's question as he suspected Doña Alomar was, judging by her momentary silence. Children! He suppressed a chuckle, lest he accidentally reveal himself. How would the señora answer this? He was more than a little interested to know.

He had drawn one of the library chairs close to the connecting door to the study and settled there, leaving the door ajar just the tiniest crack. He had been able to follow the progress of the lesson and the ensuing conversation quite well.

So far, the teacher had not been as open with her answers as he had hoped she might be. He had noticed one thing, however. She had answered Tobey's question about her husband with almost exactly the same reply that she had given him the night he had asked about her husband at Drury Lane. Not "my husband" was killed, but "my family." She had no mementos of her husband in her belongings—no miniature of him, no letters from him, no trace that he had ever existed. There was only evidence of her parents and other people.

"Your father is a fine man, young sir, very kind and generous. He has done a great deal to help me," Doña Alomar said diplomatically. Jeremy smiled, remembering the saying that those who listened behind doors seldom heard good of themselves. But the señora was not finished.

"Now, it is my turn to ask questions," she added. "You said the other day that this is not your father's house. Has he not a house of his own in London? Why does he not use it?"

This was not in Jeremy's plan at all.

"Somebody rented our London house," Tobey answered. "Papa has been away traveling. He was supposed to come home—to Hazelworth, that is—but instead he had to come here. Business, he said."

"And what sort of business do you think that might be?"

Jeremy left his chair abruptly, heading for the door of the library that opened onto the passage. It would not do to barge directly into the study, but it was definitely time for the Spanish lesson to resume, or the visit to end.

He rapped briskly on the study door in the passage and entered without waiting for a reply, smiling brightly. "And how is the lesson going in here? Ah, I see that hard work has earned you both an appetite."

Tobey and Doña Alomar both rose at his entrance. Did he see a quick flash of annoyance cross the lady's features? He helped himself to a pastry from the platter on the tray. "How is my young man doing, señora?"

"I am very impressed with him, Lord Danebridge."

If she was annoyed, she hid it well. But then, hadn't he thought from the beginning that she was a talented actress? He believed that the emotions he had seen her display this morning in St. George's were genuine, however.

"He's a bright lad. Perhaps he has had enough now for the first session, however. Run along, Tobey, and find Grandmama. Ask her to tell you what delights she has planned for you tomorrow."

"But, Papa . . ."

"No. A longer lesson next time, if the señora is willing. I wish to speak with her."

Tobey went, casting a backward glance at Doña Alomar that would have melted a heart of stone. Since Jeremy already suspected her heart was fire, he could well imagine the effect Tobey's silent appeal might have.

"Sir, it was a rather abbreviated lesson," she began.

"I know. But it is growing late, and we have no right to impose upon you. However, I would like to invite you to stay and dine with us, if it pleases you." Suddenly they were alone together in the study, and all he could think of was what had happened between them the last time. Was she thinking of it, too?

"Thank you, no. The others will be expecting me back. I made no plans . . ."

"That is easily remedied by sending a note."

"Thank you. You are very kind, but I think not." She turned hastily to gather up her shawl from the chair behind her.

She is nervous, he thought. *By George, she is thinking of last time! She does not trust me in the least.*

He had given her no reason to trust him, of course, and well he knew it. But why had she been asking Tobey questions about him? He wondered what other questions she would have asked if he had let them go on. He had not dared to, not knowing what sort of answers Tobey might give. He was determined this time to behave with the utmost decorum and propriety.

"There is one thing I need to ask you," she said in a rather apologetic tone. "The purse that was in my trunk is full of bank notes drawn on a Spanish bank. Can you advise me as to which bank I should go to tomorrow to try to have them converted? I know I may have some difficulty just because the war has left things in Spain so unstable."

If he told her that she would have difficulty for more reasons than that, would she believe him? It was perfectly true. Most respectable London ladies would send their man of business or have their husbands do their banking for them, if they were so positioned to have any financial transactions of their own. The señora, unknown in London and without a man to represent her, would be at a decided disadvantage.

"The Old Lady of Threadneedle Street—the Bank of England—is the best choice for what you want, Doña Alomar. However, might I suggest that you consider allowing me to represent you, or at least accompany you? At the very least I could vouch for you."

He could see plainly that she was reluctant. She did not reply at once, but took a moment to drape her shawl gracefully about her shoulders. Then she looked up at him, her face earnest.

"I believe I have already accepted far more help from you than may be wise, Lord Danebridge. You have been kind and generous well beyond what I am in a position to repay. I do thank you, more than you can know, especially after what you did for me today. But I also fear that misunderstanding may be growing between us. I think perhaps that I should face the bank without you."

Had he overplayed his hand? He had made the offer to help quite sincerely, out of his concern for her. She thought he only wanted to bed her and she was telling him no.

At least she understood that he wanted her. But what was the truth? Was it all still a game? At his end the stakes seemed to have gone considerably higher.

Chapter Fifteen

"Madam, I believe you must not have seen this morning's newspapers," the man at the Bank of England told Falcon the following morning. He was a pink-faced older man whose bushy white eyebrows moved expressively as he talked.

"No, I have not, that is true," Falcon responded with sudden apprehension. *What could have happened?*

She had bravely ventured forth to Threadneedle Street with both Maggie and Triss to escort her, marveling not only at the handsome, massive structure that housed the bank but also at the busy intersection where it stood and the equally impressive Mansion House across from it. Lost at first among the throng of money dealers, merchants, stockbrokers, and jobbers crowding the bank's columned courtyards and rotunda, they had eventually found their way to the hall where banknotes were issued and exchanged.

"It is reported that Spain is in a terrible state of upheaval," the man said. "Your King Fernando has returned, but he has suspended the constitution your countrymen enacted in his absence and has arrested hundreds of people as traitors against the Crown. You are asking me to honor banknotes drawn against a bank in a country tottering on the verge of chaos. Would you think this wise, if you were in my place?"

Falcon paled at the implication behind his words. To have recovered the notes only to find they were worthless was disaster enough, but she feared greatly for Don Andrés and his family. The don had been an open supporter of many of the reforms put in place by the Cortes and the constitution. Had he been among those arrested? What of Ramon Alonso, his son, who had shown such interest in her? And if they had been thrown in prison, what would become of Doña Luisa and Carmen?

"I am sorry, I can see that I have upset you," the man said, not unkindly.

"It is a shock. Forgive me." Falcon tried to pull herself together, but she felt dizzy, as if she had been spinning in circles and suddenly stopped. Her adopted world had just suddenly crumbled from beneath her as surely as if an earthquake had shaken it to bits.

"Oh, dear me. Oh, dear." The man looked around, as if seeking some remedy for her. She realized that he thought she was about to faint.

She, faint? She was made of stronger stuff than that. With a Herculean effort she straightened up in her chair. "I am all right."

The man regarded her thoughtfully. "It is too soon to know how these events in Spain will affect our foreign banking interests, I must admit. Have you any resources that we might consider as a guarantee against the funds should we run into difficulties? You understand I must protect the interests of the bank."

"I have some jewelry that belonged to my mother. Pearls and emeralds."

"Anyone who could serve as a reference for you?"

Lord Danebridge had been right, she hated to admit. Shaken as she was, she wished he were here with her now. She had struggled for so long, having his help since she had arrived in London had been in many ways a blessed relief. But the price! Her doubts about his interest in her had been confirmed when he began making advances. She did not think she could live with herself if she gave in and repaid him in the way that he obviously desired.

Quite unhappily, she named him as her reference.

"Lord Danebridge? Hm."

She waited while the banker consulted a list among the vast piles of paper on his desk. Finally he looked up and with a lift of his eyebrows informed her, "I think we can do business, madam, after all."

Jeremy had spent his morning making lists of his own. One listed all the reasons that convinced him Doña Alomar de Montero was not who she claimed to be. Another set out everything he had learned about her business in England, and a third assembled the bits and scraps of information he had left over.

Having thus prepared himself, he set off late in the morning for Hatchard's Bookshop, where he intended to purchase a copy of the most recent guide to the Peers of England. If the current Earl of Coudray had inherited two years ago, his background should most certainly be included in the latest edition.

Hatchard's, as always, was busy; as many people congregated there for social reasons as they did to buy books. Jeremy managed to catch the attention of a clerk, who directed him to the proper shelf for the popular and essential peerage guides.

"Conyngham, Cornwallis, Cottenham," read Jeremy, leafing through the newest volume. "Coudray, Earl of." He quickly scanned the pages outlining the background of the sixth earl. What information he found there confirmed what he had gleaned from the solicitor, Mr. Fallesby. The current earl was the son of the fifth earl's brother. He had come into the title two years ago. Jeremy did not care what schools the man had attended, that the family seat was in Kent, or that the earl had a house in Bedford Square near the British Museum. However, the book did mention that the original heir to the title, one Myles Anthony Colburne, son of the fifth earl, had died in 1808—in Spain.

There had to be more to the story than that. Surely Colburne had a family. If the señora was his daughter, that would make her the present earl's cousin. But the book was focused upon the peers of the realm, not those who had failed to achieve that status. Obviously Colburne had left no male heirs.

Frustrated, Jeremy snapped the book shut and replaced it on the shelf. He was not in a buying mood. Why would Miss Colburne, granddaughter of the fifth Earl of Coudray, masquerade as a Spanish doña?

He decided to try going back to his club. Perhaps today some of the older members who had known the old earl or who paid more attention to ancient gossip would be there.

"Danebridge! You devil. Thought you were still gadding about the Continent in the company of generals and statesmen," called an acquaintance from the middle of a knot of gentlemen near the bookshop door.

Damn! Jeremy was also not in the mood to trade quips with a bunch of idle gents who had nothing to do with their time. But they caught his attention with their next words.

"What do you make of the news about Spain this morning? You are usually quite expert on the state of foreign affairs."

"What news?" Today Jeremy had not even glanced at any of the morning papers.

They told him, and Jeremy slowly shook his head. "I believe, gentlemen, that King Fernando is making a bigger mistake than may ever be realized in his lifetime. It is a sad day for Spain."

The gentlemen nodded, sobered by his response. One perked up again immediately, however, saying, " 'Spect we'll be seeing you about town then, eh, Danebridge? Going to the ball for the Wallinghams' chit? 'Sposed to be a new crop of charmers in attendance—good chance to look 'em over."

"P'rhaps he's not interested, gents," said another of the company. "I've heard he's been seen escorting the beautiful Spanish Spitfire."

"I will be there, gentlemen." So saying, he took his leave. He saw no point in mentioning that he would be escorting the lady in question and had no interest in looking over the "new crop." He decided to stop in at Mrs. Isham's before going to his club.

Falcon had made ambitious plans when she'd set off for the bank that morning. Optimistic that she would have reasonable funds once she finished that first errand, she had told Triss and Maggie that when they were done at the bank they would visit the Royal Exchange and perhaps several other nearby "sights of London," such as the city's famous Guildhall.

She had it in mind to stop at Rudkin and Bowles to check on the repairs to her mother's harp, and as they would not be far from St. Bartholomew's Hospital, it occurred to her also to check on the progress of Corporal Pumphrey, although she had not made up her mind about that. She did intend to redeem her looking glass, and she wanted to arrange at last to

have boots made for Triss from the Spanish leather she had
brought to him.

Dazed by what she had learned at the bank, however, she
was inclined to cancel most of these plans by the time the trio
left that august institution. She explained to her companions
the news she had received.

"Sure and everyone's thinkin' 'tis such a grand thing to
have their king back, and he goes and does this," said Maggie,
shaking her head. "Poor lambs, what will become of them?"

Falcon was despondent. "Nothing good, of that we can be
certain. Maggie, I feel so helpless, and cut off as well."

Triss said, "Missy, there's naught 'ee can do about it, terrible though it be. We can go back to the lodgings, and you can
be miserable all day, or we can get on with the plans 'ee
made, which might lighten yer 'eart a bit despite 'ow 'ee
feels."

"Whisht, you're only after havin' your boots made, old
fool. Sure and she has reason enough to feel miserable."

Falcon hardly heard them. "I wish I had written more than
one letter to Don Andrés since my arrival off the ship. I pur-
posely delayed, hoping that we'd recover the stolen banknotes, so I would have better news! Now that I have, the news
from Spain is disastrous. What if he needs the money now
more than we do? What if there is some way we could help
him? I do not know if he will receive any letters I send now."

"Never you mind, lass. You'll write to him anyway, and to
Carmen and to Doña Luisa." Maggie said. "Someone will see
the letters delivered. Don Andrés and Doña Luisa have many
loyal friends. Let us go see this Royal Exchange—'tis only
right there by the corner!"

Falcon allowed them to persuade her, although her heart
felt like lead. She could only hope it would prove as sturdy as
that metal; she was not certain she could bear losing a family
all over again.

Jeremy, of course, was disappointed to learn that the señora
was out when he called at Charles Street. He had better luck
at his club; less than an hour after he settled himself in the
coffee room of Brookes's to peruse the morning newspapers,
old Lord Saltersby came in. The venerable viscount was ex-

actly the sort of character Jeremy was seeking—a man who could not always remember his way home, but whose mind was a veritable catalog of the past triumphs and tragedies of the *ton*. He was exceedingly thin and moved with such stiffness to his limbs that one expected to hear an audible creak with each step he took. He had probably known the old Earl of Coudray quite well.

Opening conversation with the news of the day about matters in Spain, Jeremy had no difficulty bringing up the topic of the late earl's lamented heir.

"Lamented? Huh! No such thing. Never forgave the boy for marrying an Irish chit," Lord Saltersby informed Jeremy. "Not until it was too late, anyway."

So, Colburne had indeed married. Jeremy was already pleased. He could quite see where his mystery lady got her beautiful coloring—her Irish mother, the lady in the miniature. "What do you mean by 'not until too late'?" he asked the viscount.

The elderly lord shook his head. "Lad and his family were all killed in Spain during Moore's retreat early in the war. Lord Coudray never got over it—'twas too late to give forgiveness then, you see."

"Do you recall any details of what happened?"

"Should never have bought the boy a commission in the first place. Foolish business! Ought to have a law against firstborn sons in the military. You drinking coffee?"

Jeremy sighed. "Tea," he said, signaling to a waiter who was lurking by the door. "Now then, Lord Coudray's son . . . ?"

"I have it. Captain Myles Anthony Colburne, late of the Forty-third Regiment, his wife and daughter . . ."

Jeremy's heart beat a little faster. *Officer of the Forty-third. And there was a daughter!* This was just what he wanted. The fellow sounded almost as if he were reading it from the day's paper. Jeremy had heard of people who could remember anything they'd seen just once. Perhaps the old viscount was one of them.

"It happened just before the turn of the new year. I can't seem to recollect where . . ."

Jeremy leaped into the breach. "Astorga?" It was only a guess.

"Astorga. That could be it." The old man paused as if searching for information from all that was stored in his brain. "Was it a battle? I don't recall . . ."

"No, no battle there."

Jeremy decided to try a different tack. "What about the Irish wife? I take it that Lord Coudray opposed the match?"

"Stubborn fool, he was. Runs in that family. I met the girl once—charmer, she was. Strong-minded, too. Anyone could see they were inseparable, those two. The boy met her in Ireland while posted there with his first regiment. Moved up to captain when he came into the Forty-third."

It all fit. The uniform and regalia she had, the miniatures. Except for the one thing. "You say the whole family was killed? How many children had they?"

"Only the one daughter."

"So the title would have gone to the present line within a generation anyway, if he had lived."

"Oh, no. Wrong on that point. Lord Coudray disinherited his son when the boy married. The current earl, his cousin, was in line for the title from that day on. He waited eighteen years before the old earl died."

Jeremy sighed. He still did not have all the pieces. But he had moved a giant step closer. "Thank you for talking with me, Lord Saltersby. Care for a newspaper? I think I see the waiter coming now with a fresh pot of coffee just for you."

Jeremy stopped by Mrs. Isham's late that afternoon on his way home, and twice the next day, all without seeing Doña Alomar. She did not wish to see him until they were due to go to the theater, she insisted, according to Mrs. Isham's footman.

Jeremy wanted to know how she had managed at the bank, and he wanted to know if she was aware of the upheaval happening in Spain. More than that, he wanted to know what she thought about it, how she felt about it, and how it affected her. He wanted to know if she would give Tobey any more lessons. He wanted to know if she was Miss Colburne. He wanted—devil take it, he most wanted just to be with her. He finally admitted it to himself as he dressed for the theater Tuesday evening. He had not realized how difficult it would be to spend an entire day without her, let alone nearly two. It was a very bad sign.

For once, she was not quite ready when he arrived at the lodgings in Charles Street. Mrs. Isham's footman invited him to take a seat in the small parlor off the entry passage, but Jeremy did not sit. He prowled the perimeter of the room, fidgeting with the single cream-colored rose he had brought as a peace offering. Had Anne ever reduced him to such a state of nervous anticipation? She must have, although he did not recall it. At any rate, he had been younger in the days when he had courted her. To be feeling this way now was quite ridiculous for someone of his age.

A few minutes later he heard the señora's light tread on the stairs and went out into the passage to meet her. Really, if she was Miss Colburne, he must stop thinking of her as a señora. But that was not yet proven.

Whoever she was, she looked more magnificent this night than he had ever seen her. Under a lightweight opera cape of gray cloth lined with rose, she was wearing the green evening dress that had been in the missing trunk, along with the pearl and emerald jewels. Her black lace mantilla fell straight down her back from the high comb in her hair. She held her head proudly.

"You look stunning," he declared when she reached the last step. "All of London will fall at your feet tonight, without a doubt."

"All of London cannot possibly fit in the Covent Garden Theater," she replied. With a graceful movement of her head, she adjusted her mantilla so it fell forward over her shoulders. He noticed, however, that she could not help smiling.

"They may be lining the streets clamoring for a glimpse of you. May I be the first to pay homage?" He bowed and presented her with the rose. "I thought it was precisely the color of your skin." The smooth softness of its petals had put him in mind of her skin as well, but he did not say so. It might be too much. He wanted the evening to go well, and was very pleased he had dissuaded his mother from accompanying them. "Now that I have put you and the rose together, I see that I am mistaken—you are fairer still than this poor flower."

"And you have primed your tongue with silver to speak like

a bard. It is lovely, thank you. Are we seeing Shakespeare again this time?" She touched the rose against her cheek for just a moment, softness touching softness. Then, she tucked it behind her ear beneath the mantilla. The effect was very dashing.

"We will see Shakespeare, but not his work." At her puzzled look he laughed. "A statue of Shakespeare guards the stairway at Covent Garden, so we will undoubtedly see him. However, the play is a tale adapted from the Arabian Nights, called *Shahzeman and Gulnare*."

"Goodness! It sounds quite exotic."

It also sounded like something far less likely to take up all her attention as *Richard the Third* had done, Falcon thought. She had wondered more than once if she might not have found Sweeney the first time at Drury Lane if she had been less absorbed by the drama on the stage. *But I was not expecting to see him then,* she reminded herself. This time she had an advantage; she knew he had purchased tickets and she would be actively seeking him.

She had vowed before God to find these men, trusting that she would know what to do when she found them. After her failure to exact retribution from Timmins and Pumphrey, Sweeney was the only one left. She had buried her rage so deeply during the years when she could do nothing, she dared not predict now what might occur when she allowed it to come out.

There would be no compassion for Sweeney. He had been a leader. He had been her father's fellow officer. His betrayal of that trust was nearly as shocking as the savagery of the crime he had committed. Even death seemed too easy a punishment for him. He did not seem human.

Distracted by these thoughts in the carriage as it made its way to Covent Garden, she did not notice Lord Danebridge speaking to her.

"You are lost in thoughts this evening," he said, taking her hand to catch her attention. "I have asked you three questions and you have not responded to one of them. May I surmise that you are thinking about this fellow that you hope to find? Perhaps if you were to describe him to me, I would be better able to help you look for him."

How could she describe Sweeney? *He is a monster disguised as an ordinary man.* Yet of course the baron was right—it made sense to have two pairs of eyes searching the theater, for she had seen how large a place was Drury Lane, and she assumed the Covent Garden theater was equally grand.

"He is not terribly distinctive," she began. "He is perhaps a little tall—in fact, I suppose he would be said to possess an elegant figure. His hair is blond, or at least it was—how fortunate we are that it is the custom for the men to remove their hats! He is about your age. Do we know what sort of tickets he purchased? There are so many places to look! If we only knew whether he was to be seated in one of the galleries, or the boxes, or the pit . . . If he has seats above ours, we might never see him at all!"

He placed her hand between both of his own and looked at her consideringly. "I can see how much this means to you. Have no doubt, if he is here, we shall find him."

His eyes held such strength and confidence, she could not help but believe him. She hated to admit that during her self-imposed separation she had missed him. She nodded. "Forgive me. What were the questions I so rudely ignored?"

He chuckled. "I had asked if you met with success at the bank yesterday, and if you spent your time enjoyably these past two days."

That was only two. "You were right that I was viewed rather dubiously at the bank, but I am happy to report that I was successful in the end. I did give your name as a reference."

Had she spent her time enjoyably? She could not say so. After visiting the Royal Exchange and the Guildhall yesterday, she had stopped in briefly to check on her harp and tried unsuccessfully to redeem her looking glass from the pawnbroker. She had then retired to Charles Street, lacking the heart to do more. Today she had stayed in, pondering the turn her life would soon take once she succeeded in finding Sweeney.

"I thought I would find you in better spirits after our success on Sunday, señora. You must know by now that if there is any service at all that I may perform to help you, you need only speak."

Yes, she knew that. Perhaps his third question had been inquiring why she was so dispirited. "Some things have no remedy," she answered, unwilling to address it. "It is not your fault, or anyone's."

They arrived at the theater some minutes later, but due to the traffic, they were not as early as they had hoped to be.

"Let us descend from our carriage here and walk the rest of the distance—it is only a block or two. We will get there much sooner than if we wait here in the carriage until we reach the door," Lord Danebridge said.

He then revealed to her his plan: he had extravagantly purchased box seats on both sides of the theater. They would sit in one set of seats for the first half of the program, studying the theater and hunting for her quarry. They would change to the other seats during the interval, if they had not yet met with success, and study the audience again from the other side. This answered the problem of not seeing the galleries and slips situated above their own boxes.

She should have known he would think of that. He was attentive to details and strategy as well as to her, although once again he had not consulted her. He was intelligent and competent—in fact, a very fine man, if at times overbearing. She supposed that was the cost. Would she admire a man who did not know his own mind?

They settled into their box a few minutes before the first performance and began their study. Covent Garden was if anything even larger than Drury Lane, and equally magnificent. It was quite difficult to make out anyone who occupied the slip seats under the roof, but at least most of the rest of the audience, from the pit to the shilling gallery at the back, could be seen.

"If I spy anyone whom I think comes even close to fitting your description of Sweeney, I shall point him out to you," Lord Danebridge said.

"Do you begin looking at the top of the theater, and I will begin with the pit," she suggested.

"If we see him, what then?"

"I shall have to go to him at once."

The performance was a spectacle, very much expanded from the story of Gulnare in the *Thousand and One Nights*. An elaborate setting of the magical undersea world where

Gulnare lived opened the performance, which then detailed her misadventures until she was brought to King Shahzeman as a slave in the world of men. The oriental splendor of Shahzeman's palace and the glittering opulence of Gulnare's chamber and gifts from the king pleased the audience greatly.

"Now there is a man who knows how to court a woman," commented Lord Danebridge.

"He cannot give her the one thing she desires most," Falcon replied.

"Which is?"

"To restore her to her home and family."

The baron seemed to study her. Indeed, his gaze remained on her so long she began to feel uncomfortable. He said nothing more, but finally returned to his study of the audience.

Several times he pointed out gentlemen who were tall and blond, but none were Sweeney. Falcon, too, failed to find the man and pinned her hopes on switching seats after the interval.

"You are certain we have come on the proper night? Was it Tuesday for which he purchased tickets? Perhaps the theater clerk could have given you false information," she said much later in the evening when their search had still proved fruitless.

"I am sorry, my dear. The information that we had was correct. Perhaps he just decided not to come—changed his mind, or received a better invitation."

"There are places in the shadows we could not see. Could we keep a watch by the door when people are leaving?"

"If you wish. The problem is, which door? Some may not leave by the main entrance."

She sighed. There had to be another way to find Sweeney. But this time she had allowed herself to hope too much.

They exited with a crush of other people from the boxes, and Falcon had difficulty maintaining her grip on the baron's arm.

"I do not think you would expect to find him in this!" he called to her as they were swept along toward the stairway.

Jostled by the crowd, Falcon lost her footing partway down the stairs and slipped. Terrified that she was about to fall

under the feet of the herd, she instinctively reached out for the
railing or anything to hold onto.

"I have you," came Lord Danebridge's comforting voice.
He had reacted instantly as she started to go down, grasping
her and pulling her to safety against him.

She stared up at him, lost for a moment in his gray eyes,
alone as if hundreds of people were not swarming past them.
In his eyes she thought she could read a fierce protectiveness
along with desire, a possessiveness that warmed her like fire.
Would it be so wrong to become this man's mistress? His
need touched needs of her own that she could no longer deny.
But she was not who he thought she was. And she could read
doubt in his eyes along with everything else.

"I wish I had you," he whispered, releasing her carefully to
make sure she had regained her balance.

She did not know how to answer.

They made their way out of the theater, only to face the
crowd waiting for carriages in front of the building.

"Shall we wait, or shall we walk?" the baron said. "I have
no doubt we can find my carriage in the line somewhere."

She rubbed her arms and drew the sides of her cape down
to cover them. "It is chilly and a bit damp. Let us walk."

The street in front of the theater was nearly filled with carriages, waiting in rows two and three deep in places. Lord
Danebridge scanned the line ahead of them as they walked.

"As I recognize the crests on these different carriages I realize I know exactly where in the theater each of their owners
was sitting tonight," he said with his characteristic chuckle.
"Never have I spent an evening in such concentration upon
the audience instead of the stage!"

She chuckled, too, despite her disappointment. He was
holding her very close as they walked, and she felt warm and
protected. There were many more people about than mere theater patrons—even at this late hour there were street vendors
and beggars and women selling their favors.

The baron spotted his carriage and guided her toward it. Although another carriage on the outside of the row blocked it
in, there was room enough for them to walk between the vehicles and attempt to get in.

"Won't be moving for a bit yet, your lordship," said the baron's coachman, tipping his hat as they came up.

"That's all right, John Coachman. We'll just get ourselves out of the night dampness and wait."

Lord Danebridge opened the door for Falcon and let down the carriage steps. As he straightened up and took her hand to assist her, she saw a look of alarm suddenly cross his face.

"No!" he shouted. He threw his body against her.

Falcon felt his weight crushing her back and down against the side of the carriage. At the same instant she heard the explosive report of a pistol. Her nostrils filled with smoke and the smell of burnt powder. She felt the carriage lurch as the horses whinnied and the coachman cursed, trying to hold them back. A woman screamed. The coachman on the carriage next to the baron's whipped up his horses and pulled away. It happened all in an instant.

Chapter Sixteen

For a moment, neither Falcon nor Lord Danebridge moved.

"My God! Are you shot?" she asked.

"No. Are you?"

She shook her head. She was sitting on the pavement, her back pressed against the wheel of the carriage. The baron still half covered her with his body.

"Are you all right, my lord? Is the señora?"

"We are all right, Coachman. Did you know that driver?" Lord Danebridge shifted his weight from her and began to get up. As he used his arms for leverage he suddenly groaned and sat back on the pavement beside her. Putting his hand to his right arm, he brought away gloved fingers covered with blood.

"You *are* shot!" she said in alarm.

"Ruined a perfectly good coat, it would seem."

Falcon struggled to get to her feet, aware that by now people had begun to congregate. The coachman had climbed down from his box.

"Please, help me to get him into the carriage," she said to the man urgently. "Take us back to my lodgings."

"What happened here?"

"There's been a shooting!"

"By Jove! Has there, then?"

Indeed, Falcon thought—disbelief had been her first reaction, too. Only now was she beginning to tremble in response to the shock of what had occurred. The coachman helped her up the steps after Lord Danebridge and quickly climbed back on his box.

"Make way, if you please, sirs and ladies. The man needs a doctor," he called to the curious onlookers. Somehow he managed to maneuver the horses and coach out of the squeeze and away.

Falcon closed her eyes in relief, only to see again stark images from the instant of the shooting. Smoke from the pistol's charge hung in the air. At the carriage window opposite theirs she had seen the gun barrel withdrawn and caught a glimpse of a face—one mostly hidden in the darkness of the carriage compartment. In that split second of suspended time, however, light from the street had reflected off his hair. Blond hair. With a mixture of anger, frustration and alarm, she realized that Sweeney had found her.

"I am all right," Lord Danebridge said, wincing as the motion of the carriage jostled him. "Could you just . . . give me a hand? My handkerchief is in the inside pocket of my coat . . ."

Falcon turned to him, collecting herself. She must not think about Sweeney now. Lord Danebridge had been shot. He had thrown himself between her and Sweeney's pistol—he could have been killed! Blood was oozing between his fingers as he kept his hand over the wound. A small trickle ran down his sleeve.

"Right-hand side. If you please," he said.

Reaching inside his clothes seemed to Falcon a very intimate thing to do, but it was no time to be missish. She found the bit of linen and gave it to him.

"Is it very bad?"

"I shall live—'tis a mere scratch. Do you intend to tell me what is going on? That pistol was aimed at you."

"Are you so certain? What if . . ."

"No, no more lies. I have invested my blood in this now, and I have a right to know."

Did he? She hesitated.

He was regarding her with a steady gaze. "Talk. I want the truth, Miss Colburne, and I want it now."

Falcon was too shaken by what had already happened to be able to hide her shock when he used her name.

"I . . . why did you . . . how long have you known?"

Jeremy felt a little surge of triumph. He was right! And if he had made a mistake by revealing his guess, it was too late now. "I did not know for certain until just now. I have known something was not right from the beginning."

"And yet you have helped me! I do not understand you."

"This is not about me. You are the one whose life is apparently in danger. Why?"

She sighed. "Sweeney murdered my parents. He also left me for dead—I do not know how he has discovered that I am not. I have been hiding my existence ever since it happened."

"So you are a threat to him. That explains the masquerade. And the other two men, the one at the Tower and the other one?"

"Participated in the murders." She looked at him with anguish in her eyes. "They were never even suspected of any wrongdoing. I swore to avenge my parents and see justice done."

"Would you tell me what happened?" He asked very gently.

She bit her lip and looked away, but not before he saw the pain that crossed her face. *She is in far greater pain than I,* he realized.

She began to talk haltingly, in a ragged voice, telling him things he had already learned about her father—who he was, his officer's rank and regiment. She described the beginning of Moore's retreat to Corunna—the snow and ice, the roads like quagmires, the deprivation, suffering, and frustration of the troops who had wanted to fight. Chaos had reigned when they reached Astorga only to find Romana's starving, typhus-infected Spanish troops already there before them. Homes and storehouses were pillaged; drunkenness and disorder claimed the day.

"Six of us became separated from our battalion—my parents and me, and Sweeney and the other two. They were drinking. They went a little ahead of us, and when we caught up to them they had stopped at a church and were looting it. My father—my father tried to stop them."

She paused, and he could see she was fighting for control, her fists clenched tightly in her lap and her lip quivering. He waited.

"My father and Sweeney started arguing . . . they were both angry. And then—then Sweeney pulled out his saber and struck my father down. He killed him. My mother started screaming, and Timmins pulled a pistol out of his belt and shot her . . . just like a suffering animal."

Tears had started to flow down her cheeks, and now great

wracking sobs began to work their way up from deep inside
her. He wanted to take her into his arms, but how could he?
He was bloody and would be even more so if he released the
pressure from his wound. That was not likely to give her comfort. He felt helpless.

She hugged herself, as if she were suddenly freezing.
"Pumphrey said, 'What about the girl? She saw.' You could
hear the panic in his voice. Sweeney grabbed his own pistol and
fired at me . . ." She waited until she could control the sobbing,
then continued in a hollow voice. "I hit my head when I fell,
and they apparently believed I was dead. I remember little
more. Triss found me and took me to the local priest. The good
padre hid me from the French who came through Astorga the
day after our own troops and he tended my wounds until I
could be moved to a convent up in the hills to finish my recovery. I was weak from the loss of blood and became very ill
from the infection. I should never have survived."

She was calmer now; her anguished grief was subsiding.
Indignant anger was slowly building in its place.

"The Spanish were so generous to me and yet our deaths
were blamed on them! Triss wrote me. No one considered that
our own soldiers might be capable of such a monstrous deed.
It was assumed we had been attacked by townspeople in-
censed by the rampaging soldiers or by desperate soldiers
from Romana's army. 'An accident of war,' Triss says they
called it. Even he did not know the truth until he received my
first letter to him. That was many months later."

"Why did you not go to the authorities?"

"We were in the middle of a war. The regiments were constantly moving, I was moving. It would have been almost impossible. But more, what Sweeney did, as an officer, defies
every principle and assumption on which our army is founded.
Our military protects itself. Do you think they would have appreciated my opening their eyes? They would not have believed me. Yet I knew if I revealed myself, I would be in
danger."

"You came back to England to track the men down."

"The war kept me trapped in Spain. I have waited almost
five and a half years for this. How could I live, knowing what
they did?" She hesitated. "Now I expect you are appalled."

"By what you are doing? No." How could mere words begin to convey his feelings? "What you have been through appalls me. It is almost unimaginable, unbearable. I am so sorry." His voice might carry his concern and sincerity, but only action could show her the true depth of what he felt. And he could not move.

"I thought I could continue to conceal my identity until I had found each of them and brought them down in my own way," she said bitterly. "Oh foolish hope! I could not even do that! But I did not think I had revealed myself to anyone."

But she had. As soon as she spoke the words, he realized there had been one person to whom she had revealed the truth. Her father's solicitor, Mr. Fallesby. Surely there was no connection between the lawyer and Sweeney! It made no sense.

"I do not know how Sweeney could have found me out. Even Timmins and Pumphrey do not know who I really am."

"Could they not have reasoned it out? Guessed?"

"Pumphrey is in St. Bartholomew's Hospital with no idea of who put him there. He never even saw me. Timmins said he did not know where Sweeney was. I believe he was too upset to lie."

"That does not preclude the possibility that Sweeney knew where Timmins was. Perhaps he could have contacted him after your visit."

"But why would he?"

Despite his own pain, Jeremy fixed his mind on the question. "I do not know." Perhaps Sweeney had been reading the papers, and had seen the speculations about the "Spanish Spitfire." Would that alone be enough to start the man making inquiries? It did not seem likely.

There was another question puzzling him that she had not even thought to ask, and that was how Sweeney knew she would be at the theater. "You are certain your assailant was Sweeney?" he asked. "Could it have been anyone else?"

"I did not get a close look, but there is no one else who would have reason to kill me."

If she was telling the truth, finding Sweeney had suddenly become urgent, only now the man would be more difficult to find. *If only I had pursued the search more diligently before this!* Jeremy thought. But then, he had not known the man was a threat to the señora—Miss Colburne. He would have to put all his available resources to work on it now.

"Tell me everything you can about this fellow Sweeney."

Falcon ushered Jeremy up the stairs to her rooms at Mrs. Isham's, where she and Maggie and Benita tended his wound. It was a task she was well familiar with, but not one she had ever expected to practice in England. They set to work at once and soon had the wound cleaned and the arm neatly bandaged. He was fortunate. The ball had only grazed his flesh.

While they worked, Jeremy looked about him thoughtfully, trying to keep the pain at bay. Never before had Miss Colburne allowed him into the sanctuary of her rooms. Dared he to hope that he had gained a step in her trust by offering his life for hers? Or was he only so privileged due to the practical demands of the present situation? He was pleased that she had not wanted him to walk bleeding into the house at Fitzharding Street. But what encouraged him was the fact that she had finally shared a part of her story with him.

There was still much more to learn. His first order of business in the morning would be a stop at the office of his superiors. He would see what information they had uncovered for him, and he would set in order an intensified hunt for Sweeney.

The ladies sponged off his coat sleeve as best they could, and when he was once again fully dressed, his appearance was considerably improved. Still, he hoped his mother would not see him when he got in. Thank God she had not been with them!

"Remind me not to dance any vigorous dances that require use of the arms at the ball tomorrow night," he said glumly.

"Ball?"

"Have you forgotten that when we were at Drury Lane, Lady Wallingham invited us to the ball for her daughter Penelope? You should have since received a written invitation."

Miss Colburne was clearly dismayed. "Oh dear. We have received a number of cards and invitations. I suppose I hoped that if I ignored them they might disappear and at the same time I would be considered so rude no one would send any more." She looked at him appealingly. "Must I go? You understand now the reasons why I did not wish to join in social events."

He did. He also realized that it had been his doing that she had been pushed into the glaring light of the *ton*'s attention. Had his own actions contributed to putting her in danger? It was a painful thought.

"Could we not simply send apologies?" she asked. "How do you intend to dance without using your arm? I know of no dance that can be done so."

"After what has happened I think it more imperative than ever to make an appearance there. The gossips will have spread the story of the shooting all over town. For the sake of your reputation, we must convince them it was nothing, perhaps an accidental discharge during an attempt to thwart a robbery. I will have to give my family the same story, lest they worry."

"Well, perhaps the ladies will fall all over you with sympathy if they think you were injured, and you will be spared the need to dance."

His gray eyes were dark when he replied. "You may rest assured that I will claim at least my two dances with you. And one of those had better be the supper dance."

To create a space large enough to accommodate their guests, the Wallinghams had transformed their large town house garden into a huge pavilion with four rooms. Opening into each other, these were draped in rose-colored muslin and hung with handsome pier glasses which reflected the light of many chandeliers. Swags of perfumed flowers crowned the draperies and ornamented the imitation columns that supported the roof. Colored lamps glowed like jewels along the walkway from the house, adding to the magical effect. It was obvious to all of the guests at the ball on Wednesday evening that no expense had been spared.

Falcon felt as if she had stepped into the center of an enchantment or an elaborate theatrical production. "How beautiful!" she could not help exclaiming, although she noticed that the people around her seemed to take it all in stride.

Benita had labored valiantly to clean and repair Falcon's green evening dress so that it could be worn again this evening.

As she had on the previous night, Falcon wore her mother's jewels. Not yet ready to give up the persona of Doña Alomar de Montero, she wore the black lace mantilla in place of an evening headdress. Maggie had insisted on adding a cluster of black plumes and green satin ribbon to the back of this in order to improve the elegance of the effect.

Lord Danebridge looked as handsome as ever in his dark evening coat and snowy linen. Falcon noticed a number of ladies turning to look his way as he escorted her and his mother through the house and out to the pavilion behind it. As a supposedly widowed lady, Falcon did not require a chaperone, but the baron's mother had been too delighted by the prospect of attending to be left behind.

He was right, of course, about the gossip. Many people approached them, curious to know what had really occurred at Covent Garden the previous night. Lord Danebridge repeatedly told the story they had decided upon, assuring all comers that it was nothing of importance.

She was right that many ladies showered him with attention and sympathy, clucking over his injured arm. Despite the stiffness and pain he professed to feel, he did dance, although he avoided the liveliest country dances.

"It is absolutely obligatory that I dance with young Penelope," he said early in the evening. "This is her ball." And later, "I cannot be seen only to dance with you and Miss Wallingham—people would most definitely talk." But she had yet to dance with him. She knew it should not bother her, but it did.

Falcon found that she had no lack of partners. She had not realized that in the course of barely a week she had become a celebrity. She was appalled to learn that huge sums had been wagered over her in the men's clubs; in one someone had won five hundred pounds for being the first to report her Spanish name and someone else had won eighty guineas by guessing correctly when that name would first become known. Her dance card was more than full, with gentlemen seeking to subscribe even for moments of time with her between the dances. She found it all too absurd to be flattering.

"I do not understand it," she said to Lord Danebridge when

they found a few minutes to speak between dances. "They know nothing about me."

He touched her veil lightly with two fingers. "Ah, reclusive Lady of the Mantilla, you are beautiful, mysterious and unattainable. That is more than enough to make men mad."

The number of guests in attendance continued to swell as the evening wore on. The frequent announcements necessitated by their arrivals might have become annoying if anyone had paid much attention to them.

"Some have been at other parties, some probably at Almack's," the baron told Falcon when they next stood together. "Almack's is a stuffy weekly assembly with bad food and bad music. All the high sticklers go there because it is so terribly exclusive."

She giggled. Perhaps she had had enough champagne. "You must have been there to know so much about it. Are you a 'high stickler'?"

He gave her a long look. "I have been, at times, both a high stickler and at Almack's. That is where I met my wife."

She had opened her mouth to reply when the announcement "Lord Coudray" caught her up short. Closing her mouth, she stared at Lord Danebridge. The baron stared back.

Her first instinct was to flee. She did not even want to see the man who was her father's cousin. She did not want to hear the earl's voice or know if he resembled her father in any way, and she did not want to risk meeting him face-to-face, lest he somehow recognize her and betray her masquerade. Something of her feelings must have shown on her face, for Lord Danebridge put a hand on her arm.

"My father's cousin," she whispered. "I do not wish to meet him."

"Even so, you cannot simply dash out of here all of a sudden. Nothing would be more certain to draw attention to you."

He was right, of course. She was trapped there for now. She could not help glancing at the elegant man who entered the pavilion and stood just inside, surveying the crowded scene before him.

"Let me see your dance card. Look. There are only two more dances before the supper dance, which is mine. If it is what you wish, perhaps we could slip away then. My mother will protest, but at least you need only contrive to avoid him until then."

Falcon's next dance partner came to claim her, and as she took her place in the set she felt relieved that it was forming farthest from where the earl was standing. He made no move to find a partner or join in the dancing. He watched.

Falcon watched, too, wary of any circumstance that might bring her too near the man. She was unable to keep her eyes off him for long. He appeared to be perfectly comfortable just standing there; numerous people came over to speak with him, which showed Falcon that he was reasonably well known at least among certain circles within the *ton*.

He did have a look of her father about him. Part of it, she decided, was the way he held himself, but part of it was the trim shape of his body, the long shape of his face and the way his dark hair was graying at the temples. Seeing him was very unsettling.

When the dance ended, Falcon begged her partner's pardon for the mistakes she had made and searched for Lord Danebridge or his mother. Seeing neither, she agreed to accompany her partner to the refreshment table on the other side of the pavilion. She was sipping delicious champagne punch and struggling to make conversation directed carefully to harmless topics when she saw Lord Coudray heading toward the table. She set her cup down abruptly.

"I believe they must be setting up for the next dance," she told her escort pointedly. "Would you take me back?"

Jeremy, too, was watching the earl, trying to determine if the man had any inkling of who the lovely Spanish lady gracing the ball really was. Was he watching her in particular? Had he come here looking for her? Or was it merely coincidence that had brought them all here? Jeremy assumed that after his visit Mr. Fallesby must have communicated with the earl. What had he set in motion, if anything?

Miss Colburne's reluctance to face her cousin puzzled Jeremy. Had she ever written to the earl, as she had told Mr. Fallesby she would? After hearing her extraordinary story, Jeremy could not believe that she would not welcome the existence of some remnant of family. The information he had found waiting for him at his superior's office this morning had corroborated everything she had told him, from the disorder and disaster at Astorga to the respective ranks of Sweeney, Pumphrey and Timmins in the Forty-third. At his club old Lord Saltersby had said that the former Lord Coudray, her grandfather, had rejected her mother and cast off her father. But the current earl was not the one who had done these things.

Jeremy kept an eye on Miss Colburne as well as her cousin. So far, she was managing to keep well clear of the earl. He could tell that she was distracted by the man's presence even though she moved gracefully through the dance figures and seemed to learn quickly any patterns that were apparently unfamiliar to her. She did not pay quite such rapt attention to her partners' remarks nor did she laugh or smile as readily as he knew she might. It did not displease him. He was suffering a relapse of the jealous feelings that had attacked him at the Giddings' dinner party.

When the dance ended, Jeremy lost no time heading toward her.

"My dance, Doña Alomar?"

"Yes, so it is." She took his good arm and allowed him to lead her out. As they walked, she whispercd, "Just in time. I think he was going to come over to me with Lady Halstead."

Jeremy thought it was just in time simply for the reason that he could not stand to watch her dance with one more man. Despite the pain in his injured arm, he wanted his turn. He had never dreamed it would be so difficult to wait until the supper dance. It looked as if he never would be able to claim his second dance—he had signed her card again for a dance even later in the evening, and now it appeared that they would be leaving early.

This dance was a gentle progressive country dance performed in a longways set for as many as wished. The line of couples stretched the entire length of the pavilion. As the music began, one more couple hurriedly joined the line.

"Do not look now," Jeremy said.

"Oh no."

"It is too late to drop out. Perhaps the music will end before we ever get to them."

"He was not dancing before this. Why did he have to decide to do so now?"

Jeremy tried to reassure her. "Perhaps he only wanted to ensure that he had a partner for supper. You must try to relax."

They began the dance, touching, parting, returning, turning. The light from the chandeliers cast changing shadows and highlights upon Miss Colburne as she moved. Jeremy could hardly take his eyes off her long enough to acknowledge the other dancers with whom they came into contact. She managed to smile at him, although he could tell she was nervous. Every little while she would dart a glance down the line to check on the position of her cousin. As the alternating couples variously moved up or down the line, Lord Coudray and his partner came closer and closer.

Inevitably, the music continued. When finally the two couples were face-to-face, Jeremy tried to give Miss Colburne's hand a reassuring squeeze. She had talent as an actress. Now was a very good time to use it.

Chapter Seventeen

Riding home in the baron's carriage, Falcon hoped fervently that she had passed the test. She had danced with her cousin, dutifully going through the figures nodding and smiling politely, and she thought it was not until afterward that a slight trembling had seized her limbs. But the worst moment had been when Lord Danebridge went to seek his mother in the card room so that the trio might leave. With perfect timing Lady Wallingham, beaming benevolently, had brought Lord Coudray over "at his specific request" to present him to Falcon. No doubt the delighted hostess had expected the señora would feel honored.

In truth, Falcon had felt decidedly peculiar. Meeting the earl had produced a strange sensation of being introduced to her own father. Guilt over her attempt to deceive him had mixed with a kind of horrified yearning to have her real father back and resentment that this stranger should be so much like him.

She had not been able to judge whether the man's interest in her was anything different from the curiosity shown by all the other gentlemen she had met during the evening. He had bowed graciously over her hand and peered intently into her face. She had hoped with her mantilla covering her hair her resemblance to her mother was not obvious.

The carriage arrived at Mrs. Isham's lodging house and Lord Danebridge saw her to the door. She knew he had been watching her intently during the drive home all the while he was pretending to listen to his mother's assessment of their evening.

"Perhaps it is just as well that you finally met your cousin," he said in a low voice as they approached the door. "You could not have avoided him forever."

Yes, I might have, she thought, *if I could have finished this*

business and returned soon to Spain. But she did not say so.
She merely nodded.

"Will you trust me to pursue some additional measures to
track down this Sweeney? I thought you would be safe enough
at a private event like tonight's, but I do not want you to go
out and about in the city until we know you are out of danger.
Promise me?"

She nodded again. In truth, she was at a loss to know how
to proceed, now that there seemed to have been such a turnabout of events. The hunter had become the hunted. If Lord
Danebridge could help her to turn it around again, she would
be foolish to refuse. Yet she was reluctant.

"What about you?" she asked. "Will you not be in danger?"
The thought that any further harm might come to him filled
her with dread and served only to underscore how much she
had come to care for him.

He raised her hand to his lips and kissed it. "Have no fear
for me, Miss Colburne."

Behind her, Mrs. Isham's footman opened the door, curtail-
ing any further discussion.

In the morning, Falcon fretted over her promise to stay in.
The man at Rudkin and Bowles had indicated that her
mother's harp might be ready by today, but keeping her word
to the baron meant that she would have to send Triss. It also
prevented her from visiting Pumphrey at St. Bartholomew's
Hospital. During her restless night she had become convinced
that seeing him might be worth the risk of adding to her danger if the former corporal had any information about Sweeney.
If only she had not agreed!

Frustrated, she decided to write a letter to Carmen. She had
written to Don Andrés and Doña Luisa during her self-imposed
solitude yesterday afternoon, pouring out her anxieties about
their state of affairs but saying very little concerning her own.
To Carmen she could unburden herself; Carmen had become
a sister to her during their years together in Spain. Falcon
could not know if the letters would reach them, but the mere
act of writing made her feel better.

She sent Triss and Maggie off to Cheapside and settled at
the small writing desk by the window in the sitting room. She

had covered both sides of one sheet, crossed it, and had gone on to a precious second sheet of paper when she was interrupted by the announcement of a visitor. A glance at the clock told her it was barely noon—perhaps her visitor was Lord Danebridge! But she was wrong. It was Lord Coudray.

"I do not wish to see him," she told the footman in rather panicked tones. "Tell him I am not at home."

"He said to tell you he would wait as long as necessary, señora. Suggested you might as well see him now as later."

What could he want? Had she not passed the test after all? Falcon looked about the sitting room as if it might offer some clue to what she should do. It was an ordinary room in perfectly good order and inspired no solutions. She sighed.

"All right. Give me a moment to call in my maid and then send him up. I suppose I have no choice." She did not relish seeing the earl alone, for she did not know him. Was she receiving him as the widow Doña Alomar de Montero, or as his unmarried cousin Falcarrah Colburne? Maggie had gone with Triss, so Benita would have to play chaperon.

"You have a snug little place here, small but not really objectionable, I am pleased to see," the earl said, looking about the room as he made his entrance. He carried a huge bouquet of hothouse flowers which he presented to Falcon with a bow.

"I thought these were beautiful and exotic, like you, my dear. You should have them. You were the belle of the ball last night, despite the fact it should have been Miss Wallingham. But it made me proud to see a Colburne conduct herself with such grace and elegance."

So, he knew. She had not fooled him at all. Something of her dismay must have shown on her face, for he laughed.

"Now, do not be alarmed! Did I betray any sign that I recognized you last night? Surely that should tell you that I mean you no harm. May I sit?"

She nodded, too numb to apologize for her poor manners. He seated himself on the small settee across from where Falcon was standing, still holding the flowers.

"From what Mr. Fallesby has told me, I rather think I am your legal guardian, or will be. We are family, my dear. I think it little short of a miracle to find you here! If only you knew the grief that followed the reported deaths of you and your parents! But we can speak of that later. What I must know is why in the name of heaven you did not write to us, now or even long before this. Why are you masquerading as this Doña Alomar de Montero?"

Falcon watched his face as he spoke, trying to gauge his sincerity. Mr. Fallesby had written him. She had tried to circumvent that, but obviously she had failed. The simple fact that the earl was here must count for something. If the family despised her, as she had expected, he could easily have ignored Mr. Fallesby's communication, rather than coming to London to seek her out.

"Does it surprise you so much that I would hesitate to approach my father's family?" she asked quietly. "Consider how he and my mother were treated."

"That was your grandfather's doing. Your grandmother never forgave him for it. Everyone blamed him for driving your father away, and ultimately for the tragedy that befell you all."

"I—I did not know." It was difficult to absorb what he was saying. "I always thought everyone blamed my mother for capturing my father's heart—that they thought she ruined him."

"Your grandmother is a very elderly lady, but I know she would like to see you. It would do her so much good. I believe she continued to send your father money from time to time, during all those years of service. I said nothing about you before I left for town. I wanted to see you for myself. I did not want to build her hopes up. But come, you must tell me why you are pretending to be Spanish! You have created quite the stir among the *beau monde*."

"That was never my intention. Prudence has dictated that I pose as a Spaniard since the day my parents died. I have had to conceal my identity from the French, who were everywhere, and also from the men who did the killing, as long as they were still in Spain. For most of these years I was Señorita Alvez Bonastre, a relation of the Serrano-Bonastres who took me in. It seemed safer while traveling here to pose as a Spanish widow and infinitely easier than to resurrect a young Irish-English woman thought dead for half a decade. I had hoped to quietly attend to some unfinished business here and then return to Spain as soon as it was finished."

Only, now Sweeney knew of her presence here, and she was not certain what might await her back in Spain. She sighed, looking down at the flowers.

The earl asked, "If your business was simply to find out about your inheritance, why not write? Or did you think Mr. Fallesby would not believe in your miraculous survival?"

"When I went to see him I admit I was concerned about that. But to be honest, I did not even know of his existence until after I arrived here in England. It was other business that brought me here."

She hoped that he would sense her reluctance to discuss it and would not pursue the subject further, but in that she was disappointed.

"If I am to be your guardian, any business that concerns you must also become my concern. Will you tell me about it? I have many resources and contacts—perhaps I may help."

She had been standing rooted in one spot from the moment he came in. Now she moved, giving the flowers to Benita and then seating herself in a chair placed at right angles to the settee.

"I must warn you that I have no intention of giving it up, although I doubt you will approve of it," she said, folding her hands in her lap.

How different this was from telling Lord Danebridge! He had demanded truth and she had given him everything, not just what happened but her grief and anger, her deepest emotions. Here was Lord Coudray, asking politely, and she felt cold and calm, entirely as if what she was about to relate had happened to someone else.

"I expect you were told my parents' deaths, and mine, were an unfortunate accident—a by-product of the war in Spain and the chaos that went with it. Unfortunately I must tell you that is not so. My parents were deliberately murdered, and not by Spaniards, but by three men from our own regiment."

"Murdered!" He stood and moved stiffly to the fireplace, staring at the floor. "And by our own men?"

"When it became clear that I would live, I made a solemn vow that my parents would not go unavenged. Despite having been trapped in Spain by the war for these intervening years, I have come to England to track down those men. I have found two of them. It is only the third one who keeps eluding me."

"Would this have anything at all to do with the shooting I heard rumors about?" He turned around to stare at her.

She evaded his question. "I knew you would not approve. But if I do not undertake this task, who is to do it? I am the only witness. I am the one who lost her parents. I am the one who was left for dead, who lost the only life she had known. I am the one who made a solemn promise to see justice done!" She had meant to stay calm. She stopped herself before she became too angry.

He came to her chair and reached down to take her hand. "I lost a cousin whom I regarded as an older brother. I thought I had lost a young woman, his daughter, who might have become the pride and joy of our family. Did you not think that we, too, might have been angry, if we'd but known? You must not carry on this mission all alone. You must let me help you, Falcarrah."

She shivered involuntarily at the sound of her name, and he released her hand. "You do not mind if I call you by your Christian name? I thought as we are family . . ."

"Please. I do not use it. I suppose, if you are to be my guardian . . . perhaps Sophia? It is my middle name. Or Falcon? That is the nickname I came to be known by in the regiment."

He resumed his seat on the settee. "All right, then, Sophia. Your grandmother will like that—it is her name. About this shooting . . . ?"

"Somehow the third man I was hunting—a fellow named Sweeney—has learned of my existence. I believe he tried to kill me. I was very lucky to escape."

"Good Lord! And I imagine he is quite chagrined to think that now you have escaped his designs twice. Obviously it is not safe for you here. It adds all the more reason to what I would propose—that you, and your servants, of course," he added with a nod toward Benita, "should come with me back to Kent to Colburne Hall. There you could meet your grandmother, and you would be safe! Perhaps you would entrust the task of finding this fellow to me. I am unknown to him and would be in no danger, I suspect. We can turn all three men over to the proper authorities. This kind of thing is best left to a man, my dear, and you know now that you are not alone in the world."

Falcon wanted to say that she had never felt quite alone, with Carmen's family behind her in Spain and Triss and Maggie and Lord Danebridge here in London, but she refrained. She was a little shocked to realize that the baron had truly become part of her trusted little circle. When had he? She also did not say that she thought it far too late to bring this case to the "proper authorities."

The earl, it seemed, was offering her a home, a family, a place to belong. Was it what she wanted? Would forming a connection to these unknown relatives be disloyal to her parents' memory? Perhaps it would only be a certain path to more pain.

She rose, extending her hand to her cousin. "You are very kind and generous, Lord Coudray, and I do thank you. You have given me a great deal to think about. I need some time to consider your invitation."

"Of course." He rose, taking her hand again in parting. "You have suffered terribly, and I would like to see the family make it up to you. If you are in danger from this man Sweeney, I urge you not to take too long to think. I believe you would find Colburne a fine sanctuary indeed. In the meantime, you may trust that I will not betray your identity."

He bowed over her hand and then, as he straightened, he touched her cheek. "You are far too young and charming, my dear, to have to struggle with such burdens. I just want you to know that you need not."

Jeremy, meanwhile, had been summoned to the office of his superior. He thought perhaps it was because the man had not been able to see him yesterday, when he had stopped in to pick up information.

"There you are, Lieutenant Major. Do sit down," his officer said. "Sorry I was in a meeting when you came by yesterday, but you should find the results quite happy. You no longer have a case."

Jeremy stared, dumbfounded. "I beg your pardon, sir?"

The fellow laughed. "You can go home, man! Your lady from Spain is no longer a suspect in the spy case we were investigating. We are convinced that the real culprit has been apprehended. There was indeed a plot against Lord Castlereagh, but we have names now and shall have it all unraveled before today is through. Your suspect is not involved in it. You have found no evidence of her involvement in any other political matters?"

"No, sir." *Not political.* Only an apparent personal tragedy that was putting her life in danger. That, of course, was not the concern of this department.

"Well, I must say I expected to at least see a smile on that face of yours, Danebridge. I know you were reluctant to take this last case. If I may say so, I sensed a bit of resentment, at first, that you were asked to postpone your retirement for this. You have been at this game too long for me to have to tell you that not every case is concluded with the glorious satisfaction of action. Every investigation is important to our nation's security, no matter what the result. Think if she had turned out to be the one."

"Yes, sir. I know." Jeremy felt as if his feet had been cut out from under him. He had wanted this, of course, but then the timing had been his own choice. Now he needed the resources of the office and the help of Nicholson and the rest of his men more than ever—this was the worst possible time. Was he simply to abandon Miss Colburne to her fate?

He could pick up his family and go home to a settled life in Hertfordshire. It had been his driving goal for the last year, the one that had kept him careful while he finished his assignment in France. But one green-eyed enchantress had changed all that.

She was not a spy. And by his own actions he had complicated her life incalculably. Perhaps it was even his own fault that she was in danger now.

"Are all of my assistants to be reassigned immediately?"

"Why do you ask?"

He sighed. It galled him to admit he had become personally involved. "I have run into a nonpolitical situation that still involves criminal activity. I do not feel that I can simply walk away from it, sir."

"I see. I did hear your name connected with a shooting the other night. Nicked your arm, eh? You thought that if any of the men were willing to volunteer . . ."

"I would pay them myself. Just for a few days." It would put a major hole in his finances, but he saw no choice. He was in love with the woman—that was very clear to him now.

Falcon's second visitor that afternoon was Lord Dane-bridge, who arrived carrying a package and looking very sober indeed.

"Something is wrong," she guessed immediately, ushering him into the sitting room.

"Yes and no," he replied, refusing the seat she offered him. "I have as yet no news of Sweeney. I do have something else I must tell you, however." He suggested that she, at least, might like to sit down.

She took a seat on the settee and looked up at him expectantly. Even the sight of him looking so serious had the power to lift her spirits.

He thrust the package into her hands. "This belongs to you."

The parcel was surprisingly heavy, although it was not large. As she undid the paper wrappings he went to the hearth and stood there staring into the fireplace, leaning his uninjured arm upon the mantel.

The shape of the object had a familiar feel to it. She caught her breath as she removed the last bit of paper. "My looking glass! But how . . . ?"

He turned to face her. "It was thanks to my doing that you were forced to part with it. I felt an obligation to make certain it was returned to you. I cannot even ask that you consider it a peace offering."

"Whatever do you mean? You and I are not at war. I do not understand. How did you know this looking glass was mine? Where did you come by it?" She wondered which one of them was going mad.

He sighed. "I will explain it all. You may condemn me, and I would not blame you, but hear me first."

He began at the beginning, and told her everything—how he had seen her in Portsmouth on the first day she arrived in

England, how he had followed her to Wickenham, and how he had arranged to have her trunk stolen in London before he had even arrived himself. He told her of his visit to Mr. Fallesby and of his investigations at his club; he mentioned the men he had assigned to keep watch over who she saw, where she went and what she did.

As she listened, she felt an icy coldness creep into her soul. What she was hearing was so much worse than the worst suspicions she had harbored about him. This was the man she had come to trust! Much more than trust in recent days, she had realized, although she had not wanted to admit it.

As he explained the reasons for his actions, the coldness inside her began to crystallize into anger. All of his help, all of the concern she thought he had shown for her—all had been part of performing his duty. And she had thought he wanted to make her his mistress! What an incredible fool she had almost made of herself.

"I wondered why a man just returned from the Continent would be in Wickenham," she said in an utterly emotionless voice. Her choice was that or to rage and scream at him, revealing the full force of her pain and anger. She clenched her fists. She would not let him reduce her to such a state.

"It explains why, when I first saw you, I took you for a military man, even though you wore no uniform. I suppose you have been paying Mrs. Isham a premium to rent me these rooms—I wondered how the price could be so little different than what we had paid in Covent Garden! Did your spies tell you which pawnbroker had my looking glass? Did they also report to you my distress when I tried to redeem it on Monday, only to find that it was already gone?"

She thought of the pleasure she had found in his company and of the kisses they had shared. She had even spent time with his son. Had it all meant nothing?

"Your government demands much of you, assuming you ever were a man of honor. How can you live with yourself, knowing your life's work is nothing but deceit? How do you look your son in the face?"

She felt the tears beginning and she dashed at them angrily with her hand. She would not cry in front of this man.

"It is over, now," Jeremy said gently, holding out his hands
as if to show her he had nothing more to hide. Her words hurt,
but he understood her anger. He only hoped she would keep
listening to him. He loved her. He could not go on deceiving
her.

"The assignment is finished. They know now that you are
not a spy. My involvement with the department is finished,
too. I was on my way home to begin a new life when this case
was given to me—one last investigation, they said."

"That is very well then. There is nothing to stop you from
going now."

"Yes, there is. You. I wish to make amends for any harm I
may have caused you. I care about you and I want to see you
safe. I cannot abandon you. Sweeney hopes to kill you! I have
the resources to find him and to protect you."

She rose. The lack of expression on her face struck him
with a cold, nameless fear. "You do not need to trouble yourself," she said in a tone as sharp as a saber edge. "Someone
else has now offered me assistance."

"Who?" Even to his own ears, the word came out sounding
harsh and demanding.

"That is no longer any of your concern, is it? But I will tell
you. My cousin, the earl. It seems I did not fool him last night
at the ball—he recognized my resemblance to my mother. He,
too, has resources and has offered me protection. So you may
take up your plans with—I will not go so far as to say a clear
conscience. Say, with no further thought of me."

"That would be impossible." He took a step toward her. He
had to make her understand! "I think about you constantly,
whether we are together or apart. You haunt my dreams at
night. You—"

"No!" She turned and walked away from him, putting her
hands over her ears. "No more. Why should I believe anything you say? How could anyone trust you, when to you the
truth is only a tool to be manipulated to achieve your ends!"

She had finally raised her voice in anger. She was flushed
now instead of deathly pale, and Jeremy thought that this was
better. But she was not finished.

"You may discontinue paying Mrs. Isham; I shall be quitting these lodgings immediately, perhaps as soon as tomorrow."

"To go where?"

"My cousin has offered me a sanctuary, perhaps even a home. So you see, I no longer need your help. Have you not done enough? At least I am now spared the great burden of debt I thought I owed to you. Please, just leave."

Chapter Eighteen

"I never expected to hear from you so quickly," the Earl of Coudray told Falcon the following afternoon. "I should not have been surprised, however. Your parents were both strong-minded people, and it is very clear that you are their daughter. You have shown good judgment."

I hope so, thought Falcon, acknowledging his compliment with a silent nod of her head. They were settled in his large traveling coach, headed out of London—for better or worse. Maggie and Benita rode with them, for Carlos and Triss and the earl's own servants filled the baggage coach which followed.

Falcon had sent a note to the earl in Bedford Square as soon as Lord Danebridge had left her the previous afternoon. Then she had set Benita and Maggie to work helping her pack.

"I'm hopin' you're that certain about what ye are doin'," Maggie had said then. "Runnin' away is the last thing I'd ever have thought ye would do."

"I am not running away! From what?" Falcon had caught the look that passed between Maggie and Benita, and it rankled her. "I am pursuing a new course, one that leads *towards* something—the same goal I have sought all along."

"Oh, and is that right, now?" Maggie had countered. Since then she had said nothing more on the subject, but Falcon had continued to catch Maggie giving her the eye at odd moments. She was certain that if she looked up at the older woman now, she would see the same dubious expression on her face.

Bother Maggie, anyhow! Why did it sometimes feel as if she were Falcon's own conscience? Falcon had been asking herself if this was the right course from the moment she had so impulsively chosen it, but that was different from having someone else question it.

Of course she was not running away from Sweeney. Hadn't she come here pursuing him? A different tack was needed to catch up with him, that was all. She was not afraid of him, even if he had almost succeeded in shooting her. She just wondered if leaving London really made sense.

If Maggie meant that Falcon was running from Lord Danebridge, that notion was ridiculous. Why should she need to run from him? He had deceived her shamelessly. She was done with him; she had chosen to put him out of her life. All she had to do now was put him out of her mind and her heart as well.

Falcon tried to focus her attention on the scenery they passed and on her cousin's occasional attempts at conversation. They had left London by Westminster Bridge and had headed southeast through the southern outskirts of the city until they joined the Kent Road amidst flowering fields and meadows. She knew she should be trying to be more sociable, but the sudden upheaval of events was taking its toll on her. She felt tired and very disinclined to talk.

They left the Kent Road at Lewisham Bridge and took a more directly southern route, stopping to rest in Bromley in midafternoon and passing through Keston and a few other prosperous-looking villages. In this western part of Kent the scenery was delightful; tracts of spring woodlands carpeted with bluebells and alight with hazel and dogwoods in bloom were interspersed between new-green fields and blossoming orchards and every so often the grand entrance to an estate. Falcon's appreciation of what her father had sacrificed for the love of her mother grew stronger with every passing mile.

Colburne Hall was east of Westerham, a busy little market town about twenty miles south of London. The half-timbered buildings and small village green looked gilded in the fast-departing light of late afternoon, and Falcon gazed out at them while her cousin talked about the town. He was just mentioning its pride in being the birthplace of the hero of Quebec, General Wolfe, when she noticed a man emerging from a building labeled the "George and Dragon" who looked remarkably like Sweeney.

Nonsense, she told herself even as she pulled back from the window. There was no possible reason for him to be in this place! *I am becoming obsessed—I think every tall, blond man is Sweeney.* Perhaps it was just as well that she had left London after all. In the city she might have begun to see Sweeney everywhere! The events of the past three days must have rattled her a good deal more than she had suspected.

The last long shadows of the day were giving way to dusk as the carriages turned in under the archway of the impressive brick gatehouse at the entrance to Colburne Hall. They proceeded through more woodlands and rolling fields until finally the hall itself came into view at the top of a slight rise.

Falcon could not help catching her breath at the sight of her ancestors' home. The hall was an imposing structure of rose-red brick with tall windows and many gables and chimneys. At one side stood a huge old beech tree and an ancient brick wall sheltering a garden of spring flowers. To the other side at a slight distance from the house stood what were undoubtedly the stables and a collection of other outbuildings and offices. Rolling lawns surrounded the house like an ocean of green, and beyond it lay a sweeping view of the Kent Weald to the south.

"Welcome to Colburne, my dear Sophia," said the earl.

By the time the carriages drew up at the front entrance of the house a veritable army of servants had gathered there to greet their master. Once the formalities were taken care of, Falcon was escorted into the house itself, where she met another cousin, the earl's sister Lady Rawlings, whose husband was a baronet, and a variety of houseguests. Eventually she was forced to ask her cousin about his wife. She had assumed he had one and yet no one among the group had been so identified.

"Ah. My wife and son are not in residence at the moment, although you may be sure that I will send for them now that you are here. I do not think there is any breach in propriety with my sister here. Otherwise, I would have you put up at the dower house with your grandmother."

"When will I meet her?" Falcon had not actually seen the dower house, but the lane that led to it had been mentioned when they passed it on the main drive. She felt eager to meet the grandmother who apparently had never completely severed ties with her father. She also felt at this moment much more disposed toward dealing with one person at a time—she supposed it was only natural that she should feel a bit overwhelmed amongst so many strangers encountered all at once.

"The very minute she feels up to it," replied her cousin. "She is not well, you know." The earl smiled reassuringly at her. "Meanwhile, dinner will be a little delayed by our unannounced arrival. You should have time to retire to your rooms for a brief respite. After dinner perhaps you would like a preliminary tour of the house? We can conduct a more thorough one in the morning."

Jeremy had spent the afternoon in the company of his son and mother, who had taken over his schedule at the first hint of his availability.

"You are not occupied with business matters today?" Lady Danebridge, ever the shrewd observer, had asked this morning.

"No, not today," he had replied without thinking. Miss Colburne had been taking up all his thoughts from the time he had parted with her the previous afternoon. He had slept very little and he knew he was listless and obviously at leisure.

"Were you not engaged for a musicale last night at Lord and Lady Kedsley's? You did not attend, I noticed."

"No, I canceled that."

"And tonight?"

"I have no current commitments." He had sent notes to all of the people who had invited him to attend their functions with Doña Alomar de Montero, informing them with apologies that the lady had been called out of town and that he was unable to attend.

"Why then, you are available to escort Tobey and myself today, Jeremy." If Lady Danebridge suspected the reason for her son's sudden availability, she was too wise to mention it.

"Oh, jolly! You can go out with us this afternoon, Papa!" Tobey's eagerness had made it impossible to refuse.

They had first gone to Haymarket to view the mechanical birds and animals exhibited at Week's Museum. Ready for live animals that moved on their own, they had next proceeded to the Exeter 'Change in the Strand, where Tobey was delighted by the tigers and aging lion. Finally they had returned home by way of the Egyptian Hall in Piccadilly, where they studied the real but perfectly static preserved animals and curiosities in Mr. Bullock's exotic displays.

Tobey's joyful enthusiasm might have been a balm to Jeremy's deep pain, but the boy could not seem to keep Doña Alomar out of his conversation any more than Jeremy could keep her out of his mind.

"Doña Alomar would not be afraid of that mechanical tarantula, would she, Papa? She is not afraid of anything."

"Do you think Doña Alomar would have liked to see the tigers? Why could she not have come with us today?"

"When is my next Spanish lesson, Papa?"

Hiding his discomfort, Jeremy had answered these and all the other endless questions as best he could.

Animals proved to be the theme of the day. That evening Jeremy accompanied his mother and Tobey to Astley's, where they witnessed a spectacle of human and equestrian acrobatics that was lively indeed. But Jeremy was no better able to keep his attention focused on what was in front of him than he had been all afternoon.

He had known that confessing his interference in Miss Colburne's affairs carried a risk that she would be angry or even would reject him altogether. He had seen no choice—he could not further their friendship without honesty. He had believed that she cared for him, perhaps not as deeply as he cared for her, but at least enough to feed his hope that she might have forgiven him. Had he so deceived himself?

He had been wrong. She had not even heard him out completely. So why, after arguing with himself for some thirty-six hours, could he still not bring himself to let her go? Was he so much worse off than he was before he'd met her? Why could he not simply return to his original plan to settle down and find a nice, commendable, comfortable woman to fill the void in his life and Tobey's?

Lady Danebridge, the soul of forbearance all day, finally spoke to the matter after they returned to Fitzharding Street and Tobey had been sent off to bed.

"Whatever is troubling you, my son, is less likely to resolve itself it you do nothing but mope," she suggested. "I will not press you to confide in me if you are not so inclined, but it is very difficult to be in your company when your heart and soul are apparently a thousand miles distant."

She was right, of course. Jeremy had found no comfort in the solitude he had sought last night, nor in the busy activity with his family today. He was fighting against his instincts, something that as a rule he never did.

"Not a thousand miles, Mama," he replied with a rueful smile. "Probably less than fifty."

What had really caused Miss Colburne to decide so suddenly to go with her cousin? Jeremy's instincts were screaming at him, telling him that something in the picture was wrong. Could he truly have so misjudged her feelings? Such judgment was part of his work, a skill that had sometimes meant the difference between life and death. Had love made him so blind?

I am not ready to give her up so easily, Jeremy decided. He might no longer be officially investigating her, but that did not mean his hands were tied. There was still so much for him to learn! He could be stubborn and determined. In the morning he would pay a visit to St. Bartholomew's Hospital; it was time to discover what Corporal Pumphrey knew.

Falcon spent much of the following day touring Colburne Hall, settling into her room, and exploring the gardens and grounds of the estate. The other guests tried to entice her into joining their various activities, but she was of no mind to do so. The estate was beautiful, yet it felt strange to walk on the pathways and pass through the rooms where her father had spent his childhood. Had he played in the rose garden? Had he spent his days confined in the nursery? She longed to ask her grandmother such questions, but the earl delayed the visit, saying that the dowager countess was not well enough.

Maggie and Triss did not exactly fit in the order of the house—Falcon saw them as friends rather than servants, and yet they could not be presented to the earl's guests. After some confusion, they had been relegated to the domain of the upper servants, but Falcon worried about them. When she spent time alone in her room, she had Maggie keep her company.

"Are you and Triss comfortable enough, Maggie?" she

asked. "It does not seem fair to have you tucked away like servants."

"Whisht, don't ye be worryin' over us," the Irishwoman replied. "To be sure, the housekeeper Mrs. Brock and that uppity butler Forbes don't condescend to speak to us, but the steward treats us right enough. Truth is, we are what we are, and no better than we ought to be."

"Are Carlos and Benita all right?"

"Fine, child. The younger servants are in awe of them. His lordship may soon find all his grooms speakin' Spanish, and 'tis a charm to see the other ladies' Frenchified abigails makin' a study of Benita's Spanish habits."

Falcon smiled at that report, but she could not find it in her heart to actually laugh. Despite her elegant and comfortable surroundings, she was blue-deviled. She hated to admit it, but she missed Lord Danebridge. When she closed her eyes she saw his face, his gray eyes serious as at their last meeting or filled with warm humor as she had seen them so often. She wondered what he was doing and where he was. Had he packed up his family and left London? She had been so angry with him—he who had used his own body to shield her from Sweeney's gun. How ungrateful he probably thought her!

Snatches of their last conversation haunted her. He had told her he cared, and she knew it was true. As much as he had interfered in her affairs and deceived her, he had also taken care to see that she had whatever she needed. Why else would he have come to her and confessed what he had done? What else would he have said if she had let him finish?

When she considered that, she thought perhaps it was just as well she had treated him so shabbily. Despite what he may have thought, she was not a fit companion for an English peer. Her experiences in Spain had separated her from that forever. If she had hurt him, surely he would recover from it soon enough. She only wondered if time would heal her own pain.

On Sunday it rained, forcing the earl's guests to amuse themselves within the confines of the house. They seemed bored and world-weary; apparently even the whirl of the London Season held no interest for them, else why would they rusticate in Kent at this time of year? None of them attended church. Falcon was hard-pressed to avoid them, but she had no wish to gamble at cards, gamble at charades, or gamble at any other diversion they thought up. The only activity they indulged in that did not appear to involve wagering was music, and she did not want to play her mother's harp for people like them. She did not like the way the gentlemen looked at her, like cats looking at cream. She wondered what her cousins found to like in them. She wondered, too, if the earl's wife preferred to live elsewhere because such guests came too often.

On Monday the weather cleared. Like children released from school the houseguests reclaimed the garden and the park; Falcon stayed inside. She hoped that she would be given permission to visit her grandmother, but still her cousin said no. What if her grandmother's health only got worse instead of better? Was waiting for a better day the wisest course?

From her bedroom window Falcon could see the dower house chimney stacks rising just above the distant trees, a constant reminder of her grandmother's near presence. She tried to imagine the house or her grandmother in the house, but the exercise was futile. The portrait of her grandmother in the long gallery showed her as a much younger woman.

Falcon wrote a new batch of letters to send to Spain and spent part of her day playing her mother's harp, practicing and filling the house with a soft melancholy sound.

Tuesday's bright sunshine brought with it plans for an outing to the North Downs. Lady Rawlings tried her hardest to persuade Falcon to accompany the group.

"It is the nicest of spring days, Sophia, and the picnic site has the most beautiful views," she wheedled. "We have an excellent stable—I do not think you have yet been out? If you do not care to ride, a few of our guests are taking their carriages. I'm certain we could fit you in with them, or take out one of ours."

Falcon apologized but remained steadfast in her determination not to go. At breakfast the earl had suggested she accompany the group; he himself planned to be closeted in his study all day tending to business matters. His unavailability made it quite clear that there would be no official visit to her grandmother again today. It also suggested the perfect plan to Falcon, who had run out of patience.

She watched from her window as the group gathered in front of the house and the chaotic mixture of houseguests, grooms, horses, and carriages eventually sorted itself out. It appeared that everyone was going. That suited her perfectly. She hoped that the earl would assume that she had gone with them.

Shortly after the picnic procession departed, Falcon dressed to visit her grandmother.

"If she is entirely too ill to see me, I'll simply come back," she explained to Maggie as Benita helped her into her black silk pelisse. "I do not know if my cousin has even told her of my presence here. If she seems too weak to withstand the shock, I shan't tell her at all. I just want to judge for myself."

She had borrowed Maggie's bonnet once again and had just put it on when she heard the sound of a horse cantering up the drive to the house. "Oh no. I hope that isn't one of them returning." Looking out again, Falcon was the one to be shocked. "Sweeney?" She did not believe it until the tall rider dismounted and removed his hat as he approached the front entrance.

"It is!" She stared in horror as the man moved beyond her line of sight. "How can he be here? This time I know I am not imagining it." As she accepted the reality of his presence there, her horror gave way to firm resolution. "I don't know how he found me, but that is the biggest and last mistake he'll ever make. Quick, Maggie. You keep watching here by the window!"

Falcon hurried to the wardrobe and began searching in the bottom of it.

"What are ye doin', child?"

"I am finding Papa's pistol."

"Oh no. Now what exactly do ye figure to be doin' with that?"

"What I came here to do, Maggie. See justice done." Falcon found the pouch and removed the pistol and ammunition. "He hasn't left, has he? Keep watching."

At the sight of the gun Benita began to protest in Spanish, but Falcon shook her head and warned her maid to silence.

Working carefully, she loaded and primed the weapon, set the safety catch and then looked around for her basket. She put her reticule and the pistol in it and covered them with the linen towel from her washstand. Then she went to her door and opened it just enough so she could listen for sounds from the ground floor. She heard voices but she could not make out the words.

"I am going to slip out and go down the drive and wait for him," she told Maggie. "It is better this way."

Maggie wrung her hands. "Oh no, it isn't, child. Think what ye are doin'."

"Oh, I have, Maggie, I have. The thought of this kept me alive for a long time. The time for thinking is over."

Chapter Nineteen

Falcon was surprised at the calm determination she felt as she hurried quietly down the stairs and through the entry hall of the mansion. She even managed to smile as she put a finger to her lips to silence the footman waiting by the door. *Once I am out of the house, I should have the upper hand,* she thought.

A groom was walking Sweeney's horse in the drive just outside the entrance. That was easy enough to fix. It suggested a change of plan to Falcon.

"The gentleman who rode this horse will be staying longer than he thought," she told the groom quietly. *Much longer.* "Would you take his mount down to the stables, please?"

Now all she had to do was wait. Positioning herself to one side of the door, she took the pistol out and set her basket down on the stone step beside her.

Sweeney came out a few minutes later. Falcon was ready. As soon as the door closed behind him, she spoke.

"Looking for your horse?"

He swung around, startled, and at that moment Falcon raised the pistol. With satisfaction she watched the expression on his face change from surprise to confusion. But she wanted to see fear. And she wanted to be very certain that he knew why he would die.

"You know that I know how to use this," she said. "Don't make a sound." Gesturing with the pistol she indicated that he should open his coat. "I have no doubt that you are armed—take your weapon out slowly and place it on the ground. Now back away slowly—a little farther—good, that's far enough."

She would take no chances. Without taking her eyes off him she reached down and retrieved his pistol. Once it was in her hand she noted that the safety catch was engaged.

"All right, now turn and walk. "I'll be right behind you."

She marched him away from the house past the beech tree and the spring flowers, across the lawn toward a patch of woods that remained as part of the grounds surrounding the artificial lake. An earthen path led through the trees.

"That's far enough," she said once she felt certain they could not be seen. They were in a small clearing.

"This is all a mistake," Sweeney said.

"Is it? Are you going to tell me that I have mistaken you for someone else, or that you did not come here looking for me? Would you claim that you are not the man who butchered my father in the snow at Astorga? That you never led your men to kill my mother? Never shot me and left me for dead as well? You, an officer. And all for a few ounces of gold and a handful of holy relics!"

"You don't understand."

"Understand? What? What it is like to hover near death for weeks, in such pain that death would be welcome? To battle the nightmares from memories too vivid to ever be escaped? To lose a loving family and a familiar world all in the space of two brutal minutes? What do I not understand?"

Of course she did not expect him to answer. Once she had opened the door on her bitterness and anger, she could not stop the tirade that came out.

"Do *you* understand what it was like to be fourteen years old, hiding and trying to travel over brutal terrain under the cover of night? You know what Spain was like! French soldiers and Spanish bandits were everywhere. The only safe place was in the south and later, not even there. Some people would only help if they were paid, and how was I to do that? It was all your doing—all of it. Throughout it all I thought of you and planned and waited for this day. I vowed my parents would not go unavenged. And because I lived, I pledged my life to find justice for their deaths."

The pistols were heavy. She would have to shoot him before her arms grew weary of keeping the guns aimed at his heart.

"If I shoot you through the heart, will you die? Likely not—I am convinced that you do not have one. Perhaps I should aim a little higher . . ."

Sweat was pouring down his pale face, and fear showed on it now. "Wait. It wasn't for the gold. It wasn't only me. I am not the one you really want," he stammered. "It was your cousin. I owed him. He arranged it."

"What?" Did Sweeney truly expect her to believe him? "We were in the middle of a war, in Spain. My cousin was in England."

She heard a twig snap behind her, but she did not dare to take her eyes off Sweeney. She did not have to.

"Yes, I was in England," said the earl.

Falcon glanced at him quickly as he stepped into the clearing and she saw that he also had a pistol. Her pulse began to pound in her ears.

"This is not working out the way I'd hoped," her cousin drawled, his tone as cool as if they were taking tea in the drawing room. "The two of you were not supposed to meet today. I did not know she was here. But when I didn't hear you leave, Mr. Sweeney, I looked out and saw her taking you across the lawn. Since you have found it so difficult to kill her, failing twice, I thought it still might work out if she simply killed you. But you had to go and open your mouth. Now I'll have to kill both of you."

"Then it *is* true," Falcon whispered. *But how? Why?* Had he been behind both attempts on her life? She looked at the earl. "I have two shots to your one; I think you will have difficulty carrying out that threat."

She should never have taken her eyes off Sweeney. At that moment, he leaped at her. He moved so fast that he shoved her and grabbed one of the pistols from her hand before she realized what he was about. He fired at Lord Coudray. As the earl fell backward and hit the ground, his pistol discharged. The ball whizzed past Falcon's cheek, missing her by an inch.

Shaken but still in control of her wits, she backed away from Sweeney, training her remaining pistol on him once more. To her left the earl lay still and silent.

"I think you have killed him," she said, risking a quick glance. Her heart filled with a peculiar mixture of horror, relief and dismay. The earl looked so much like her father lying there. He would give no answers to anyone now. "But why? Why did he want my parents dead?"

"If you kill me, you'll never know," Sweeney said.

"Do not count on that to save you. Seeing you dead means more to me than knowing why my parents died. I can begin to guess."

"He would have killed you. Do I get no thanks for this?"

"You would kill me, if you had another shot."

"What about the others—Timmins and Pumphrey? Timmins shot your mother. I did not act alone." Even now Sweeney would argue against his fate.

"Both of them were under your influence and your command. I have seen them—they are pathetic wrecks of the men they once were. They are punished enough."

She recognized the sound of footsteps hurrying toward them along the path. Whoever it was might try to stop her. Sweeney's face showed that he heard them, too.

"You won't do it," he said. "I don't believe that you can bring yourself to shoot."

"Then you will die surprised." She steadied the gun with both hands. This was the final moment. Now she would fulfill the promise she had made, achieve the purpose that had given meaning to her long ordeal. The hard, bitter stone buried in her heart would give her the strength to carry out his sentence.

"Miss Colburne!"

It was Lord Danebridge's voice. But how could that be? Where had he come from? Falcon was tempted to look as the baron arrived in the clearing, breathing heavily, but she did not dare to take her eyes off Sweeney again. She heard more people coming now along the path behind the baron.

"Miss Colburne, stop. You do not need to shoot him. Are you all right? I heard the shots . . ."

"I must finish this."

"No. Please. Give me your gun." He moved beside her. A glance from the corner of her eye told her that he had a pistol in his own hand, aimed at Sweeney. "Listen to me. I love you. I will never deceive you again as long as I live, if you will only forgive me and give up this course."

"This man killed my father! I have lived for this. I made a vow . . ."

"It appears that this man has now also killed the one most responsible for your parents' deaths. After he faces a coroner's jury and a King's Bench justice, he'll face the gallows. Is it not enough? Do you believe that your mother and father would have wished you to bloody your own hands in their name?"

"Will you take away the only thing that has made sense of my life—of my survival?" She was beginning to tremble.

"Is it the only thing?" He sounded utterly despondent. "What about love? Could not God have saved you for that instead of vengeance, Miss Colburne? I never thought I would love another woman after Anne, until you came into my life. I never expected to love you, but you changed all that. You reawakened me to what that kind of love could be. I had not realized how desolate my life was without it. I love you more than life itself, Miss Colburne. Do you feel nothing for me in return?"

But she did, of course. Life was so unfair. Tears welled in her eyes, and she realized that she could no longer hold her pistol steady.

Lord Danebridge lowered his voice almost to a whisper. "If you choose to kill him, you throw away any chance for happiness that we might find together. I could tell you I love you a thousand times, but in the end you still must make the choice."

A sob escaped from her throat. "We have no hope of happiness together!" But her will to kill Sweeney was gone. For a moment longer she pointed the gun at him. Then she lowered it and dropped it into the grass at her feet. She could not look at Lord Danebridge.

"Sergeant!" called the baron. "If you would, please?"

Triss appeared from behind him and took his pistol, aiming it at Sweeney with a determined and fierce look on his face.

"You!" exclaimed Sweeney in recognition. His body seemed to sag in defeat.

Lord Danebridge reached down and picked up Falcon's weapon. As he straightened up, he turned to her and put two fingers under her chin, gently raising her face to his searching gaze.

"We have much to talk about," he said. "First we must see Sweeney secured and put under guard until the constable can be brought here, and we must do something for Lord Coudray. But then will you consent to walk with me?"

She nodded, looking at him through eyes blurred by tears. Despite her best effort to control herself, she was shaking so hard now that her teeth were chattering.

"Devil take it," the baron growled softly. In full view of their audience, he stepped up and took her into his arms.

There would be many more explanations needed later, but the only one Falcon wanted right away was Lord Danebridge's. He had brought Mr. Fallesby with him from London and the two had arrived at Colburne Hall just in time to find a distraught Triss and Maggie in front of the house with Benita and Carlos.

"Your Maggie was as near to hysterics as I imagine she ever gets," the baron was saying. He and Falcon were now walking alone along the gravel pathways in the garden behind the mansion. The earl's body had been removed to the house and Sweeney was tied to a chair in the earl's private study awaiting the constable.

"She told me you'd gone down the drive to try to kill Sweeney, but I knew that you were not there. Mr. Fallesby and I had just driven up the length of it and had seen no sign of you. They did not know where Lord Coudray was, either, and I feared the worst. That is when we heard the shots coming from the grove."

He stopped walking and turned to face her, his eyes full of pain. "I thought I was too late. I thought I had lost you. I have never run so fast in my life."

Falcon could not give him the reassurances that would ease his pain. How could he lose what he had never had? But she did not say that. Instead she began walking again and steered the conversation back to questions.

"How did you come to know that my cousin was involved in what happened? I did not know it myself until Sweeney told me. I might not have believed it even then, if the earl had not arrived and confirmed it himself."

"I went to see your Corporal Pumphrey at St. Bartholomew's Hospital. He did not know where Sweeney could be found, as I gather you suspected since you did not visit him. But that is not what I wanted to learn from him. I asked him to talk about his army days in the Peninsula, and whenever he mentioned Sweeney, I would ask a few extra questions."

"Are you never direct?"

"I promise in the future I will be as direct as you wish, if you will only be a part of my life."

She shook her head. "What did you learn about Sweeney?"

"I discovered that he was a younger son of gentry and went into the army to escape his creditors."

"How does that involve my cousin?"

"I'm getting to that. My kind of work requires patience. You must have some for the telling." He gave her a crooked smile that took away any sting in his words.

They were close to a bed of wallflowers and Falcon breathed in their sweet scent, willing it to overpower the haunting smell of gunpowder that she fancied still clung to her. Lord Danebridge was hard to resist when he looked at her with just that expression. She wished he wouldn't.

"That information from Pumphrey meant I could look up Sweeney's family in the guides to the gentry. Do you know what I discovered? His family is from Kent—from the same area as your cousin. Sweeney's eldest brother attended Harrow with your cousin. So you see, the families knew each other even then."

"How can you know all this?"

"This has been my career—matching up information and paying attention to details. If you look at birthdates, and where the candidates in question went to school, you can quickly discover if they were classmates."

"But that still does not link my cousin with Sweeney. Why did you look at my cousin's information?"

"There was something Mr. Fallesby said when I visited him. It slipped past me at first, but when I discovered the geographic link between Sweeney's family and your cousin, it came back to me. Mr. Fallesby was impressed that you knew your father was supposed to have been disinherited. Not 'was disinherited,' but 'was supposed to have been.' So he never was. Did you know that?"

"Only when Mr. Fallesby told me. We never knew. Everything could have been so different!"

They had reached the fountain that stood at the center of

the garden where the paths intersected. Falcon stopped in front of it and stared at the trickling water, a huge lump in her throat. "If only they had told us!" she whispered.

"Did it never occur to you that if your cousin knew of it, he would have ample reason to wish your father dead?"

"But no one knew!"

"Your grandfather knew. And Mr. Fallesby, his solicitor, knew. Perhaps your grandmother knew, also. It does not seem impossible to me that your cousin might have found out."

He turned her to face him and took her hands in his. "I went back to Mr. Fallesby and asked to see his records of disbursements made when your cousin came into his inheritance. Miss Colburne, he had a massive number of debts. It looked as if he had been living on his expectations for years. If I am right and he discovered at some point that he was not in line to inherit after all, can you imagine his desperation?"

"But we are only guessing . . ."

"He might have known for some time, not knowing what to do about it, hoping your father would die in a battle. But think of the temptation and opportunity that presented themselves if he then learned that Sweeney had been commissioned into the same regiment as your father? Sweeney went into the army to escape debts—how easy for your cousin to take on some of those to gain leverage over him! Do you recall when Sweeney first joined your battalion?"

"Not precisely. It was after we came back from the Copenhagen campaign. Perhaps early in 1808? It was some months before we were shipped out to Spain."

"Did your father's battalion see action any time after Sweeney came?"

"No. Not really. We just marched all over half the Peninsula, or so it seemed."

"If Sweeney had hoped to kill your father under the cover of a battle, he must have felt very frustrated."

"When General Moore decided we must fall back to Corunna, everyone felt frustrated."

"Think how Sweeney must have felt. No opportunity had presented itself, and suddenly the whole army was turned back, destined to return home. He must have become very desperate indeed."

She shivered. "We do not know that this is true."

"I will put some of these questions to Sweeney before they take him away. One thing is certain; there were payments made to Sweeney from the earl's accounts. I think that your cousin never thought anyone would connect them. I believe that Sweeney was blackmailing him."

"How shall I ever be able to tell my grandmother? Or even Lady Rawlings, Lord Coudray's sister?"

"Your grandmother?"

"My cousin said she would want to see me, but he kept putting off the visit, saying she was not well enough. Today I had decided to go to her without his permission. That is why I was here when Sweeney came."

"And where exactly did he say this grandmother was supposed to be?"

Something like dread began to uncurl in the pit of Falcon's stomach. "In the dower house. Why, what do you mean?"

Lord Danebridge spoke very gently. "Your grandmother died a year ago, my love. Mr. Fallesby told me."

Falcon's control finally crumbled. She felt as if her cousin had performed another murder at that very instant, robbing Falcon of one more family member. One huge sob rose up out of her throat. Then, like a flood through a breaking dam, her grief poured out. Awash in tears, she grieved not only for the dead, but also for the living, the lost possibilities and hopes, the dreams that could never be fulfilled. Overwhelmed by emotion, she hardly noticed when the baron took her into his arms again and tried to comfort her with gentle strokes and soothing words.

"Cry," he murmured. "You have more than ample reason. It is all right. Everything is going to be all right."

Chapter Twenty

Falcon knew in her heart that everything was definitely not going to be all right. Lord Danebridge was in love with her. That he had said so openly in front of witnesses mattered less to her than his actions. He was here. He had pursued his investigation despite her cruel rejection and he had come here to find her. That alone proclaimed his love to her beyond any doubting. If it had not, the look in his eyes when he had finally released her from his embrace would have told her as much.

What was worse, she knew now that she loved him, too. Only love could have caused the great anger she had felt when he had confessed his wrongdoings and the unassuageable longing she had felt after she had dismissed him from her life. Only love could cause the terrible grief she felt now. She knew he was going to offer for her. Because she loved him, she knew that she would have to say no.

She stared into the fire in her cousin's study, a room only recently vacated by the constable and Sweeney. She was alone now, grateful for the solitude after the turmoil of the day. The earl's houseguests had returned from their outing before the constable arrived. Fortunately they had all retired to change out of their riding clothes almost immediately. The constable and his assistant had presented themselves minutes later and managed to slip Sweeney quietly out of the house without alerting anyone beyond the circle of those who already knew what had happened.

Lady Rawlings had to be told of her brother's death, of course. The poor woman had fainted at the news, but after she revived she had shouldered the responsibility of sending off the guests quite admirably. The scandal might not break until the inquest, but surely there would be no avoiding it then.

Falcon sighed. If she had not already had reason enough to refuse the baron's offer, the coming scandal surrounding her cousin's death would have provided it. As much as she dreaded the painful scene ahead of her, a part of her wished she might just get it over with. The loneliness of her future hung over her now as surely as the shadow of the gallows cast its pall over Sweeney.

Her gloomy thoughts were interrupted when Lord Danebridge knocked on the study door and begged admittance.

"You have been through so much today, I do not think it best for you to sit in here alone," he said, entering. He went straight to the hearth and stirred up the fire into a lively blaze. "There! That is more the thing. As the day wanes, it is growing dark and chill."

He turned to look at her and thought that she had never looked so lost and sad and beautiful. "Miss Colburne—"

"Lord Danebridge—"

He chuckled when they both spoke at once. "You see? I warned you once that if we were not careful, this might become a habit." He stepped closer to the chair where she sat looking up at him with a guarded expression in her exquisite green eyes.

He lowered his voice. "We must not have been careful enough, Miss Colburne, because you have certainly become a habit with me. One that I cannot live without."

She stood up abruptly and moved away from him. "Please, Lord Danebridge, do not say so."

"It is true." He stood perfectly still, willing her to turn and look at him. Now above all times he wanted her to know that he was serious.

She did turn, and for a fleeting moment he saw a look of despair cross her face before her expression hardened into a mask of indifference. He knew then, before he said anything, that she was going to refuse him. But why? He was more convinced than ever that she cared for him.

He ploughed ahead, hardly knowing what words to choose. "Did you believe me earlier today when I said I loved you?"

She nodded.

"Good." That was a start. "I believe that you care something for me also. Do you deny it?"

Her voice was a whisper. "No. I cannot."

"Good, again. You see? Already we have more of a foundation on which to build a marriage than many couples have." He advanced toward her. "Please, Miss Colburne. Please say you will consent to be my wife."

It was a very backward proposal, not at all what he had planned. He was trying to build a case against her refusal, when what he really wanted to do was simply kiss her and keep kissing her until she said yes.

"No. I am sorry," she said, her lower lip quivering. She bit it and turned away from him again, as if she would stop it. But her next words came out in a rush of anguish. "I would say yes if I could! I do care for you. But there are too many reasons against it."

"Tell me what they are. I think I have a right to know."

This was not going to be easy for her, he could see. She raised her chin and straightened her back in the way he had seen her do every time she faced a challenge. He loved that about her. God help him, he loved everything about her.

With fists clenched she turned back to face him. "Yes. I suppose you do have a right." She took a deep breath. "I do not know what will come out at the inquiry into my cousin's death. Mr. Fallesby explained to me about the process. But the murder of a peer is bound to shake the very roots of society at his—your—level. My name will be caught up in the scandal. To be associated with me is the last thing you need."

"What I need is you. I care nothing about the scandal."

"And what of your London friends? Would you give them up so easily? They are likely to recognize that I am the Spanish lady they entertained so happily. I have no doubt that they will feel they were intentionally duped and will take offense."

"You do not give my friends enough credit. They are loyal and capable of understanding more than you suppose."

"That is easy to believe as long as they are not put to the test. You might find yourself disappointed."

"I might, but I would be grateful to learn their true colors. You are worth a hundred of them to me, even if they are true friends."

Why was this so difficult? She faced him across a space of half a dozen feet, yet there might as well have been a yawning chasm between them. He was determined to bridge that chasm.

"What else?" he said. "If those are the only reasons to keep us apart, I blow them away like fragile cobwebs."

Her chin went a little higher, he thought, and suddenly she could not look at him. "I may be the granddaughter of an earl," she said, "but I was raised in my father's regiment. I was only fourteen when my parents died. Even as an officer's daughter, I lack the training and social graces that you should require in a wife. You might not think that matters now, but later, perhaps in a year or two, when you are relying on me to run your home and be your hostess, you will find me wanting."

"It is never too late to learn those skills. My mother would gladly teach you. But those do not matter to me now or later. My first wife had those skills. What I want from you is your company, your precious laughter, your love. These are gifts that need no training to bestow."

At his words her eyes filled with tears. Had he somehow hurt her? But no. Whatever it was, her deepest reason was still buried in her heart. They had only scratched away the superficial layers of her reluctance.

"If you truly knew me, you would not want those," she whispered. "I am unfit." Closing her eyes, she bowed her head and shook it.

He went to her then, wanting to comfort her, uncertain of her meaning, but when he tried to put his arms around her, she pushed him away. "Do you not understand?" she said angrily. "I am impure—unclean. I have been with another man!"

He was shaken, although he tried not to show it. For a moment he thought of all his original suspicions about her. "When was this? In Spain I thought you had stayed in a convent!"

She laughed a brittle, bitter laugh. "Yes, that is true, once I reached the south. But it is three hundred fifty miles from Astorga to Seville. Sometimes we had to pay our way."

"We?"

"Carmen and I. She was only a year older than I, staying in a convent school in the mountains near Astorga. Her family had sent a trusted friend to bring her to them in Andalusia,

where many of the landed class took refuge. She insisted that
I go along with her, to find safety. But we ran into many trou-
bles, and eventually the man abandoned us. We made our way
the best we could, two young girls. It took us months. At
times I had to steal food, money, valuables. One time nothing
we had was enough to pay the men who helped us."

Tears were running down her face unheeded. He wanted to
dry them and offer her comfort, but he did not know whether
to touch her or not.

"They said one of us had to go with them. I had so much
less to lose than Carmen, it only made sense that I should be
the one. She is a Spanish nobleman's daughter. She would
have been unmarriageable. For her to be defiled that way
would have been the same as death."

"So you offered yourself to save her."

"I was a foreigner, an orphan without prospects. They did
not hurt me."

"I can see that they did, even if you cannot."

"After I had done it, it did not seem quite so terrible. We
had no choice! I knew I had sacrificed my chance to ever
marry. But marriage did not fit into my plans to seek revenge
on Sweeney and the other two men. I could not imagine then
that it would ever matter."

Her face was averted, her eyes closed. He moved as close
to her as he could without actually touching her.

"And if I said it did not matter, would you marry me?" he
said very softly.

She opened her eyes. "I would think about it, if I believed
you."

"Then allow me to convince you that it does not matter."
He put one hand behind her head and the other behind her
waist and drew her gently to him. Just before he kissed her he
said, "I love you. If there was any way I could take away the
pain you have suffered, I would do it gladly. But if you let me
I will give you a future more full of happiness than you ever
knew was possible."

Falcon's heart was still full of anguish when the baron's
lips touched hers. His kiss was tentative at first, a question
posed in physical terms. But the intensity grew as he sought

her answer in the exchange of their warm breath and the beating of their hearts.

Her heart and soul knew what her mind had not yet accepted—that indeed, love was the destiny God had intended for her. She could not help responding honestly to the message he was sending to her, a message of love so great that all of her past mistakes and suffering could be swept away by it.

As he enfolded her deeper in his embrace and allowed his passion for her to show the way, her own passion began to shake loose from the restraints she had built around it. The hard, bitter stone of vengeance in her heart cracked apart into dust. Joy and wonder rushed in to fill its place. She did love this man, and it felt right—so right. In his arms now she felt a sense of belonging, of having come home, of having found what it was she was supposed to have been seeking all along.

Tears of gratitude and happiness began to spill down her face. A little sigh escaped her when he nuzzled her neck and planted a warm kiss on the collarbone exposed by the neckline of her dress. "Say you'll marry me," he murmured. He stopped suddenly and fixed his gaze upon her, his gray eyes dark as a storm and more intense than she had ever seen them.

"Say you'll marry me," he repeated. This time it was a command.

A log shifted in the fire, sending up a shower of sparks and momentarily brightening the room.

"Yes," Falcon whispered, echoing the sound of the fire. Then louder, more certainly, "Yes! Yes, I will marry you!"

Lord Danebridge whooped in joy and spun her around, laughing. She laughed, too, until he slowed down and kissed her again, this time a long, lingering kiss full of promise.

"I think, in this case, it is high time that you begin calling me Jeremy," he said when he was finished.

Falcon paused, facing one more decision. But this time there seemed to be no question. "In the regiment my name was shortened to Falcon. I had sharp eyes when we were foraging, and they teased me about my stubbornness—they said I never let go of an idea once I seized it." She smiled into his eyes. "I cannot promise that that has changed. Fair warning! But I was named for the village in Ireland where my mother was born. My name is Falcarrah."

"It is beautiful," he said, repeating it. And it did sound beautiful, on his lips. Falcon did not feel the rush of pain that had accompanied it ever since her parents' deaths.

"I hope you like the sound of it combined with mine," he added. "Falcarrah Coleburne Hazelton, Lady Danebridge. I do not intend to give you long at all to get used to it. I hope and pray that you will live with it for a very long time."

True to his word, Lord Danebridge obtained a special license and he and Falcon were wed within a fortnight. The Dowager Lady Danebridge and young Tobey were as thrilled as anyone, except possibly Maggie and Triss. Those two, if anyone had asked, would have insisted they were even happier.

Falcon's only regret was the exclusion of her Spanish friends from the new direction in her life. She continued to send letters regularly, never knowing if they were received. That is why, three months later she was both excited and fearful to receive a letter sent from Cadiz.

She was playing her mother's harp softly in the comfortable and well-stocked library at Hazelworth when the footman brought her the letter. Jeremy was reading in his favorite chair nearby.

"It is from Don Andrés," she told the baron, opening it with shaking fingers.

Jeremy had long since come to know a great deal more about the Spanish family that had taken Falcon in after she had reached the south of Spain. He left his book to come to his wife's side.

"Don Andrés writes that they have evaded Fernando's pogroms and that they are emigrating to the La Plata provinces in South America," Falcon said, her eyes skimming over the page eagerly. Then she lifted them to look at Jeremy. "They will be farther away than ever, but at least they will be safe. Don Andrés hopes to purchase a large tract of land for a ranch. Oh, how I hope they will be happy."

"At least as happy as we are?"

"Oh, at least," she agreed, rising from her chair to embrace him. As she felt his warm, strong arms around her, she sighed contentedly. "If that is possible. Or at least as happy as Maggie and Triss."

The prickly Irishwoman and the crusty Cornishman were as unlikely a pair as honey and vinegar, but they had decided they had grown so used to each other's company that they would make their testy partnership a permanent one. Wedding plans were already afoot to celebrate their union in a month's time.

"I will have to ask Carlos and Benita if they would like to go to Carmen's family. Those two have done well enough here, but when winter comes the difference between the English climate and what they are accustomed to will be worse than anything they've yet encountered.

"There have been so many changes," Falcon murmured as Jeremy's embrace began to turn into something more.

"Yes," he agreed softly, slipping one hand between them to feel her breast through the fabric of her dress. "Although I have to say I am only just beginning to notice some of the changes in you."

"Can you truly notice a difference already?" She smiled dreamily. "Tobey was so delighted with the idea of our adding to the family. We must tell him soon, although I can hardly imagine how he will survive the suspense of waiting to know if it is a boy or a girl."

Jeremy kissed her nose. "Perhaps, in time, we can give him one of each, if we conduct ourselves appropriately."

"Mm-m," Falcon replied as he drew her up into a deep kiss. "One of each, or even more. There's your mother to make happy, too, you know."

"Not to mention you and me," he said, putting his lips back on hers. "I love you," he whispered against the softness of her mouth.

"I love you," she whispered back.

They finished the conversation in a way that needed no further words.

① SIGNET REGENCY ROMANCE

ENDURING ROMANCES

☐ **THE GYPSY DUCHESS by Nadine Miller.** The beautiful young widowed Duchess of Sheffield Moira knew all to well why Devon St. Gwyre hated her so: she shattered his younger brother's heart, driving him to throw away his life in battle. And now she was asking the Earl to take charge of the child of a forbidden love and loveless marriage. But soon she discovered that this man had a weapon of vengeance she had not dreamed of—his desire. "A charming new voice in Regency romance."—Anne Barbour, author of *Step in Time*   (187288—$4.99)

☐ **THE DUKE'S DILEMMA by Nadine Miller.** Miss Emily Haliburton could not hope to match her cousin Lady Lucinda Hargrave in either beauty or social standing. Certainly she couldn't compete with the lovely Lucinda for the hand of the devastatingly handsome Lord Jared Tremayne who was on the hunt for a wife. The duke couldn't see Emily as a wife, but she did manage to catch his roving eye as a woman.   (186753—$4.50)

☐ **THE RELUCTANT HEIRESS by Evelyn Richardson.** Lady Sarah Melford was quite happy to live in the shadow of her elder brother and his beautiful wife. But now she had inherited her grandmother's vast wealth, all eyes were avidly upon her, especially those of three ardent suitors. She had to decide what to do with the many men who wanted her. For if money did not bring happiness, it most certainly brought danger and hopefully love.   (187660—$4.99)

☐ **THE DEVIL'S DUE by Rita Boucher.** Lady Katherine Steel was in desperate flight from the loathsome lord who threatened even more than her virtue after her husband's death. Her only refuge was to disguise herself as the widow of Scottish lord Duncan MacLean, whose death in far-off battle left his castle without a master. But Duncan MacLean was not dead.
                                                                                        (187512—$4.99)

☐ **THE RUBY NECKLACE by Martha Kirkland.** Miss Emaline Harrison was the widow of a licentious blueblood after a marriage in name only. Around her neck was a precious heirloom, which some London gentlemen would kill for. So it was difficult for Emaline to discern the true motives and intentions of the seductive suitors swarming around her. Such temptation was sure to lead a young lady very dangerously, delightfully astray.   (187202—$4.99)

*Prices slightly higher in Canada

Buy them at your local bookstore or use this convenient coupon for ordering.

PENGUIN USA
P.O. Box 999 — Dept. #17109
Bergenfield, New Jersey 07621

Please send me the books I have checked above.
I am enclosing $_____ (please add $2.00 to cover postage and handling). Send check or money order (no cash or C.O.D.'s) or charge by Mastercard or VISA (with a $15.00 minimum). Prices and numbers are subject to change without notice.

Card #_____ Exp. Date _____
Signature_____
Name_____
Address_____
City _____ State _____ Zip Code _____

For faster service when ordering by credit card call **1-800-253-6476**

Allow a minimum of 4-6 weeks for delivery. This offer is subject to change without notice.

ⓘ SIGNET REGENCY ROMANCE

DILEMMAS OF THE HEART

☐ **AN AFFAIR OF HONOR by Candice Hern.** The lovely Meg Ashburton finds herself in quite a dilemma when the dazzliing Viscount Sedgewick is recovering from an accidental injury in her country manor. All too soon, though, he would be on his feet again, able to once more take Meg in his arms, and this time not to dance. . . . (186265—$4.99)

☐ **A TEMPORARY BETHROTHAL by Dorothy Mack.** Belinda Melville knew it was folly to be head-over-heels in love with Captain Anthony Wainright, who made it clear that he far preferred Belinda's heartbreakingly beautiful and calculating cousin, the newly married Lady Deidre Archer. Should Belinda hold out for a man who would be hers and hers only? Or was being second best to a man she adored at first sight better than nothing? (184696—$3.99)

☐ **THE AWAKENING HEART by Dorothy Mack.** The lovely Dinah Elcott finds herself in quite a predicament when she agrees to pose as a marriageable miss in public to the elegant Charles Talbot. In return, he will let Dinah pursue her artistic ambitions in private, but can she resist her own untested and shockingly susceptible heart? (178254—$3.99)

☐ **LORD ASHFORD'S WAGER by Marjorie Farrell.** Lady Joanna Barrand knows all there is to know about Lord Tony Ashford—his gambling habits, his wooing a beautiful older widow to rescue him from ruin, and worst of all, his guilt in a crime that made all his other sins seem innocent. What she doesn't know is how she has lost her heart to him!
(180496—$3.99)

☐ **LADY LEPRECHAUN by Melinda McRae.** When a lovely, young widow and a dashing duke are thrown together in a cross-country hunt for two schoolboy runaways, they are both faced with an unexpected pleasurable challenge. "One of the most exciting new voices in Regency fiction."—*Romantic Times* (175247—$3.99)

*Prices slightly higher in Canada

Buy them at your local bookstore or use this convenient coupon for ordering.

PENGUIN USA
P.O. Box 999 — Dept. #17109
Bergenfield, New Jersey 07621

Please send me the books I have checked above.
I am enclosing $_____ (please add $2.00 to cover postage and handling). Send check or money order (no cash or C.O.D.'s) or charge by Mastercard or VISA (with a $15.00 minimum). Prices and numbers are subject to change without notice.

Card #_____ Exp. Date _____
Signature_____
Name_____
Address_____
City _____ State _____ Zip Code _____

For faster service when ordering by credit card call **1-800-253-6476**

Allow a minimum of 4-6 weeks for delivery. This offer is subject to change without notice.

① SIGNET REGENCY ROMANCE

WHEN LOVE CONQUERS ALL

☐ **ROGUE'S DELIGHT by Elizabeth Jackson.** The handsome and heartless Viscount Everly needed a wife for the sake of show. So how could an impoverished orphan like Miss Susan Winston say no? But playing the part of Lord Everly's pawn was one thing—and becoming a plaything of passion was another. (182774—$3.99)

☐ **LORD CAREW'S BRIDE by Mary Balogh.** When the beautiful Samantha Newman is faced with a marriage proposal and new feelings that have been stirred by the charming Marquess of Carew, she must decide if she can resist her strong attraction to the Earl of Rushford, the notorious libertine who betrayed her six years ago—or ignite the flames of a new passion. (185528—$3.99)

☐ **LADY KATE'S SECRET by Marcy Elias Rothman.** Lady Katherine Grovenor was faced with a devilish choice. She could give her hand to a man she did not know—Nicholas Monroe, the stranger from abroad whose past and fortune were cloaked in sinister secrecy. Or she could yield to her father and wed Lord John Peterbroome, the most infamous rake in the realm. Kate stood at the crossroads between the way of the world and the path of desire—with no guide but her own wildly wavering heart. (185021—$4.50)

*Prices slightly higher in Canada

Buy them at your local bookstore or use this convenient coupon for ordering.

PENGUIN USA
P.O. Box 999 — Dept. #17109
Bergenfield, New Jersey 07621

Please send me the books I have checked above.
I am enclosing $_____ (please add $2.00 to cover postage and handling). Send check or money order (no cash or C.O.D.'s) or charge by Mastercard or VISA (with a $15.00 minimum). Prices and numbers are subject to change without notice.

Card #_____ Exp. Date _____
Signature_____
Name_____
Address_____
City _____ State _____ Zip Code _____

For faster service when ordering by credit card call **1-800-253-6476**

Allow a minimum of 4-6 weeks for delivery. This offer is subject to change without notice.

ROMANTIC TIMES MAGAZINE
the magazine for romance novels
...and the women who read them!

Also Available in Bookstores & Newsstands!

♥ *EACH MONTHLY ISSUE* features over 120 Reviews & Ratings, saving you time and money when browsing at the bookstores!

ALSO INCLUDES...
♥ Fun Readers Section
♥ Author Profiles
♥ News & Gossip

PLUS...

♥ Interviews with the __Hottest Hunk Cover Models__ in romance like Fabio, Michael O'Hearn, & many more!

♥ Order a __SAMPLE COPY__ Now! ♥
COST: $2.00 (includes postage & handling)
CALL 1-800-989-8816*
*800 Number for credit card orders only
Visa • MC • AMEX • Discover Accepted!

♥ BY MAIL: Make check payable to: **Romantic Times Magazine,** 55 Bergen Street, Brooklyn, NY 11201
♥ PHONE: 718-237-1097   ♥ FAX: 718-624-4231

♥ E-MAIL: RTmag1@aol.com

VISIT OUR WEBSITE: http://www.rt-online.com